'I shall never be your lady.

'I shall inform my father that I have rejected your proposal. It will disappoint him but he will accept my decision. I trust you will not approach me again.'

Lionel was blocking her escape from the arbour. 'I am not disappointed. I knew you had spirit, had no wish for some tame little country milkmaid. You will grace my house well, my lady.' His long lips parted in a smile of pure sweetness. 'I do not give up what is mine. Remember that, Corinna Webster.'

Dear Reader

In COUNTRY MOUSE, we have the latest Regency by Petra Nash—a treat! Joanna Makepeace leaves Richard III for the Monmouth Rebellion in CORINNA'S CAUSE, an action-packed plot. Our American authors are Patricia Potter and Lucy Elliot, with THE ABDUCTION, set in the Scottish Borders of 1550, and PRIVATE PARADISE, featuring New York in the 1880s.

See you next month!

The Editor

Joanna Makepeace taught as head of English in a comprehensive school, before leaving full-time work to write. She lives in Leicester with her mother and Jack Russell terrier called Dickon, and has written over thirty books under different pseudonyms. She loves the old romantic historical films, which she finds more exciting and relaxing than the newer ones.

Recent titles by the same author:

RELUCTANT REBEL
BATTLEFIELD OF HEARTS

ᵉ

CORINNA'S CAUSE

Joanna Makepeace

MAY 1994   JUNE 1994(A)
AUG 2010
JUNE 2012
MAR 2017

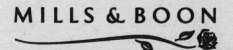

MILLS & BOON

MILLS & BOON LIMITED
ETON HOUSE, 18–24 PARADISE ROAD
RICHMOND, SURREY, TW9 1SR

First published in Great Britain 1993
by Mills & Boon Limited

© Joanna Makepeace 1993

Australian copyright 1993
Philippine copyright 1994
This edition 1994

ISBN 0 263 78245 X

MAY 1994 — JUNE 94 (A)

Set in 10 on 11½ pt Linotron Times
04-9402-80170

Typeset in Great Britain by Centracet, Cambridge
Made and printed in Great Britain

CHAPTER ONE

CORINNA sat with her back pressed firmly against the bole of the old oak tree, her eyes scanning the river path for signs of the men. Clytie, the small brown and white spaniel, frisked about nosing tussocks of grass in search of elusive rabbit smells. Corinna watched her indulgently. The June sun was hot on her face, and she pushed aside a straggle of fair hair from her perspiring cheek. She had hurriedly put on her old brown house gown before dashing off in pursuit of her brother and Oliver. They had left immediately after dinner, carrying their fishing-rods, and Corinna had declared her intention of joining them, but her mother had stopped her in her tracks, for once adamant.

'No, Corinna, not this afternoon. You know well enough Lionel is expected. It is bad enough that Julian should be missing, but you must be here when he arrives.'

Corinna had murmured, mutinously, that there was so little time to be with Julian and Oliver before they returned to Oxford, and the day was so lovely that she could not be expected to sacrifice the opportunity of spending it with them.

'Nonsense, Corinna. By the look of things the weather is set fair for the next day or two. There will be plenty of time for you all to ride out together. Sir Lionel comes specifically to celebrate your birthday with us, and you cannot insult him by being absent on the very day we expect him.'

Corinna had faced her mother sulkily. 'The last time

5

he was here he showed very little interest in the horses or dogs, let alone the fishing. He won't want to go out on the estate and we shall all be forced to wait attendance on him.'

'Lionel's father had only recently died on the last occasion. Things may be different now. Now go up to your chamber and change your gown, child. He comes from court, and I do not wish him to report to his mother that you have been allowed to become a hoyden.'

Corinna had sighed and gone up to her chamber as ordered. She had watched as Joan, her mother's maid, had searched through her clothing chest for her most fashionable gown, then had abruptly seized her oldest one, the most suitable walking shoes, had insisted on being laced into them, and had escaped from the manor house while her mother was interviewing Cook about her plans for supper. Corinna's father was busied in the stable, where his favourite mare was soon to foal, and so she hadn't been seen as she'd whistled Clytie and made for the river path.

Now there was no sign of either her brother or her cousin. Clearly they had crossed the stepping-stones and gone further afield. There was little point in walking upstream when they might well have headed for the water meadows, and she dared not be too long absent from the house. She sighed. Like it or not, she must be gowned in her best and at her mother's side when Sir Lionel Summers rose across the moat bridge. It was rare that Corinna's father showed his anger with either of his children, but, on those occasions when he *had* done, both Corinna's and Julian's backs had smarted from the feel of his riding whip, and, loving him dearly though she did, Corinna had no intention of defying him today.

Clytie barked excitedly and Corinna looked up expectantly to see her cousin, Oliver Hunt, crossing the broad, flat stones across the river towards her.

'I see you managed to get out. Julian was so anxious to get to the river we could not wait, and I saw Aunt Dorcas was intent on talking to you. Hey, there, settle,' he said sharply to the silky little dog who ran yelping between his legs. 'Bart came over to join us, and he and Julian are engaged in one of their ardent discussions about politics. No chance the fish will bite with that in progress, so I left them to it and thought I would try my luck upstream.'

He sank down at Corinna's side, and her heart leaped with her delight at his nearness. She loved to be with her younger brother, Julian, of course, whenever he was down from university, but it was Oliver she had most hoped to see during this short vacation. She had been overjoyed when he had accompanied Julian to Leicestershire for her birthday celebrations, but disappointed to find he had in tow another student companion, Bart Spicer, who seemed to take all his attention, and was obsessed with talk of court affairs.

In this year of 1685 when King Charles had only recently died this February, and the new King, James, his brother, was so newly crowned, it seemed that the thoughts of all the men in the household were focused on the thorny problem of the new King's strongly held devotion to the Catholic faith.

Corinna was well aware that, despite his concern, her father would be fiercely loyal to James, as he had been to the late King. He had known both men personally, had fought at Worcester and waited on the royal brothers during their period of exile in both France and Holland. Oliver's father was puritanical to the core, as were Corinna's mother and her Aunt

Tabitha, who had been brought up by their tyrannical father. Self-opinionated and dictatorial, Saul Hunt would allow no fears of determination to express his doubts about the safety of the Protestant faith in the hands of his new sovereign. It seemed that Bart Spicer was another of the same kidney. Corinna could well understand that Magdalen College was a hotbed of intrigue and rashly expressed rebellious views. Only this morning when her brother Julian had held forth on this theme Corinna's father had sharply bade his son hold his tongue.

'I'll have no treasonable sentiments arrogantly spouted at my table,' he'd thundered.

Julian had found it politic to obey him. Corinna found court affairs fascinating enough, but, today of all days, she would have preferred Bart Spicer not to monopolise the attention of her menfolk. Opportunities to ride and fish with them or simply walk leisurely through the summery fields and lanes, as they had done so often together as children, seemed likely to be in short supply now that Lionel Summers must be fittingly entertained at Manor Court.

Oliver put a strong brown hand on her knee.

'What is it, Corin? Is it that you detest Sir Lionel Summers so much?'

She turned wide blue eyes on him. 'No, why should I? I hardly know him. It's just that I would have preferred to have you and Julian to myself for my birthday and the short time before you're back at Oxford.'

He grimaced comically. 'Am I to understand that you resent Bart's presence as well?'

Corinna sniffed. 'The man's much too full of himself. I wonder that you and Julian give his opinions so much attention.'

'He says only what we all think — that the late King's eldest son would have been more welcome on the throne.'

'But James, Duke of Monmouth, is illegitimate. The late King named him his loved "natural" son on the occasion of the Duke's marriage. He could not inherit. Since the King died without legitimate heir, the Duke of York succeeded by due process of law.'

'But what if Monmouth could prove King Charles had legally married his mother?'

'But everyone knows Lucy Walter was not married to the King.' Corinna's tone was incredulous.

'Bart says otherwise.'

Corinna laughed. 'And, of course, Bart would know.'

He grinned back at her quick riposte. 'Each day you show very clearly how much you dislike poor Bart. His opinion of you is not so scathing, I can assure you.'

Blue eyes flashed fiery sparks at him. 'You have discussed me with Bart Spicer? Shame on you, Oliver.'

His brown eyes clouded with concern. 'Corinna, no insult was meant. Bart merely expressed his sincere admiration.' His lips twitched teasingly. 'If he saw you at this moment he would excel himself in praise of your beauty. Would you have me deny it?'

Her cheeks were stained scarlet at his casual reference to his own appreciation of her charms. Oliver was almost a full year younger than herself and, at twenty years of age, Corinna thought herself considerably more mature than her cousin and her brother, who were much of an age. She tossed her tangled fair curls angrily.

'I'd have you keep me well out of your conversation, sir.'

He began to laugh again, then his brown eyes softened.

'You have become very lovely, Corin. I suppose you always have been and I've only now realised it. I can understand why your mother is not anxious for you to be roistering round the estate so much these days.' He sighed. 'We have all been so comfortable together. Why do things have to change?'

She smiled faintly at the slight petulance of his tone. Oliver was as dear to her as her brother, Julian, but sometimes he seemed so very much younger than herself. She glanced towards the river.

'I must be getting back to the house. I think Julian should come home now. Father will not be pleased if we are not there to welcome Sir Lionel.'

Oliver stood up and offered her his arm to help her rise. She brushed frantically at the grass and earth clinging to her dusty skirts.

'I really must hurry and change. Where is Clytie? That spaniel is never where she should be.'

'I'll go and find Julian and remind him of his duty, and send Clytie back to you. I imagine she's trying to nose out some water-rat from his hole in the bank.'

They stood facing each other, and, again, Corinna felt herself blushing uneasily. He seemed to have grown several inches at Oxford and now towered over her, a sturdy figure, well built, loose-limbed, a comely young man with a mop of curling brown hair cut unfashionably short, with a square chin, slightly snub nose and wide-spaced velvet-brown eyes. He bent and made to kiss her, and she moved back apace.

'Corin?' He looked at her wonderingly. 'Do you grudge me a kiss in parting? We are kissing kin.' Then, abruptly, the genial smile faded. 'But we aren't cousins, are we?'

His hand reached out and imprisoned hers, then he bent and kissed her palm, turned, and was off along the river path again.

She watched him go, her eyes troubled. Recently she had become very aware that she and Oliver Hunt were not related in blood. She had always known that Sir James and Dorcas Webster were her adopted parents, but they had loved her as a true daughter, never once shown any distinction between their dealings with her and Julian. They had told her little about her parentage. Lady Webster had been staying in London with Sir James's mother and her own sister, Tabitha, during that terrible summer of 1665 when the Great Plague had taken its terrible toll. The dowager Lady Webster, whom Corinna had known as her adored grandmother until her death three years ago, had lost a dear friend to the horrifying disease, Lettice Graham, a young widow who had possessed no near kin to care for her surviving child. The Websters had returned to Leicestershire that autumn with the baby—christened Corinna, because her mother had so admired the pretty poem by Mr Herrick—and Sir James and Dorcas had brought her up as their own child. When Julian had been born in the following year, Dorcas had been delighted to give Sir James an heir to his estate near Barrow-upon-Soar, and Corinna had wanted for nothing, certainly not companionship, for her adopted brother and her aunt Tabitha's son, Oliver, had always played beside her. The three had rarely been parted until Julian and Oliver had departed to Magdalen College, Oxford, only last year.

No, she had barely given her true parentage a thought until talk of Sir Lionel Summers' visit had been mooted. She had met the Summerses on several occasions when they had come visiting from their own home in the Yorkshire Dales. With them had been their only child, Lionel, a quiet, reserved boy who had always seemed to Corinna a trifle out of place during their boisterous country pursuits. Corinna had an uneasy feeling that a match might well have been broached some years earlier if Lionel's father had not died prematurely and he been forced to take on the management of the Yorkshire estates, like the Websters' at Barrow, sadly run down and neglected during the years of the Commonwealth and Protectorate when Sir Richard Summers and Sir James had been forced into exile. Sir Lionel had recently spent a year in Paris at the court of Louis XIV. But for that he would have come more often to Barrow, Corinna felt sure. She had been glad of the respite, conscious that many girls in the country had been wed well before their nineteenth year, but strangely unwilling, as Oliver had only just now confessed, to put an end to her own easy, comfortable life at Manor Court.

On Lionel Summers' last visit with his mother he had, again, seemed uninterested in the hunting and fishing Julian so enjoyed. Corinna had been out and about with the men, and found now that she had taken little note of his appearance. She remembered he was taller and slighter than Oliver. His conversations with Sir James had centred on the thorny problems of court and the difficulties of making ends meet on his own estate, where costly repairs to house and estate buildings were in progress. Corinna, with Julian, had taken little note of any of it. Now he had returned from Paris, and she wondered if his sojourn at the most fashionable and dissolute court in Europe had changed him from the quiet, unsmiling boy she remembered.

There was no sign of Clytie and, before setting off back to the house, Corinna moved down to the river, calling the puppy by name. She frowned, uncertain whether to return without her mother's favourite pet in the hope that Julian or Oliver would come across the spoiled little creature, or search further. Clytie was descended from another loved spaniel, given to Lady Webster by King Charles himself when she had expressed her admiration for his favourites. Charley, as she had daringly called him, had been the delight of all their lives. The King had sent Corinna's mother a pretty bitch, Cassandra, five years later, and Clytie was the grandchild of the original pair. Lady Webster doted on the silky creature, as Corinna did herself, but the spaniel resisted all efforts to train her to heel and could prove maddeningly disobedient.

Glancing up at the position of the sun, Corinna knew she should certainly be returning to the house. She had no wish to get Joan into trouble, and her mother would certainly be angry with them both if Sir Lionel arrived before the younger members of the family were waiting to welcome him. She gave one last call and reluctantly turned from the riverbank. It was then that she heard the frantic scrambling and paddling sounds that turned her body cold and made her lift her skirts high and dash southwards along the path. Here the bank was exceptionally steep and sheer. Now she could see the little dog desperately trying to scramble from the water, but the slippery mud resisted all her efforts to get a purchase. Corinna came to a slithering halt and peered anxiously round for sight or sound of the men. Had the puppy had more sense she would have swum further upstream, where the bank was lower and easier of access, but obviously Corinna's imperious calls had frightened her, and she was frantic to climb from the water and come to her mistress.

Corinna bent down and called to her urgently,

fearing the little dog would utterly exhaust herself
vainly and drown.

'Clytie, good dog, good dog. Come further along,
then. Come.'

She started back up the path, hoping the spaniel
would swim alongside, but Clytie gave a frightened
whimper and redoubled her efforts to climb the bank
with no success.

Muttering anxiously beneath her breath, Corinna let
out an unladylike yell, hoping Julian or Oliver would
hear and come to her help, then she went as near the
bank as she dared and slipped to her knees. Somehow
she must get hold of the dog's leather collar and yank
her clear of the water, but would Clytie stop her
struggles and allow her to do so? Impervious to the
mud and grass stains, Corinna took a firm hold of a
grass tussock and leaned over still further, encouraging
the little dog to come closer by clicking her tongue.
She was intent on her task when she was suddenly
seized from behind and dragged firmly from the water's
brink. Impatiently she turned to snap at her brother or
cousin, when she found herself staring into a pair of
golden-hazel eyes flashing with fury.

'God in heaven, wench, what do you think you're
about, endangering yourself like that?' a masculine
voice snapped. 'That bank could give way and have
you in.'

Angrily she tore herself free. 'Can't you see I'm
trying to save my dog? Let me alone, you fool. I know
what I'm doing.'

'Idiot.' He gave her shoulder a hearty shake. 'Dogs
can swim by instinct. The little beast will be all right.'

'Not if she can't climb the bank.' Corinna was
already slithering back down to the water's edge, with
her unwelcome rescuer in hot pursuit.

Her eyes scanned the river and saw Clytie was tiring, and her anxiety and anger mounted.

'If you are so clever,' she shouted at the man, 'go in and get her out. I take it you can swim.'

The man stared at her incredulously, his eyes widening.

'Jump in? For a dog which hasn't the sense to swim further along and scramble out on its own?' He looked down at his elaborately decorated riding coat of fine wool.

Corinna gave his shoulder a push. 'Yes, of course. Can't you see she's only a puppy and like to drown? Hang your stupid clothes. It's not deep near the bank. Do you want me to do it?'

He followed her gaze and seemed to realise suddenly the very real danger which threatened the little creature. He moved Corinna aside firmly and stepped down into the river.

'What's her name?'

'Clytie.'

He called imperiously, and it seemed that the spaniel instinctively recognised the voice of a master, for she stopped struggling and managed an undignified dog-paddle until he was able to wade out far enough to seize her by the scruff of her neck and dump her unceremoniously upon the bank. Despite Clytie's immediate and frantic shaking to rid herself of the river water, Corinna was able to take firm hold of her pet and scramble clear of the bank.

The dog's rescuer waded upstream to where the access was easier and drew himself up on to the path again. His boots dripped river water, and it had also soaked into the skirts of his fashionable mulberry coat. Corinna stared, horrified, at the wet turn-backs to the sleeves with their fine braid trimming and diamond-cut buttons, then back into the furious face of their owners.

'Sir Lionel . . .' Her voice trailed off unhappily. 'I'm sorry, I didn't recognise you.' She looked down at the squirming puppy in her arms and added in a sudden rush, 'I — I don't know how to thank you. I was afraid I would lose her and we — all love her so.'

He gazed back at her in exasperation; then, as he also recognised her, his eyes widened in amazement.

'Mistress Corinna?'

She bit her lip uncertainly and turned from him to the road, where she could see waiting horses and a man who held the reins of both of them. She could not have failed to mark the way Sir Lionel's gaze had travelled the length of her body, taking in her old, rubbed gown, mud-caked and grass-stained, and her scuffed walking shoes. Her hand went up to her straggling fair curls, torn free from the knot on her crown. She probably had mud on her cheeks too, and the dog was making the situation worse by her desire to lick her mistress's face in her delight at being rescued. Corinna knew her mother would be furious. She had given her strict instructions to go up to her room and change into her most fashionable gown. Not only Sir Lionel would see her now to disadvantage, but his servant as well. She squared her shoulders and turned back for a frank scrutiny of their visitor.

No wonder she had not immediately known him. His stay at the French court had changed him utterly. Gone was the reserved, slight youth she had known, and in his place stood a confident and very fashionable gentleman. Even in riding dress he looked magnificent. His long-skirted coat of mulberry wool was cut exquisitely and embossed with silver braid. His long riding boots — finely polished, she could see, despite the mud and river weed which now embellished them — were of the finest red leather. He was taller than she remembered, though he would never be great of stature. The slight form had filled out, and the cut of his coat and breeches showed her he was lithe and muscular. She lifted her eyes to meet the gaze of those unusual golden-hazel ones. In features he had not changed so much. His nose was still aquiline and well formed, nostrils flaring, she thought, in slight contempt at her rustic state of dishevelment. His own hair was now hidden beneath a full-bottomed, curling wig, and there was priceless lace at his throat and peeping below his cuffs. She swallowed hard at the thought of what damage the river had dealt that spidery web Frenchwomen had spent hours in the making. He swept off his low-crowned black felt hat, adorned with a ribbon of mulberry velvet, and swept her a mocking and courtly bow.

'I regret, mistress, I too failed to recognise you,' he said, his long lips curling into a disdainful smile.

Corinna's mouth set mutinously, and her blue eyes became steely as she dropped him a cool small curtsy in return.

'I am sorry, sir. It is not to be wondered at. I followed my brother and cousin to the river, where they came to fish. I'm afraid I forgot the time, as they must have done, and then. . .' She broke off and indicated the struggling puppy in her arms. 'Again, I must thank you. I'm afraid your fine clothes have suffered considerable damage. I'm sure our servants will be able to put some of that right.'

He smiled frostily. 'My valet has the sole charge of my clothing. We should reach the house before we both take a chill. You are getting sadly wet from the antics of that ridiculous animal. Should you not put her down?'

Clytie gave a final convulsive heave in Corinna's arms and, breaking free of her hold, jumped down, where she began to gambol delightedly round her rescuer's muddied boots. He sighed gustily and indicated that Corinna should walk before him towards the road.

As they reached the horses, Sir Lionel gestured to his man.

'Pierre, follow us to the house and see the horses are cared for. I shall need you as soon as possible in my chamber. As you can see, my apparel has suffered some slight mishap and will need attention.'

So the servant was French. Corinna had not seen the man before. Obviously he must have been engaged to wait on Sir Lionel during his stay in Paris. He was a small, dapper individual of undecided age and indeterminable appearance. He shot Corinna one shrewd glance from his small, wizened countenance, then made her a bow as Sir Lionel introduced her.

'Mistress Corinna Webster. Her spaniel was unable to climb from the river without assistance.'

The Frenchman did not show by the movement of one single facial muscle that his master's remark had surprised him. Obediently he followed behind them, leading the horses.

Clytie made every effort to trip Sir Lionel up by weaving between his legs. When Corinna hissed at the dog to come to heel she paid her no attention whatever, and she was red-faced and mortified when they came in sight of the gatehouse.

'Perhaps it would be better if you managed to go to your own chamber without it being known that we have met,' Sir Lionel said.

Corinna considered the idea and found it attractive, but dismissed it firmly.

'No, sir, that would be unfair to you. My father and mother could not fail to note your appearance and know something has happened. They might come to some unfortunate conclusions. I must explain.'

The hazel eyes narrowed slightly, as if he formed a new opinion of her character.

'If that is your wish.'

Again she bit her lip. 'It is, sir. My mother will not be pleased. She had not wished me to leave the house, but she will be overwhelmingly grateful for your rescue of Clytie.'

He looked down sardonically at the spaniel, who had sat down facing him, plumey tail wagging ecstatically, brown, protuberant eyes glistening adoringly.

Sir Lionel's former stern expression melted. Those expressive lips curved again into a smile, and he bent to stroke the silky coat.

'You are a very winning lady, aren't you? But if you were mine you'd learn to have more sense and be obedient.'

Corinna was so glad to see him relax his stiffness that she, too, managed an awkward smile.

'She is still very young. I'm afraid I'm the one who spoils her.'

He nodded.

It was at that moment that Sir James emerged from the stable where the Frenchman had led the horses. His kindly face was wreathed in smiles and his hand extended in welcome.

'Lionel, my boy, I can't tell you how glad I am to see you. We've been expecting you since dinner, but I suppose you broke your journey to dine.' He stopped abruptly, staring at his young friend. 'How elegant you've become. You make me homesick for my own youth in Paris, but, my dear fellow, you seem to have been in some accident. I hope you were not attacked, and so close to Barrow, too. We have had our own share of trouble from highway robbers as the rest of the country.' His eyes suddenly took in the sight of his recalcitrant and appallingly dishevelled daughter, and his brows twitched together in a scowl.

'Corinna, what is this? Why are you in this state, and where is your brother?'

She took a hard breath. She loved this tall, fair-haired man who had always shown her the true affection of a parent, but she respected his anger too.

'I don't know where Julian is, Father. He—he was fishing in the river with Oliver and that friend of theirs from the university.' She looked down at her ruined gown. 'Clytie fell in and—couldn't get out. I was kneeling on the bank trying to help when Sir Lionel came to our rescue.'

Sir James looked down severely at the spaniel. 'I have told you times she should be on a lead until she learns to come to heel. It was fortunate Lionel was by—you might well have joined the dog—but ill fortune that his garments are spoiled before he sets foot beneath our roof. Go, prepare yourself for supper and take that fool dog with you. If she's been in the river she'll need bathing before she is allowed in the house again. See to it.'

He hooked his arm into Sir Lionel's and, without a second glance at Corinna, led his friend into the house.

Corinna delivered Clytie to Tom, one of the Websters' grooms, and hastened into the house and upstairs before she was seen by her mother. Joan gave a startled exclamation at sight of her, and Corinna impatiently waved aside the maid's complaints.

'Get me out of this and fetch warm water. I must hurry and change. Our guest has arrived.'

She made a hasty toilette and sat down before the small Italian travelling mirror her father had bought for her on his last visit to London while Joan attempted to bring some order to the tangled fair curls.

She scrutinised her features thoroughly. Did she, indeed, look like some country milkmaid? She had the colouring for it, certainly. Her hair was golden-fair, while her eyes, large and expressive, were blue, almost violet. Corinna considered such colouring insipid, though she had heard it was considered fashionable enough at court and among some of the less respectable ladies who thronged the Oxford streets and played on the susceptibilities of the youthful students. Julian had told her with relish that many of those ladies of his acquaintance lightened their hair with the application of cow's urine. When Corinna had shuddered at the notion he had told her gleefully that she should be thankful she had no need to resort to such tricks. Her features would be considered regular, she decided. Her brow was broad, her nose small and tolerably well shaped, but her chin was almost masculine in its tendency to jut aggressively forward, and she loathed the large single dimple that adorned it. Her complexion was creamy rather than milky-white and, again, she had to thank providence that it was so, for she had not the problem with freckles which would have kept her from the sun and air she loved so much. Still in her shirt, she allowed her gaze to travel the length of her body, as Sir Lionel's had done. She flushed at the thought of that appraisal. She had thought at first he was noting her state of dishabille but now she was not so sure. Was he seeing that, despite her advanced age of almost twenty years — her birthday was tomorrow — her breasts were still small and her form boyishly slender?

When Joan brought up the gown and underskirts she rose reluctantly. Her mother wore modish gowns when she travelled with Sir James to London, but largely, round the manor, she still kept to the plain, serviceable garments her puritanical upbringing had taught her were suitable for the wife of a country landowner, and, loving the freedom of the house, gardens and stables as she did, as well as her training in still-room and dairy, Corinna was contented with similar gowns. Lately her father had summoned seamstresses from nearby Leicester to make her more fashionable ones, presumably for this very visit, and with their arrival had come the disquieting thoughts that often now filled her head. She frowned at the sight of the bright blue silk draped over the maid's arm.

Joan had arranged her hair in its usual low knot on her crown, but brushed her forward locks into long ringlets to fall coquettishly on to her shoulders. Now Corinna stood docilely while Joan hooked her into the required underskirts, the final one of white silk adorned with ruffles. Over it went the overgown of sky-blue silk, the bodice caught at intervals to show the white silken vest beneath. The neckline was alarmingly low. Her aunt Tabitha would be scandalised, and Corinna wrenched at the lace trimming in an attempt to bring it further up over her small breasts. If she must wear such a gown to please her father, and their courtly guest, Corinna could only wish her slight figure did it more justice. The mirror told her the colour set off to perfection the blue of her eyes, though she would have liked darker lashes, not those gold-dusted ones Julian termed 'sandy'. Her eyebrows, though, were well shaped and marked.

'You would look better, mistress, if you relaxed that tight set of the lips,' Joan murmured with the plain-

spoken familiarity of the well trusted servant. 'Bite
them a bit. Gives them colour.'

Corinna sniffed. 'Anyone would think I was Father's
choicest heifer trimmed up for market.'

She glanced back at Joan's expressive face and lifted
her shoulders in a little shrug of acceptance. This was
what her father required of her. She had disappointed
him this afternoon. The least she could do was try to
please him now by her docile behaviour at supper.

'Thank you, Joan,' she said with genuine gratitude
for all the woman's pains. 'You go now and get your
own supper. I shall come down in a moment. If you
see Julian, tell him I shall not be amused by any
teasing — not tonight.'

Careful of her new finery, Corinna perched
uncomfortably on the edge of her chair and regarded
herself again. She looked very different from the girl
Sir Lionel had encountered on the riverbank. A sense
of panic welled up within her that she could not subdue.
Clearly she was expected to impress Lionel Summers,
and she feared he would make the proposal her parents
obviously hoped for. Yet she could not make any
objection before such a suggestion was made. Perhaps,
after this afternoon's incident, he would not wish to
make her his wife. If his way of life matched his looks,
he would want her to stay with him in London, possibly
waiting upon Their Majesties at court. The notion was
utterly repugnant to the countryside-loving Corinna.
She sighed. Her father would not wish her to be
unhappy. If she could not fulfil his desires and accept
Sir Lionel, he would understand. He must.

She rose and moved to the door. Supper would be
served with undue formality tonight, she was sure, and
she must not incur her father's continued displeasure
by arriving late in the dining-room.

CHAPTER TWO

LIONEL SUMMERS rode out early from Manor Court the next morning. Preparations for Corinna's birthday feast were occupying most of the family, and he had breakfasted alone. He supposed Lady Webster to be busied in the kitchens, overseeing Cook and the servants in the production of great quantities of food for the evening, and he was informed that Sir James and Master Julian were at the quarry, making sure work would be completed in time for the labourers to be dismissed early. All estate and quarry workers would take part in the festivities, so it was to be hoped that the fine weather would remain set fair for the feasting and dancing, much of which would take place out of doors.

The morning was fine and sunny with a faint haze, presaging intense heat later. Lionel left the village of Barrow-upon-Soar and headed for Mountsorrel, where the family slate quarry was situated. Sir James had begun quarrying in partnership with his brother-in-law, Saul Hunt, soon after his marriage, and the business had prospered, so much so that with the proceeds he had been able to repair and refurbish Manor Court, badly damaged by Roundhead soldiers during the Civil War. Lionel envied his friend such a continuing source of wealth, but was aware that it provided Sir James with the income sufficient to offer a substantial dowry with the hand of his daughter, Corinna.

Lionel's lips curled slightly at thought of that. He could not deny that Corinna's dowry would be welcome, yet even without it he would have been willing enough to offer for her. On his last visit he had been struck by her vibrant personality and the promise of great beauty with the coming of mature womanhood. His mother had been faintly shocked by the licence afforded the girl to roam freely over the manor lands with her cousin and Julian, though she had forborne to comment on the matter to Lady Webster. Lionel sensed a streak of stubborn wildness in the golden-haired girl which did not entirely displease him. He admired her spirit, especially so now that he had come recently into contact with the insipid, spoiled beauties of the French and English courts.

If Lionel had had any doubts they would have been dispelled when he had seen Corinna sweep into the dining-room last night. In her elegant gown she was totally transformed from the sharp-tongued hoyden he had met by the river. Prompted by her mother, she had played the virginals and sung for him in a soft contralto following the meal, and her manners were impeccable. Clytie, the spaniel, freshly bathed, had insinuated herself into the dining-room, despite Sir James's wrath, and immediately sprung on to her rescuer's knee. Lionel had stroked the silky creature, aware that Corinna was mollified by his apparent acceptance of the little dog's place in her heart. This morning there had been no sign of Corinna at the table. Lionel assumed she was helping her mother in the kitchen or dairy. That, too, pleased him, as evidence of her competence to run his Yorkshire manor as he wished. His mother would have no objection to Corinna assuming command of the household. Lady Summers much preferred life at their town house to a rustic existence in the Dales.

After supper last night, when the women had left

them to their port to retire to the withdrawing-room, Sir James had given a silent signal to his son. Julian had rise at once, murmuring some excuse to visit the stable, and Sir James and Lionel had been alone together.

'Lionel, I would like to know now if it is your intention to offer formally for my daughter,' Sir James asked as he passed the port decanter to his young friend.

Lionel poured himself more wine and leaned back comfortably in his chair.

'Yes, sir. Nothing would please me more than possessing Corinna as my wife.'

Sir James moved a little uneasily. 'She has been excellently trained in housewifely skills. My wife has seen to that. And you will find her intelligent.' He hesitated. 'Possibly too intelligent.'

Lionel smiled faintly. 'You mean she is too high-spirited to accept lightly a husband's domination?'

Sir James cleared his throat a trifle nervously. 'Corinna is a good lass. It is true she has had rather more of her own way than is perhaps good for her and it might have been better had she been wed younger. . .' His voice trailed off awkwardly. 'I think your father made you aware of the unusual circumstances of Corinna's birth.'

'I understand that her mother was unwed.'

'Aye. Corinna believes that her mother gave birth to her during the plague summer, which she did, but that she died soon after.'

'Then Corinna's mother still lives?'

'Aye. Several lives would be ruined if the full truth of that were to come out, so we thought it best to allow Corinna to believe she is orphaned. Also we did not consider it needful to disabuse her of the notion that her true mother was a widow.'

Lionel nodded.

'You can be sure, my boy, there could be no bar to the marriage. Corinna is bred from healthy and honourable stock. If it is your wish to question ——'

'No, no, sir. I am perfectly satisfied. Better not to probe too closely into these affairs. What I have seen of your daughter well assures me she will make an excellent mistress of my Yorkshire manor. Two years ago, when we visited, I was greatly stricken with her loveliness, and I saw only tonight how much she has matured.'

He paused, tilting the ruby liquid in his glass to catch the light from the oriel window. 'Have you any indication that her affections might be — otherwise engaged?'

Sir James looked startled. 'Corinna? Nay, lad, what other man in the neighbourhood could be suitable? And, for obvious reasons, we have not presented her in London society. I have always believed — well, hoped — that the arrangement concerning you both, made by your father and me, would be honoured, but I would not have you offer for Corinna if your own heart is given to another. . .'

Again Lionel smiled faintly. 'You need have no fears on that score, Sir James. While I have not lived as a monk, I have always considered myself promised to Mistress Corinna, and you can be sure I would never insult her by flaunting my affairs publicly.' His golden-hazel eyes grew wistful. 'I can only hope that Corinna will agree to accept me, for her beauty has quite dazzled me.'

'Oh, she will accept you. I shall inform her of her duty. I had thought it convenient to announce the betrothal formally while the county gentry are assembled for the festivities tomorrow.'

'I had assumed that to be the case, but would you allow me to approach Mistress Corinna before any command of yours might prejudice her against me?'

Sir James looked thoughtful. 'If that is your wish. Corinna must be aware of our intentions, or, at least, the idea must be at the forefront of her mind. We have made it clear to her that she was to do her upmost to impress you.' He frowned. 'I fear she has had much freedom, no other young girl of her own age as a companion, and I think she is closer to her brother and cousin than most young girls of her age. She loves Manor Court. At first she will find it a wrench to leave Leicestershire. She has never been one to pine for life at court or even town society. It will be for you to give her time to adjust. Once the betrothal is announced I shall take her to London, and, over the next month or two, you will have more opportunity to become fully acquainted before the wedding. I had thought here, at Barrow, possibly in the autumn?'

Lionel stretched one leg comfortably over the other, absently pulling Clytie's ears as she sat very close to him. 'That would seem an admirable arrangement.'

In a mood of amiable agreement the men had joined the ladies. Once or twice during the course of the evening's chat Lionel had been conscious of Corinna's curious gaze upon him, hurriedly averted when he happened to look her way.

Now, as he rode, he was considering the best way to put his suit to her. She was nobody's fool and would not take kindly to the empty flattery and flirtatious conversation enjoyed by many ladies of his acquaintance. He was aware that he was burning with desire for her, but he wanted her to accept him willingly, not out of necessity forced upon her by her father's wishes or the conventions of county society.

His horse mounted a rise near the village of Mountsorrel. He drew rein, noting the ruins of Fitzparnel's castle, which had once dominated the surrounding countryside, a reminder of times when civil war was rife and barons found it imperative to build fortresses to guard their property. He sighed, thinking of the stories of civil strife recounted by his own father, with the knowledge that such a state of affairs could once more engulf the land if young James Scott, Duke of Monmouth, challenged his uncle for the throne. Speculation had been rife in the capital, and Argyll's landing in Scotland had been commented on with growing pessimism for the peace of the realm.

He leaned forward over his horse's withers, listening to the sound of trundling wheels and hammer blows which told him he was now not far from the slate quarry. Before him stretched an area of lush pastureland bounded by a small copse. In the distance lay the woodlands of Swithland and Woodhouse.

A sudden flurry of movement below him seized his attention. Two riders burst into view, riding full gallop, obviously making for the cover of the small copse. The woman rode fearlessly ahead. Her linen cap had slipped back, and Lionel's eyes narrowed as he recognised that glorious mane of golden hair. Corinna, then, was not occupied, as he believed, in the kitchens of Manor Court. Lionel was near enough to know that it was not her brother who laughingly pursued. Her companion was young, broad-shouldered, brown-haired, more than likely her cousin, Oliver Hunt. Lionel remembered him well from his other visits to Leicestershire.

The two drew up just outside the copse and secured

the reins of their mounts to low branches of saplings
before running into the shelter of the trees hand in
hand. Lionel's fingers tightened on his horse's mane,
and the chestnut turned his head and sidled nervously.

Was Lady Webster aware of her daughter's presence
here, unescorted? Likely enough, as a child Corinna
had been used to the company of her cousin, but she
had outgrown that state, and Lionel's thoughts were
murderously inclined towards the easygoing young
country squire he had known. Their whole attitude
bespoke pleasure in each other's company, and they
had made instinctively for the hidden depths of the
copse. Sir James had avowed that Corinna had no
other suitors, but had he realised that his nephew might
pose a threat to his hopes?

Lionel remained where he was for some time, his
attention focused on the line of dark trees, then
abruptly he turned his mount and made for Manor
Court again.

Corinna sat, leaning back against the trunk of a felled
elm. Oliver was sprawled on the grass beside her, his
head resting on her knee. She was pulling viciously at
the grass tussock near her, and Oliver sat abruptly, his
brows twitching into a puzzled frown.

'What is it, Coz? You seemed to have suddenly lost
all pleasure in the day. Was your father very angry
about that business with Clytie and Sir Lionel? Jules
told me about it last night.'

She shook her head, but her gaze was abstracted and
her mouth held in a tight line.

'Jules says the fellow has become quite the court fop.
He wondered how he had come by the gold to embel-
lish himself so grandly. We understood the Summerses'
fortune had been at a low ebb since Naseby.'

'What?' Corinna turned back to him, surprised, and he realised she had not been listening. Obviously she was disturbed, yet she had ridden over to Glebe in good spirits, delighted at her own achievement of having evaded her mother's vigilance when she should have been busy about the house in preparation for the evening's feasting. 'Oh.'

Clearly she had half heard him, for she added, 'I imagine he must have been given a grant by the King. Father said Charles had promised reparations freely, yet rarely got round to making those promises good. Possibly King James has proved more generous than his brother. He must know he needs all the friends at court he can get just now.'

'Indeed.' Oliver's tone was hard, quite unlike his usual genial speech. 'Soon it will become even more clear to His Majesty that his subjects are opposed to the religious changes he is determined to bring out.'

Corinna's eyes darkened in concern. 'You are talking of armed insurrection, Oliver. That must not be.'

'On the contrary. We must rid ourself of this usurper. King Monmouth will see to it that our rights are upheld.'

'Oliver, you cannot be serious. James Scott has no more right to the throne than any of the other numerous bastards Charles sired. The idea might be unpalatable, but King James is the Lord's appointed.'

Oliver's youthful, comely features hardened into stubbornness, and Corinna sighed. She had heard much talk about the mysterious black box which Monmouth's supporters avowed contained documents proving the late King's wedding vows with his mistress, Lucy Walters, but her father had laughed such notions to scorn. Charles's affairs with Lucy Walters had been a youthful indiscretion, but the late King, even as a young prince, had never behaved in a manner which might later prejudice his restoration to the English throne. She understood Oliver's need to believe in Monmouth's claim. Monmouth was Protestant, and the Hunts' fierce loyalty to the Puritan cause would necessitate an allegiance to one of a like conviction. Yet she was deeply concerned. Oliver had never before expressed himself so recklessly. She feared for his safety.

'You are speaking open treason,' she whispered, shocked.

He was looking at her intently now, his brown eyes pleading for her understanding.

'I have to do what I consider honourable. Do you censure me for that, Corin?'

Her own eyes were troubled as, again, she shook her head.

'No, of course I could not, but I fear for you, Oliver. Bart Spicer has persuaded you into some rash commitment which could bring you to your death.'

'You are too quick to blame Bart. Do you think I am not capable of making my own decisions? Do you think that of Jules, too?'

Her cheeks paled and she sat very still. 'Julian is involved? Dear God, Oliver, what are you all about? Don't you realise how you not only risk your own lives but ruin your families as well? How would we be able to go on living if anything happened to any of you?'

'Then you would care — if I were not to come back?'

'Oliver, you are frightening me. Argyll has landed in Scotland. The danger of civil war is miles from here. We must. . .'

He did not answer, and she broke off to lean closer. 'You have had some news. . .' Her whisper sounded chill with the suddenness of her fear.

'When we return to Oxford we shall hold ourselves in readiness for news of Monmouth's landing. It will be in the south. The men of the south and west are with him to a man. The towns there have suffered the most since the restoration. West countrymen have seen their charters withheld, their boroughs heavily fined for their allegiance to Parliament. It will be there that the Duke will find his most loyal subjects.'

'This is some foolish student activity. . .'

'No, Corinna, it is not. In fact few of our fellow students hold our views, and even if they did they would not be prepared to take up arms to uphold them. Father says he thinks our young men have been brought up soft. Their parents have told them of the misfortunes of war, and many of them prefer to remain in the comfort of their own homes rather than fight for religious freedom. Let them. It will be those of us who are prepared to fight and die for the Cause who will bask in the glory when our King James of Monmouth is crowned.'

Corinna was fully alarmed now, her mouth dry with apprehension.

'Oliver, the King is no longer a young man. His eldest daughter, Mary, is wed to Prince William of Orange, a truly Protestant prince. All will be well when she inherits the throne.'

'But the Queen is young enough to conceive a son. What if we are saddled with a Catholic heir? Where would our religious freedoms be then?'

As she made no answer he stood up suddenly and put out his hand to help her rise.

'You will not say any of this to Uncle James, not even about Jules?' he added soberly. 'They will all know of it soon enough.'

She gave a little premonitory shiver. Indeed they would.

'No,' she said quietly, 'I will not betray you; you can be sure of that. But Oliver, my dear, come back to us very soon. We love you all so much.'

He bent and cupped her chin in his palm. 'Corin?' His voice was a little hoarse, strange sounding. 'Corin, I love you. Do you know how much? These last few months I have come to see you quite differently. We have always been friends, companions in disaster some-times, but now — now that this Summers fellow has come to Manor Court — I fear I shall lose you.'

His hands had dropped to his sides again, and she was free to move away from him, but she did not.

'Oliver,' she breathed, 'if you only knew how I have waited for you to say that.' Her eyes looked into his troubled ones appealingly, and he made a little muffled sound and gathered her into his arms.

She had been longing for this, to feel safe, secure, close to him, feeling the steady beat of his heart against her own. His kiss was hard, and she answered him fiercely. This was her own cousin, Oliver, whom she had always loved, but she had been conscious of this depth of feeling for so short a time. Something had been missing from their relationship, she knew that, knew now her abiding love was answered, and she gloried in the knowledge that he shared her desire. She gave a sigh of submission, her arms stealing to his shoulders, drawing him ever closer.

Suddenly he stiffened and gently put her from him.

'We must be very careful now, my love,' he mur-mured thickly. 'If we stay here like this I shall not be able to prevent myself from taking you here on the grass, and I cannot leave you in danger of any shame an act of mine could bring you. Let us be practical, my love, and realise that I might not always be with you to protect you.'

She gave a great sob of panic.

'Oliver, you must not go into this foolishness, not now when we understand at last our need for each other.'

'Corin, if you love me, you will understand why I must go, why every honest man who thinks as I do must join Monmouth.'

Her blue eyes sparkled with tears, and her heart was pounding with suppressed fear and anger at his determination to leave her, but his gaze was steady, appealing for her trust and understanding, and she gave a little cry of frustration.

'Then I must wait — patiently, however fearfully — and pray, pray every day that the stern God you worship will send you safely back to me.'

'That's my brave girl.' He bent and claimed her lips again, but more gently now. The rigidity of his body pose told her how firmly he was keeping himself in check. 'Now what of Lionel Summers? Do you think he will offer for you — today? What can be done? Is your father determined to make this match? I cannot make you my lady, nor have I any standing at court, nor yet am like to have, even if King Monmouth should come into his own. I am stout yeoman stock, Corin, no lordling. Yet I shall inherit Glebe and the half-share in the Mountsorrel quarry. You would want for nothing as my bride. Will your father accept me as I am?'

'He *will* do for my sake,' she said stoutly. 'We are not such close kin. Even had we been truly cousins there would have been no bar to the marriage. He loves me very much. When I tell him, make him understand how I love you, he will give up this ambition to make me Lady Summers. His heart has been set on it since my babyhood, but there has been no formal betrothal. The arrangement can be put aside. As for Lionel, I think perhaps he will be a trifle relieved that he will not take a country hoyden as bride. Such a handsome courtier should choose one of the elegant ladies of St James's court for his bedmate.'

'Then I must speak to your father this morning. The matter is urgent. He will seek to announce your betrothal at the feasting tonight —— '

She put her hand gently against his mouth to stem his words. 'No, this you must leave to me, Oliver. Only feminine wiles can win this contest. My father will put forward cogent reasons for my marriage with Lionel Summers. He must understand how deeply I love you, and you alone. Only I can make him see that. Trust me.'

'Then it must be very soon. We should go back immediately. When can I see you again and know you have succeeded?'

'I'll give you some signal before the feasting, and as soon as possible we must slip away from the guests for a few precious moments.'

He put one hand on her arm. 'Will your father be brought to announce our betrothal instead?'

She gave a little frown of concern. 'I think not. He must not know that you are going into danger, and he will insist that I truly know my own mind. He will make us wait, I think, and there will be your parents to convince. I am by no means sure your mother will wish to accept me.'

He said sharply, 'Why do you say that?'

Corinna gave a nervous laugh. 'She thinks me too frivolous for a true Puritan wife, but wait, I shall be very demure and circumspect. I will make her love me.'

He drew her to him hungrily. 'I care nothing for any of them. We love each other. That is all that matters, my heart. We'll make them see it in the end.'

She drew away from him at last, saying quickly, 'We must get back to Barrow. Now, more than ever, I must try to avoid a confrontation with my parents.'

He nodded, though reluctantly, and, hand in hand, they walked back to the horses.

Corinna was flushed and excited when she rode into the courtyard of Manor Court. Looking hurriedly round for a groom, she was surprised and not a little displeased when Sir Lionel Summers came to lift her down.

'Thank you.' She was somewhat breathless. 'I stole away for an hour. I should not have left my mother with all the work. Is she still in the kitchens, do you know, sir?'

He shook his head. 'I cannot say, Mistress Corinna. I have only this moment ridden in myself.'

'Oh, I see.' She sounded flustered as he continued to hold on to her wrist. 'I'm afraid we have all been remiss in our attentions to you. We do not usually treat guests so, but, as you can see, all is in confusion before the feast tonight.'

He bowed gravely. 'I understand perfectly, Mistress Corinna, but I beg a moment or two of your time now. Your mother spoke of the beauty of the gardens at this time of year. Shall we go there?'

The last thing Corinna wanted was to accompany a possible suitor to the gardens. She needed to escape to her own chamber, where she could think over the events of the morning in privacy. She felt somewhat dishevelled, and wondered if her cheeks revealed the inward glow of exultation she was feeling. Although she had spoken confidently to Oliver concerning her

father's reaction to her proposed announcement, she
was by no means so sure that he would accede to her
wishes so tamely. She must consider very carefully how
to put forward such a momentous revelation. Her
father *liked* Oliver, but was he convinced of his suitability as her future husband?

Corinna's teeth bit down on her bottom lip as she
turned to regard Lionel.

'I regret, sir, that I cannot oblige her. I really must
go to my chamber and change my dress, then go in
search of my mother.'

His grip on her wrist did not slacken, and Corinna
was astonished, almost alarmed, to see a strange golden
glitter to his hazel eyes.

'I think you will discover that your mother would
prefer you to accompany me, mistress,' he said pleasantly, but there was a touch of cold steel in the even
tone.

It would have been discourteous to pull away from
him in full view of the two grooms occupied with
cleaning harness near the stable door, even impossible,
for Corinna thought he had no intention of releasing
her without an embarrassing struggle. She gave a little
sigh, hastily suppressed out of a sense of politeness,
watching helplessly while her mount was led away,
then she smiled up at Sir Lionel, despite a growing
sense of hostility.

He stood back at last, allowing her to lead the way
to her mother's favourite pleasaunce. The sun was
intense now, and the two made for the shaded arbour
in the rose garden. Corinna walked slightly ahead, her
riding crop swishing nervously against her skirts. She
had a horror of being trapped with this man, yet she
had nothing to fear. Her own servants were in earshot;
she had only to call. Yet she knew she would not,

whatever took place here. Her father would be furious if his guest was insulted. She swallowed back her foolish feeling of panic and turned to face him as he stood in the arbour entrance, one hand reaching up to the door lintel.

'This is more pleasant. I became overheated on my ride.' He was looking at her steadily, and she found it hard to tear her gaze away.

'Yes.' Her tongue tip touched her upper lip fleetingly. 'It is almost too hot to ride. Where did you go?'

'Just to the quarry and back.'

She started and looked down guiltily at the riding crop. Was it possible that she and Oliver could have been observed? Surely not. There had been no sound in the wood to betray any eavesdropper.

'Then you saw my father and Julian?'

'No, I thought it best to avoid hindering Sir James in his work. I know he intended to leave early.'

'Yes, of course.' As he continued to smile at her encouragingly she sank down on the rustic bench. 'Today is no day for business.'

'No, indeed, Mistress Corinna, only one of rejoicing. I have not formally offered my congratulations on your achieving your twentieth year. I had expected to see you earlier.'

If there was a hidden reproach in that last statement she offered no excuse, merely forced a smile of acceptance.

'However, now that we are alone together I beg leave to proffer my gift.'

She fumbled her riding crop clumsily and dropped it to the ground at her feet as he placed the small leather casket between her hands. She could not be under any misapprehension as to its contents. Such a box could only contain jewels, and no man would offer such a gift unless it were to the woman he expected to make his bride. She stared down at it stupidly while her mind raced to find some way of escape from the next few agonising moments.

As if from a distance she heard his words.

'I came to Manor Court to offer formally for your hand. Naturally I have your father's permission to speak with you; indeed, I am fortunate that he favours the match. If you will accept me, Mistress Corinna, the betrothal can be announced at the feast tonight. The casket contains some of the family jewels and, in particular, a necklet of pearls and sapphires I had fashioned for you in France, though no sapphires can rival the blue of your eyes.'

It was a formal speech, extravagant, one she might have expected from him. The court ladies he knew so well would have approved such honeyed flattery. Corinna was only bemused and dismayed that this should have happened before she had had a chance to speak with her father.

Desperately she sought for something to say which would not wound Sir Lionel.

'Please,' she said lamely. 'I. . .I had not expected to—I need to find my father. I regret, sir, that I cannot give you the answer you wish for. I——'

The golden eyes flashed with fury, and he advanced into the arbour, caught her by the wrist again, and pulled her to her feet. The casket fell, disgorging a glittering array of gems and gold into the grass.

'How can you say you were not expecting my proposal? You must know that it was for this reason I came to Manor Court.'

'Nothing has been said. I. . .' She jerked at her imprisoned wrist angrily. 'You are frightening me, sir.

Please release me. My father would not approve such conduct.'

'He would not approve of your secret meeting with your rustic lover in the wood either. I wager *he* did not frighten you, mistress,' he said harshly, and, before she could prevent him, he had caught her into a fierce embrace. Her breasts were locked hard against the fine wool of his riding coat and she could feel his heart racing. She struggled ineffectually to free herself, but his grip tightened. To her horror his lips pressed hard down on hers. forcing hers apart. She found herself almost unable to breathe. His being sought to possess hers utterly, and she thought she would faint under the frightening intensity of his ardour.

He murmured thickly, 'You are mine, Corinna, have been promised to me from the beginning. Last year, when I saw you had become a woman, I could hardly force myself to wait before declaring myself. Yet there were reasons, pressing reasons, why it had to be so. Your father approves the match. I will allow nothing to come between us. Understand that.' He gave her a little shake and set her at arm's length until she was gazing into his blazing eyes. 'You can forget this youthful lover of yours. I shall marry you, take you to court, then to my manor in Yorkshire, where you will prove an excellent châtelaine. It is all decided. You can fight against it however you wish, but you will see that it shall be as I say.'

With the added strength given her by her violent reaction to his arrogant and insulting words she tore herself from his grasp.

'How dare you treat me so?' she hissed. 'Shame on you, a knight of the realm, that you dare to lay discourteous hands on me. My father trusted you.'

He gave a little yelped laugh. 'Oh, I would have

treated you more courteously, mistress, had I thought
you the innocent maiden you appear, but, you see, I
saw you enter the wood with your lover, waited for
some time for you to emerge. Do you think I wasn't
aware of what was taking place there?'

She gave a great gasp of astonished fury.

'You dare to suggest that I and—and Oliver—that
we. . .?'

'Do not take me for a fool, mistress. You sneak off
from the manor without your mother's consent. You
ride alone with a man, enter a sheltered place. What
am I to believe? However, as I have said, it is of no
moment. I want you. I've wanted you since I saw you
last year. I have thought of nothing else over these last
months but possessing you. Now I shall take what I
want, and I shall not need to be so gentle and patient.'

Her hand caught him full across his sneering mouth
and, taken by surprise, he fell back apace, putting up a
hand to his smarting cheek.

'If my father or my brother were to know of this they
would demand satisfaction,' she said icily. 'Since I have
no wish to see blood spilt, not even yours, Sir Lionel, I
will keep silent on the matter and try to forget that you
offered me deadly insult. Now stand aside. I shall
inform my father that I have rejected your proposal. It
will disappoint him, but he will accept my decision. I
trust you will not approach me again today and will
take your departure early in the morning. I hope never
to see you again.'

He had recovered himself and was blocking her
escape from the arbour. 'I am not disappointed. I knew
you had spirit, had no wish for some tame little country
milkmaid. You will grace my house well, my lady.'

'I shall never be your lady, be very sure of that.'

His long lips parted in a smile of pure sweetness. 'I

do not give up what is mine. Remember that, Corinna Webster.'

'I am not yours,' she snapped. 'Am I a heifer at market to be sold without my consent? You are contemptible, sir. You know I love another, and should do the honourable thing and withdraw with dignity.'

'When you are truly mine I shall teach you what love is,' he said softly, and she deliberately turned her head from him as he moved closer once more, but this time he made no attempt to take her into his arms again, but stood aside with a mocking bow.

'Very well, Mistress Corinna. If wait I must, I will do so, but not for long. That genial young country lad is not for you. Soon you will know it.'

Her eyes were so blurred with tears that she could hardly see her way as she rushed blindly from the arbour, anywhere, so that she might be out of his hateful presence.

Once in the courtyard, she slackened in her wild rush lest the grooms or serving maids see her and gossip of her distress. Now she must seek the sanctuary of her chamber. Her tears could have full rein there and she would have time to master herself before going in search of her father.

CHAPTER THREE

IN HER chamber Corinna stripped off her riding dress,
flinging her riding crop across the room with such force
that it dislodged a favourite pottery box from her
dressing chest and smashed it to smithereens. The
maids were all occupied and she could not summon
one to help her with her riding boots, so she struggled
for some time until she stood staring at herself in her
shift, hair dishevelled and cascading down her back.
She had not realised that she was still crying quietly,
and her face was marred with ugly rivulets of dust-
stained tears. She gave a sharp exclamation of revulsion
and turned from her travelling mirror in disgust, her
fingers clenching into tight fists.

How dared the man? To force her to accompany him
to the arbour! For she had been constrained. The
presence of grooms in the courtyard had made it
impossible to refuse him. Her father had placed her in
this impossible position. Had he spoken of his intention
to allow the man formally to offer marriage earlier, she
could have forestalled him. Of course Oliver had not
declared himself then, but she could have pleaded for
time. It had been unfortunate that Lionel Summers
had seen her ride into the copse with Oliver, but to
believe that. . . Tears threatened to choke her. She
must regain control of her feelings. It would be disastrous if her father or mother saw her in this state, and
she could not reveal what had taken place between
herself and Lionel Summers. It was as she had said.
Either Sir James or Julian would feel it necessary to

defend her honour, and she could not place either man in danger. And if Oliver should hear of the encounter. . . She shuddered at the thought of his reaction. He was foolishly impulsive and would undoubtedly challenge his rival without stopping to discover if Lionel Summers was a superior swordsman. The man appeared a fop, certainly, but he had lived in France, had probably taken lessons from the noted swordsmen there. No, she could not risk Oliver's life. Lionel Summers' deadly insult to her honour must remain unpunished.

Impatiently Corinna turned to her water ewer to remove the revealing marks of her distress. She must change into a fresh gown, a simple one not requiring a maid's assistance with the lacing, and join her mother below stairs.

She had removed the worst of the ravages when one of the younger maids scratched upon the door and, without waiting for her call to enter, pushed her way nervously just inside the chamber. The girl had been dispatched hastily from the kitchen, for her face was red and shiny with sweat, and she had run upstairs in such haste that she could hardly summon breath enough to explain her errand.

'Mistress,' she managed to gasp out at last, 'Sir James is in the library with my lady and they say you are to go down to them at once, to stop whatever you be doing, that is.'

The girl's eyes were huge with avid curiosity, and Corinna swung round on her in sudden alarm.

Dear God, had Lionel Summers already reported her refusal to accept him? The command from her father was couched in so aribtrary a fashion that it seemed as if something of the friction between them had been discovered. She managed a reassuring smile to the frightened girl.

'Very well. I shall be down instantly. The library, you say?'

The maid nodded emphatically.

'Was anyone else with my parents?'

Again the gooseberry-round eyes widened in astonishment.

'No, no, mistress.' The girl hesitated, then said doubtfully, 'I reckon it be a family matter, mistress, and — and Sir James seemed mightily upset.'

Again Corinna smiled at the girl's warning, nodded her thanks, and waited while she scuttled below stairs.

Once more Corinna surveyed herself in her fine Italian mirror. She could still detect lines of strain round her eyes, but the tears were gone. She drew a hard breath of trepidation and turned to follow the maid below stairs.

'Well, Corinna,' her father barked as she entered the library, 'what is this nonsense of refusing Sir Lionel Summers out of hand? Foolish wench, you could at least have consulted me without giving your decision.'

He was in his riding clothes. The dust of the quarry still lay powdered on his coat.

Corinna threw back her head and said defiantly, 'So he has come complaining to you?'

'Watch your insolent tongue, my girl.' Sir James's eyes, as blue as Corinna's own, became flinty. 'I told you of the need to make a good impression on young Summers. Of course he made no complaint. I encountered him as I rode in and, knowing his intentions, asked him to tell me how he fared. He told me — reluctantly, I add — you had rejected him summarily. Understand this, Corinna. It is our wish that you wed Lionel Summers, and I will not be flouted.'

Corinna's knees felt weak and she longed to sit down, but stiffened her spine and faced them out, while turning appealingly to her mother for support.

Her mouth was dry, but she spoke clearly, none the less. 'Father, you gave me no outright command. I understood I had the right to answer as I pleased.'

'Lionel insisted on speaking to you before I made my wishes plain but, had you had the sense to play the unsuspecting maid and tell him you would consider, we could have dealt with this sensibly.'

Lady Webster said mildly, 'What is your objection to the match, Corinna? Sir Lionel is young and comely, and you are not strangers.'

Corinna gritted her teeth and said softly, 'I'll not wed him.'

'What?' Her father advanced on her, one hand upraised as if to strike, until Lady Webster interposed herself between them. He brushed her aside impatiently, but mastered his rage and his arm returned to his side; yet, for all that, he was having trouble in keeping himself under control.

'Now see here, my girl, you have had your own way too much. Other girls accept what their fathers decide. Am I faced now with an ingrate, a disobedient child? I have made a good marriage for you and, by God, you will abide by my wishes.'

Corinna steeled herself to face his further anger and said quietly, 'I will not marry Lionel Summers.' Her eyes filled with sudden tears. 'Father, you must listen to me. I cannot love him. I love Oliver. He has asked me to be his wife. I know he is young and impulsive and cannot make me my lady, but he is steadying down now he is at Oxford, and will inherit Glebe and. . .' Her words were coming out in a fast gabble, and she moved imploringly towards him. 'Please say you will consider the match, speak with Uncle Saul for us——'

He caught her by the shoulders and shook her until her teeth rattled. 'Oliver Hunt? When were there words of love between you? What has happened? Dear God in heaven, tell me.'

He released her and she stumbled awkwardly, so that Lady Webster came forward to support her, one arm defensively around Corinna's shoulder.

Corinna was frightened now and weeping copiously. 'There has been nothing wrong between us. We went into the wood near Mountsorrel, as we have done many times. We talked and. . .'

'And?' he demanded.

'He. . .he kissed me. I love him, Father. What difference can it make if we wed? I know you are disappointed, but——'

'You cannot marry Oliver Hunt. It's out of the question. He is your brother.'

The words were torn from him without thought and, for the moment, did not register on Corinna's consciousness. She stood quite numb, then turned, appalled, to face her mother.

'James,' Lady Webster said warningly, 'you promised you would leave this matter to me. Now what have we done?' She gathered Corinna close and led her gently to a chair, taking the girl's trembling hands within her own. 'Child, what you have told us is true? There has been no lovemaking between you and Oliver?'

Corinna shook her head. She was totally bemused and stricken. What they were saying to her was not true. It *couldn't* be true. It was a ruse, surely, to compel her to marry Lionel Summers, and she would resist it with all her might.

'I. . .I don't understand. It cannot be so; tell me it isn't.'

Lady Webster turned away, her own eyes brimming with sympathetic tears. 'Corinna, I wish I could tell you that. We hoped you would never have to know.' She was kneeling by Corinna's chair, and turned to look up at her husband. 'James, leave us alone together, please.'

He was already regretting the hastily spoken revelation and was about to resort to bluster, then, meeting his wife's eyes, blew out a sharp breath and nodded.

'Aye, very well, make her see sense.' He looked at Corinna shamefacedly. 'I'm sorry, lass. Your defiance brought out the worst in me, but you have to face facts now. Tabitha Hunt is your mother, and you must put all thought of marriage with Oliver out of your mind. Listen to your mother. I'll—I'll see you later.'

Lady Webster rose and went with him to the door. They murmured together in low tones, then he left and she returned to Corinna.

There were no tears. Corinna was too stunned. Even now she could not take it in, this terrible thing they were telling her. She gave a little intake of breath and reached blindly out towards Lady Webster, who gathered her into a close embrace.

Corinna broke down then and, at last, Lady Webster drew away slightly and cupped Corinna's face between her two hands.

'Oh, my dear,' she said shakily, 'one thing you must believe in all this is that we love you so very dearly and all was done to protect you.'

Corinna swallowed hard and gave a little tremulous nod of her head.

'Tell me,' she whispered huskily. 'Tell me everything.'

Lady Webster drew her back to the chair, but Corinna indicated that her mother must sit in it, then she drew out a little footstool and seated herself very close.

Lady Webster sat looking intently at Corinna's stricken face, then took one cold hand firmly within her grasp.

'You are saying that my true mother is — is Aunt Tabby?'

'Yes.'

'But Grandmama always said it was her friend, Lettice Graham. Did — did Mistress Graham not exist?'

'Yes, she did and, as you were told, she died of the plague. She was the dowager Lady Webster's goddaughter and had lost her own child of the sickness. She would have taken you and brought you up as her own, but — ' Lady Webster drew a shaky breath ' — she took sick herself and succumbed. You — you cannot imagine how terrible those weeks were in that abandoned, plague-stricken city. There were times when I thought none of us would survive.'

Corinna's eyes were huge and luminous, and Lady Webster squeezed her hand again and continued.

'Tabby was so very young; you must not censure her too harshly. When she discovered she was with child she was terrified. Your grandfather was like Saul Hunt, a hard, Puritanical man to be obeyed without question, and he held the strictest moral views. She was terrified and turned to me for help.'

Corinna said softly, 'I — I always suspected that my father — ' she gave a little gulp of despair ' — Sir James was my true father. I — I am very like him.'

Lady Webster shook her head. 'You are Ned Webster's daughter, Corinna. You will remember

when he came here last—you must have been about
five or six then—he took so great an interest in you.'

'Uncle Ned?' Corinna murmured wonderingly. 'Yes,
it was strange he seemed to want always to be with me.
He brought me that beautiful gown as well as the
painted doll from France dressed in the height of
fashion. I wondered that he did not prefer to be more
with Jules, though he was generous with both of us.
Then I am Sir James's niece and yours?'

'The Websters came to Manor Court in the autumn
of 1664. The place was in ruins. Your grandfather, my
father, had had some hand in that. He had been a
colonel in Cromwell's model army. For years after the
King came back from exile we feared retribution. Then
James and Edward Webster came to the village.' She
gave a little shaky laugh. 'They were so very handsome
and grand. Barrow had not seen anything like them for
years. Of course their finery was very faded and
shabby, but, to Tabby, Ned Webster was like a young
god. He wore his hair curling to his shoulders—they
both did—and she had always secretly longed to wear
the scarlet and blue colours they flaunted in church.
When those two walked down the aisle to the family
pew they held all eyes. Ned Webster couldn't take his
from Tabby. She was sixteen and so pretty, even in her
sober black gown. Despite our father's vigilance they
somehow managed to meet and—the inevitable
happened.'

'But what of you? How—how did you come to wed
Sir James?'

Dorcas Webster's expression softened and she gave
a little secret smile. 'I shall never forget my first sight
of him riding in the village, his golden Cavalier locks
and fashionable moustache. Of course I thought such
splendour ungodly. Astonishingly he came to ask for

my hand. I had quite a large dowry and he needed gold urgently for the rebuilding of Manor Court.'

'And Grandfather agreed?'

'To my amazement, he did. He knew things were changing all around us and—he had been too close to Cromwell to rest easy on his land. He realised safety for all of us lay in accepting Sir James's offer, and he made it clear to me where my duty lay. I was a dutiful daughter and wed where I was bid. I was not to know how deeply I was to come to love my husband.' She stopped and looked meaningfully at Corinna, but the girl closed her lips tightly and abruptly turned her head aside.

'I was already wed when Tabby confided in me. I begged Father to allow me to take Tabby with me to London, for James wished to present me at court. She was already betrothed to Saul Hunt. We thought she might bear the child there in secret and we would find some respectable family who could be persuaded to rear it.'

'But I don't understand. Was Ned Webster married?'

'No, your uncle—your father—never married.'

'Then why. . .?'

'He went away to sea. The Dutch wars were in progress and we believed him lost. He was held in a Dutch prison for months.'

Corinna gave a little sigh. She could see now how it had been, a naïve, pretty girl, panic-stricken in that sickness-ridden city, giving birth in such terrible conditions. She had never understood her aunt, had always felt that she disapproved of her wilful young niece. Now Corinna realised Tabitha Hunt had never dared to allow herself to show her child affection.

'So Saul Hunt never knew.'

'He must not know, Corinna. It would ruin your

aunt Tabitha's life. He is a hard man, a good man, but with rigid principles. He would never forgive her, or let her forget her shame, and—Oliver must not know it either.'

Corinna's lip trembled, and her blue eyes filled with tears.

'But he must be told—how can I let him believe I do not love him, cannot marry him?'

'I know, child. It will be very hard, but think, would it serve any useful purpose for him to discover his mother bore a. . .?'

'A bastard,' Corinna finished softly.

'A love child, Corinna, for so you are. Dear God, when Lettice Graham died I should have allowed your grandmother to find you foster-parents, as she urged me to do, but I could not part with you. I loved you then, as my own child. Rose Grimsley nursed you, for she'd recently borne her own son, Jesse, and when James came back from France—for he had been on a secret mission to France for the King, and was not with us during that terrible time—and saw you, he agreed to my request that we bring you up as ours.' She buried her face in her hands. 'I should have known, even then, that we were courting disaster, that we were too close to the others involved, that Tabby would bear a son whom you would meet and see often, that you could come to love your own half-brother so much. . .'

Corinna's cold little hands gently prised the fingers from her foster-mother's loved face and kissed her. 'You must never castigate yourself for that. I—I have been so very happy. It was no fault of yours. I can only be grateful to you both forever, despite what came of it. Had you not brought me to Barrow I should never have known Julian and—and Oliver.' Despite her effort to control her tears, she broke down again and murmured, 'How am I to let him think. . .that I have changed my mind. . .that I no longer love him? Oh, Mother, I think I can bear anything but that.'

Lady Webster sat up and resolutely dabbed her own eyes with her kerchief.

'We were considering that at the door before your father left us. We think tonight's feast must go on as planned.' She averted her eyes momentarily from Corinna's tortured face. 'If we do not, there will be gossip, ugly speculation.'

Corinna gave a shudder of revulsion. 'Yes, I understand, but how can I face them all? And Oliver will be there. We spoke of trying to convince my father. He will wish to know. . .' She broke off piteously. 'He will not believe me so fickle.'

There was a short silence, then Lady Webster said very softly, 'If your betrothal to Sir Lionel Summers were to be announced, as we planned, Oliver would believe that you lacked the courage to defy your father.' She waited, her brown eyes scanning Corinna's face intently.

'No.' Corinna's whisper was so soft and so pain-filled that Lady Webster gave a start of surprise.

'You hold Lionel so much in contempt?'

'I—I cannot like him. There must be some other way.' She was pleading as her fingers laced and interlaced distractedly.

Lady Webster frowned thoughtfully. 'Have there been harsh words between you, Corinna? Trust me, please.'

Again Corinna drew a hard breath. 'He was riding near to the quarry and—and he saw Oliver and me enter the copse. I gather he remained waiting there for quite some time,' she added grimly.

Lady Webster's eyes opened wide. 'Then he believes the worst?'

'So it would seem.'

'Yet still he wishes to marry you?'

'He is arrogant and possessive. He will not part with anything he believes to be his by right.'

Lady Webster controlled a desire to smile with an effort. This man resembled her own husband, and, though she would not admit to the fault in her own nature, Corinna herself.

'Oliver knows you were informally promised to this man. He would accept your father's decision as binding on you. He would not defy his own with impunity. Consider this carefully, Corinna. You are twenty. It is known in the county that there is mystery concerning your birth. I will be very blunt. This lessens your chance of acquiring a suitable husband. You could do worse than take Lionel Summers, since Oliver is lost to you. He wants you. I think he could come to love you, and, in all events, it might not prove necessary for you to spend too much time in each other's company. If his mother is anything to go by, Lionel will wish to spend a greater portion of his time at court rather than on his estates. Corinna, do you wish to remain a lonely spinster, living on the charity of your brother when he brings his bride to Manor Court and inherits? That time will come, my dear, however much we push the thought to the back of our minds. Just now, while you feel so wounded, you think you would prefer to remain unwed rather than cleave to a man you dislike and distrust, but I think you are wrong in that. I see Lionel Summers' character more charitably. I would not counsel you to accept him if I thought otherwise.'

It was a long speech for Corinna's usually reserved and gently spoken mother. The girl sat, looking unsee-

ingly at the folds of her country gown. What was urged
was sound sense, and she knew it. Sir James wished
her to accept Lionel Summers. If she accepted the
necessity of seeming to consent, would it not be
possible later to have the contract dissolved? Oliver
would not understand her weak compliance, yet it was
the one way she could avoid revealing the stark truth
to him. She must do it — for all their sakes — and her
father and Lionel must never come to blows over his
chillingly insulting words to her. That must be her
secret, and hers alone. She gave a great shuddering
breath.

'Send my father to me and — and I will tell him he
can make the announcement,' she said at last.

Lady Webster rose from the chair and drew Corinna
up and into her arms again.

'That's my brave girl,' she murmured, kissing the top
of her foster-daughter's bent head. 'Go now and
change into your best gown, ready for receiving our
guests.' Gently she added, 'I will try to see to it that
Oliver spends very little time alone with you. Be sure
that Lionel will remain by your side for much of the
time, and that will save the need for explanations.'

Corinna summoned a tight smile and turned from
her mother to the library door.

In her room once more she sat near the window,
staring out, unseeing, over the pleasaunce. She was
stunned and still could not quite take it in. Already,
below, she could hear sounds of arrivals. Grooms
scuttled to deal with horses, and trestle tables were
being conveyed outside to be loaded with food for the
servants. Though she took little heed, Corinna was
aware of the merriment and general good humour of
all those involved in the final preparations. In a few
short hours she would be betrothed to Lionel Summers,

a man she had so recently told, vehemently, that she would never be his. Had she too tamely accepted her mother's solution for what seemed an insuperable dilemma? She could not think. Her head ached, and there seemed to be a dull pain round her heart. This morning the countryside she knew so well had appeared lit with a new brilliance because of her love for Oliver and his avowed love for her. There was no hope now. Whatever the circumstances, she could never marry him as she had so fondly dreamed, never rule the household at Glebe. Did it matter whom she married? Her mother had been right: a household of her own, children — she winced at the thought, yet children would be a consolation, even though they could not be Oliver's — would be infinitely preferable to a life as a dependent relative of her brother, however she loved him.

The nervous little maid who had summoned her to the library knocked and entered at her toneless invitation. She carried a laden tray.

'My lady says you must eat something, Miss Corinna. I've brought you a breast of chicken and some manchet bread and fruit just to blunt the edge of your hunger, like, not ruin it for tonight.'

Corinna gazed listlessly at the food. She was about to order the girl sharply to remove it, then relented. Her mother would feel concerned if the girl reported that she had rejected food, and would doubtless hurry upstairs to fuss over her. She nodded and dismissed the girl.

She forced herself to eat a little, though she felt sickened, and choked on the food. She was grateful for the tankard of cold ale, for it seemed now that her body burned with a fever. If only she could become ill and could be spared the coming ordeal, but she knew

that whatever the outcome she must take her place at
her parents' side soon, to receive their guests. Her
emotions must be kept firmly in check. She would have
to face Oliver and her aunt, as well as her uncle Saul,
as though nothing had changed. Though her heart
would break from the pain of it, this agony of loss and
shock must be endured.

When Joan arrived to dress her for the evening she
submitted with good grace, even managed to appear
delighted with the magnificent gown her father had had
made for her in Leicester, copied from London designs.
The overgown was of gold silk, laced back with white
satin bows into a sweeping train behind. The short,
loose, fashionable sleeves were of apricot satin. She
was glad she had chosen silks rather than brocades,
since the day was so hot. Her white silk petticoat and
undersleeves were trimmed with cloth of gold, and
Joan wound a rope of pearls in her hair, her father's
gift of the morning. So she must look her best as the
sacrificial lamb on the altar of matrimony. Had her
proposed husband been Oliver, as she had dreamed,
how gladly she would have dressed for this occasion.
Her mother had made her a present of a beautiful fan,
delicately painted with flowers and leaves, while the
golden struts matched the colouring of her gown. Joan
remarked on her pallor, putting it down to the heat.

'The worst of it is already over, Mistress Corinna,'
she said cheerfully. 'The doors have been flung wide in
the hall and the screen doors too. It's well shaded.
You'll soon be feeling better as the heat lessens. Listen,
can you hear the fiddlers?' She smiled fondly. 'You
look very lovely. Your father will be proud.'

'Indeed he is.' The women swung round to the door
as Sir James entered the chamber. Corinna could detect
no sign of anger or concern on his smiling face. He

looked very grand tonight in his well cut court coat of green satin, his breeches of beige silk and his smart buckled shoes with the new red high heels he had bought on his last visit to the capital for the late King's funeral procession. He nodded his gracious thanks to Joan, who curtsied and withdrew.

Coming closer in, he held out his hand to Corinna, and she came to him with a little pitiful sob, burying her head against the cool satin of his coat.

'There, there, child, let us not spoil your finery. Joan has done so fine a piece of work.'

He tilted up her chin and looked deep into her eyes. 'Can you forgive me for my angry words, Corinna?'

She nodded, blinking back the tears. 'I know you had only my welfare at heart.'

'Aye.' He sighed heavily. 'Possibly we made mistakes that summer twenty years ago, but you must understand that you have always given us so much happiness that we could never regret our decision.'

'Nor could I, Father, however unhappy the outcome.'

His handsome face looked boyishly embarrassed. 'Your mother tells me that you are willing to accept Lionel. Is that so?'

She avoided his gaze. 'It would seem the only situation.'

'He wants you, lass. There is no question of taking you for your dowry alone. That should prove some comfort. His father was a good friend, and an honourable one. I have no doubts that his son will inherit those qualities.'

'He — he has not been told?'

'Of your willingness to reconsider?'

'He has not been told the truth about my birth?'

'Of your relationship to Tabitha Hunt? No, no, child.

He has not questioned your parentage, and we thought the secret should be kept safe between us. Your grandmother knew, of course. Now the truth is known only to your mother and me, Tabitha, Rose Grimsley and you. Your mother thinks it might be as well for you to go to Rose to stay for a while soon after the festivities, then I'll fetch you and take you to London, where you can become properly acquainted with your affianced husband.'

It was not spoken openly between them that it would be better now if she did not remain in Barrow, where she would see Oliver often when he came down from Oxford. The thought was a thorn in her heart. Her beloved home would soon be lost to her with all the hopes and dreams she had held for so long. Yes, her old nurse, Rose, who lived at Brinklow near Coventry now that her son, Jesse, was married and had inherited a small farm, would be the sole person who would understand her distress and be able to offer some measure of comfort.

Her father was moving to the door again. 'I'll speak with Lionel now that I have heard your resolve from your own lips. Courage, child. You look truly magnificent. I know that you feel your heart is breaking. You will not believe me, perhaps, but I have faced suffering as great and lost hopes, yet I found happiness at last, and I pray you, my brave, spirited daughter, will also, in time.'

He gave her a final loving glance before she heard his shoes with their distinctive clicking high heels descending the stair. She put a hand to her breast, her heart racing in sudden dread as she thought how soon she must face Lionel Summers again.

When she went down at last, Joan hovering behind

her, Lady Webster stood at the library door, smiling. She kissed Corinna and nodded to her maid.

'You look very beautiful, my darling. Lionel begs a word with you in private.' She indicated the library door.

Corinna swallowed nervously.

Her mother stood aside.

'If you need me I shall be just outside the door,' she said quietly.

He was standing near the massive fireplace, his fingers tracing the family arms above it, and turned the moment he heard the door open. As he stood waiting for her his expression was bland, totally inscrutable. Corinna thought in a sudden panic, He has agreed to this match, knowing there is bad feeling if not downright hostility between us. If I must marry this man, what measure of true happiness can I hope for?

He was making her that half-mocking courtier's bow, and she returned him a deep curtsy.

He was clad, as she expected, in the height of elegance, in an exquisitely cut coat of blue brocade ornamented with a profusion of diamond-cut buttons. His fashionable shoes had the new scarlet heels and high tongue, the buckles sparkling in the sunlight which poured through the oriel window.

'I understand you have reconsidered my proposal, Mistress Corinna, and are prepared to accept me as your future husband.'

She said coldly, 'As you know well, it is my father's wish, sir.'

'And yours?' he pressed inexorably.

'My will does not enter into this decision,' she said hurriedly. 'I will do what is expected of me, and now, sir, if you are satisfied, I'll join my parents. Our guests are already arriving.'

'Wait just one moment.' He lifted the leather box she had seen before from a nearby table and came towards her. 'I would like you to accept my betrothal ring and to wear the gift I had specially made for you.'

She murmured a quick assent.

'Allow me.' He undid the box and withdrew a necklace. 'I may put it on for you?'

Stiffly she nodded, hardly glancing at the glittering thing as he came quickly behind her and bent to clasp it round her throat. He had said he had chosen sapphires to match her eyes. She felt the cool feel of his fingers on her throat and the nape of her neck as he adroitly adjusted the necklet, then he came in front of her again.

'I was right. The colour is for you, yet your eyes, sparkling with excitement — or is it tears. . .?' He hesitated, then hastened on as she made to interrupt. 'All I meant to say was that the gems, though beautiful, are somewhat dimmed by the brilliance of those lovely eyes of yours. I decided on a family heirloom for our betrothal ring. It is not so fashionable, yet its value lies in its antiquity. It has been handed down through the generations, and my mother generously gave it to me for my bride. I trust, as you wear it, you will remember the family honour it signifies.'

She gave a little gasp at the sharp reminder of her duty. The ring was heavily chased, a blood-red ruby, supported by floridly fashioned leaf and flower shoulders, and she felt it weighed down her hand as fetters would have done, an implicit pledge and symbol of his domination.

He stooped and kissed her fingers, looking up into her face, as he was aware that they felt chilled and trembling, despite the heat.

'Thank you, sir.' Again she swept him a formal

curtsy, and he stood back to allow her to precede him to the door.

Outside her mother scrutinised her face anxiously, and Corinna lifted her hand to show the betrothal ring. Lady Webster smiled thankfully and touched the necklet appreciatively.

'Lionel, how exquisite, and it complements Corinna's gown excellently. Now, child, let us go and face them all.'

Corinna could not recall afterwards how she had managed to endure the evening's proceedings. She ate and drank mechanically, smilingly accepting the expressions of goodwill offered her by friends and neighbours. She stood stoically by her father's side as he announced, with pride, his daughter's betrothal to the son of his old companion, Sir Lionel Summers. As the toasts were drunk, the loving cup was brought to her, a family custom. As she lifted it to kiss the rim, her eyes encountered the brown ones of Oliver Hunt. She had never seen him look so utterly stunned. At her father's prompting, she hurriedly touched her lips to the jewelled cup, and handed it to Lionel Summers, who drained it.

The toasts seemed interminable, and Corinna's head ached with the effort of appearing at ease with the company. For what seemed the thousandth time she received the congratulations of one of her father's many neighbours. The man was elderly with a bluff, red-cheeked countenance and the broken veins and paunch which suggested he liked his port too well.

'He's a very fortunate fellow, your betrothed. I wish I had been ten years or so younger when I became widowed, and I'd have beaten him to it, and asked for you myself. I hope you aren't going to keep him too long before he takes you to the wedding couch.'

Wincing inwardly from such bawdiness, Corinna managed to make her escape from his company, murmuring that she had promised to dance with some of the servants outside.

The fiddlers had struck up a merry tune, and the head stable-lad, flushed with embarrassment, approached and asked permission to accompany her in the dance. The steps were more lively than complicated, but even so she found it hard to concentrate and once or twice almost fell. She thanked him warmly as the tune stopped, more because the sweating fiddlers needed to rest than that they had come to the end of their piece. The stable-boy made to lead her back to the hall, when they were intercepted by Oliver near the door, who refused to take no for an answer and led her out on to the courtyard again as the fiddlers struck up once more. Clumsy and mentally exhausted, Corinna almost tripped again, and her cousin put one hand around her waist to steady her and led her quickly from the ring of flushed dancers. She tried to pull from his hold, but he hastened her away from the courtyard towards the pleasaunce arbour.

'Oliver, no,' she begged, but he did not turn or stop, but dragged her inexorably onwards.

'We shall be missed,' she panted at last, as he thrust her inside the shaded place and pulled her to face him. 'My father will be so angry.'

'As angry as I am?' he demanded, and his voice was husky with suppressed fury. Corinna had never before seen her genial cousin so beside himself.

She was shaking and could not face his accusing eyes.

He shouted at her, 'Why, Corinna? Why did you allow him to give you to this fop from London?'

She turned desperately towards the closed door, which he had thrust to angrily with the toe of his shoe.

'I cannot talk about it now, Oliver. It is done. My father—he insisted. I could not disobey. He flatly refused to countenance our marriage.'

'And you submitted so tamely?'

'It is not easy for me,' she flashed back to him. 'You were not there. You cannot understand.

'I will never understand,' he snapped. 'You gave me no time to talk with my parents——'

'You have said nothing to them?' she pressed him anxiously.

'No, nothing. You said you must convince your father first.' He looked bewildered, as if he thought she believed him in some way to be at fault and could not explain her reasoning.

'You—you must not talk of it,' she said between her teeth. 'I must marry Lionel Summers, and you must forget me.'

'As you will forget me—easily, it seems. I had thought better of you, Corin.'

Her eyes were closed. She was near to collapse, and he must not know it. 'Please, Oliver,' she begged, 'you must accept this is for the best. You will find some country squire's daughter who will prove a more satisfactory mistress for Glebe than I could ever be.'

'Then it's true what I dreaded? You want much more than I could ever give you—London society, to be presented at court, the admiration of other town fops.' He was hurtfully contemptuous. 'Well, at least let me give you this as a reminder to compare with Summers' embrace on your wedding night.'

His mouth came down hard on hers and she swayed within his grasp, feeling herself fainting under her desperate longing to tell him the truth, make him understand the agony of her surrender to her father's will, and not condemn her further. She was swooning in his arms, pressing ineffectually at his shoulders to push him away from her, when a hatefully familiar voice sounded from the doorway.

'I thought I might find my betrothed here and in such company. I think the lady wishes you to release her, sir, though I confess I find it hard to understand why she accompanied you here in the first place.'

Corinna wrenched herself free and turned to face him.

'Oliver had the right to know from my own lips what prompted my decision.'

Lionel Summers' lips curled derisively. 'And he needed to taste the sweetness of them before accepting the inevitable?'

Oliver cut in, 'I will give you satisfaction, sir, but it must be first thing tomorrow, soon after dawn.'

Lionel drawled, 'I never open my eyes at such an hour, let alone rise.'

Oliver's fists clenched, and Corinna interposed herself between them.

'I will not have this.'

'"Will not", mistress?' Lionel Summers' eyebrows rose interrogatively. 'And how, pray, can you be concerned in this matter between Master Hunt and myself?'

Corinna's cheeks were dyed scarlet with anger. Lionel's very mode of address for Oliver implied he was no gentleman. As if to confirm that, Summers added, 'I do not take or give satisfaction to one who is not my equal, sir. If you insist on importuning my betrothed I shall be forced to take my riding whip to your back.'

Corinna stormed, 'Get out of here, Oliver. Allow me to deal with this.'

'I refuse to leave you alone with this insolent brute.'

Gently she put a hand on his arm. 'Please go. I shall be quite safe with my affianced husband.'

She knew that would strike home, and intended it to achieve that very purpose of sending him from her without further explanation. He flinched as if she had struck him, then made her a truly elegant bow, stiffly did the same for Lionel Summers, then stalked from the arbour.

Corinna lifted a defiant chin and faced her betrothed.

'There was nothing between us which could impugn your honour. Oliver, I'm sure, is inexperienced, and would be outmatched in swordsmanship in any duel between you. If you were to challenge and kill him, understand, sir, that nothing my father could say or do would make me marry you.'

A cold little smile played about his well chiselled lips. 'I have said I have no intention of brawling with that overgrown child. He *is* a child at heart, Corinna, despite his height and brawn. I shall teach you what it is to be loved by a man.'

'So you have bragged before, sir. It will be for me to recognise what, in truth, makes a man. I have discovered, despite my youth, that it rarely consists of an ability to wound with words, sir, or to frame empty compliments.'

He moved a fraction nearer to her and, as in the morning's encounter, she noted that chilling glitter in those strange golden eyes of his.

'You believe yourself to be in love with that fellow.'

'I *do* love Oliver Hunt,' she said. 'My father has explained why we cannot be wed. I have accepted you. There is nothing more you need to know. If, in the circumstances, you wish to withdraw from this betrothal, I shall make no complaint. After this incident I must confess you would have good cause.'

His grip tightened on her wrist. 'Know now, Corinna, I shall never release you.'

Meaningly she looked down at her white flesh, where bruises would form later. 'I am pledged to you, sir. That is your privilege.'

He released her wrist and lifted it to his lips. 'We must return to the feasting. Your parents will be concerned at your absence.'

She allowed him to lead her back to the hall. Though he remained near her for the rest of the evening, he did not once seek to talk with her again.

CHAPTER FOUR

CORINNA was wakened by someone entering her bed-chamber and closing the door. She had fallen into sleep very late, despite her utter exhaustion. The momentous revelation and the encounters with both Oliver and Lionel had preyed on her mind, and she had tossed and turned for hours. Her final instruction to Joan had been to leave her strictly alone until she herself summoned a maid, and now she was angry that her orders had been disobeyed and still half bemused with sleep.

She called crossly, 'Go away. I said I was not to be disturbed,' aware that it must be almost noon, since sunlight was pouring into the chamber. The intruder must have summarily pulled back the curtains. Corinna sat up in bed, pushing back her disordered hair, and ready to do battle. She checked as she saw that it was Lady Webster who came to the bedside.

'Oh, Mother, I'm sorry, I thought it was Joan.'

Her head ached abominably, and she looked heavy-eyed and miserable.

'I know you had planned to sleep late, child. After all that happened, I cannot censure you. I would have left you, but your aunt is here and wishes to see you.'

Corinna went white to the lips. The events of the feasting and the announcement of her betrothal seemed vague to her. Her suffering had been so great that she had gone through the evening without being entirely aware; now she recalled that her aunt had been missing from the celebrations, and realised that she should have registered that fact. Before joining their guests she had dreaded to see both Oliver and the woman she now knew to be her mother, and she had been spared seeing Tabitha Hunt at least.

Lady Webster explained, 'I went over to Glebe and managed to see Tabitha alone.'

'You told her that — that I know the truth?'

'Yes, I thought it best. She was very frightened. Fortunately Saul was busy about the fields, so we were able to talk. She confessed her terror at facing you and she said she would inform Oliver and her husband that she was ill, so that she would not be forced to come to your birthday celebration. It seemed the most sensible course. Saul has gone to the quarry early this morning and she has ridden over to see you. She is still upset, but more controlled. Oliver has left Glebe already, it seems. She is anxious to know what passed between you.'

Corinna leaned back for a moment against the pillows. Her eyes appealed to her adopted mother.

'Must I see her — now?'

Lady Webster took Corinna's hand, which was grasping convulsively at the coverlet.

'She is your mother, Corinna. Will you not try to understand?'

'She knows about Oliver — and me?'

'Yes. I had to give my reasons for telling you the truth.'

'Yes, of course. I must come down. There has been no change of plan? I am going today to Brinklow to Rose?'

'Yes, Jules will escort you. It is on his way. He, too, is sleeping late. I'll send your aunt up to you here and give strict instructions that none of the servants is to come to your chamber until given leave to do so.' She hesitated. 'You and — your mother will be private here,

less likely to be overheard.' At the door she paused.
'You will be gentle with her, Corinna?'

Corinna drew a hard breath. She must be the strong
one, it seemed. Through her lack of moral fibre Tabitha
Hunt had ruined the lives of Corinna and Oliver and
threatened the security of her own marriage, to say
nothing of bringing about the possibility of a family
quarrel between the Websters and Hunts. The partnership in the quarry could well be at stake if the truth
were to come out. Yet she, Corinna, the innocent pawn
in all this intrigue, was the one to suffer most and the
one who must be 'gentle' with Tabitha Hunt.

She forced a smile. 'Yes, of course I will.'

She rose and put on a bed gown, and was busied at
bringing some order to her tangled hair when Tabitha
Hunt bustled into the chamber. Corinna had rarely felt
at ease with her, had told Oliver that she believed her
aunt did not like her, certainly disapproved of her
freedom to roam the countryside at will with the boys.
Tabitha had often said, her mouth in a tight line, that
Corinna should have been more firmly disciplined had
she lived at Glebe.

There was a cool glint in her eye as she turned to
face the woman who had been so lax in her own
behaviour that she had brought this disaster on them
all. She left her mother to make the first move.

Like her sister, Dorcas Webster, Tabitha Hunt was
brown-haired and -eyed, smaller in stature than Dorcas
and thin almost to the point of emaciation. Corinna,
looking at her intently now, saw that she must have
been very pretty, but disappointment had soured her
expression and painted lines of dissatisfaction around
eyes and mouth, so that she looked years older than
her older sister.

To her horror, Corinna realised that there were tears

in her aunt's brown eyes and the usually tight mouth was trembling.

'Aunt,' Corinna said awkwardly, 'I — that is — Mother says you wished to see me urgently.'

Tabitha Hunt came very close and put a hand appealingly on Corinna's arm.

'It's Oliver. He's gone.'

'Back to Oxford, yes, Mother told me.'

'No, no.' Tears choked the habitually peevish voice. 'Not to Oxford, to Plymouth. He's gone to join this ridiculous rebellion. We tried to stop him, but he was so distressed by the news of your betrothal that he was beside himself. Even his father could make no impression on him. He rode off last night without even letting Julian know what he was about. He will be killed, Corinna, and he is all I have.'

Corinna's heart missed a beat. Dear God, what had she done? Oliver had rushed off in an agony of disappointment and anger at her seeming betrayal and would throw himself recklessly into the thick of this doomed endeavour.

Realising their shared anxiety, she reached out blindly to the weeping woman, and Tabitha Hunt clutched her daughter desperately. All these years she had not dared to show her any demonstration of affection; now the dam had burst and she was able to reveal her love.

'If you only knew how often I have wanted to tell you, wanted to hold you in my arms. I've longed for a daughter, and there you were, so very beautiful, and resembling your father, and I had to pretend that you meant no more to me than any other child of my acquaintance. Is it any wonder that I have so doted on Oliver? And now he could be lost to me through my own wickedness.'

'Hush, hush.' Even now Corinna found it almost impossible to address Tabitha Hunt as 'Mother'. 'This is not your fault. Oliver intended to join this rising from the first. He told me as much yesterday. He is in a passion now, but he will calm down and become more clear-headed when he has time to think. I know Julian intends to join him, and Bart Spicer, also. They will seek him out and bring him to a more equable frame of mind.'

'What passed between you last night? You did not tell him?'

'No, I could not. That could prove disastrous.'

'He is furiously jealous that you have accepted Sir Lionel Summers.'

'It seemed the only way to convince him that we must stay apart.'

'Yes, of course.' Tabitha Hunt dabbed ineffectually at her reddened eyes with her kerchief. 'Corinna, I feel for you. I, too, was sold into a loveless marriage.' Her lips curled into the familiar bitter line, and Corinna's eyes softened.

'Uncle Saul is a good man. Have you never — come to love him?'

Brown eyes met her blue ones directly. 'No, I cannot love him. Respect him, yes, accept gratefully his care of me, and — and I have Oliver. . .' She broke off and turned away. 'I shall pray for you, Corinna, that you will be more blessed than I, that you will come to love your husband as Dorcas cares for James. In that she is fortunate, though she had no more say in the matter than I did.'

Corinna squeezed her mother's hand in understanding, and Tabitha looked hurriedly towards the door.

'I should be returning to Glebe. Saul will demand to know where I have been.'

Corinna watched her go, her teeth worrying her bottom lip. She longed to assure Tabitha that she would contrive to send a message to Oliver by Julian, which she was sure Tabitha had hoped for, but she dared not. She must do nothing now to bring Oliver hastening to her side again. Her only hope in coming to terms with this problem was to remain apart from him for as long as possible.

Both her adopted parents were present in the court-yard when she and Julian departed for Brinklow. They took no groom or maid, for the ride was short and Rose would see to it that her nursling was well provided for. Sir James promised to take her to London soon, and Corinna tried to look suitably enthusiastic. Sir Lionel arrived in the doorway as they were about to ride out. He came to her side and, meeting Sir James's eye, she offered a cool cheek for him to kiss.

'I shall see you in London very shortly,' he reminded her, a little smile curling his long lips.

She made no answer but a little mutinous lift of her chin.

Neither she nor Julian were burdened with much baggage. Most of his clothes and personal possessions were at his lodgings in Oxford, and Corinna had made frequent visits to Brinklow, so there were country gowns and a quantity of underlinen she could use at her nurse's home. The greater part of her baggage would be brought in the coach to Brinklow when her father came to escort her to London next month.

Julian was silent for the first few miles, and Corinna glanced at him sharply. His features were set in a sullen cast, and such an expression was alien to her usually good-humoured brother. Corinna sighed.

'I imagine you are about to take me to task too. Out

with it, Julian. You blame me for this break with Oliver. Is that it?'

Boyishly he burst out, 'What are you about, Corin? Poor Oliver is heartbroken. I saw him last night just before he dashed back to Glebe. I thought there was an understanding between you two. How could you bring yourself to accept that extravagantly dressed town fop? Surely you do not hanker for a title, and for the life of court and society, that you would break Noll's heart over it?'

Another dagger to her heart. Corinna looked stead-fastly ahead, avoiding her brother's gaze.

'It is Father's wish,' she said listlessly. 'When it is your turn, you will find it harder than you think to gainsay him.'

He rode up close, his eyes troubled.

'Did Father put so much pressure upon you?'

'He impressed on me the suitability of the match.'

'It is just not like you to give way so tamely,' he grumbled, 'and Noll needs so much encouragement now when he intends to. . .' He broke off, reddening, in sudden confusion.

'When he intends to risk himself in the dangerous enterprise in which you intend to join him,' Corinna finished drily. 'Have you thought this out carefully, Jules? Do you realise how your behaviour could rebound on our parents? It might be as well if I am wed to someone with influence at court, should the need arise.'

He frowned and blinked unhappily, made as if to speak, then swallowed hard and fell silent for the next few miles.

Rose greeted Corinna warmly, and it was balm to her hurt senses to know that her nurse knew the truth

about her birth and disastrous relationship to Oliver
and that it was not necessary to keep her distress to
herself. The little farm was prosperous, and Jesse
ideally happy with his rosy-cheeked wife. Her father
owned a larger farm at Wellsbourne and had made the
two newly-weds a present of this smaller one set across
the old Roman Fosse Way. Corinna bade a tearful
farewell to Julian, knowing he was going into unknown
hazards, and aware of the rift between them which was
none of her making.

Rose's mother had been of gypsy stock, and both
she and her son were dark and swarthy-skinned. Jesse
had a shock of black curls and he was tall and heavy-
set, yet, for all his size and prowess in the wrestling
ring, he was gentleness itself both with his young wife
and the young woman he still regarded as his foster-
sister, both of them nursed at the breast together by
Rose. His mother, also, was still a comely woman, tall
and spare and carrying herself with the unconscious
grace and regality of a queen. Since there was no
husband in evidence Corinna had once ventured to ask
her mother about it and been told sharply not to plague
Rose with questions. The last time she had visited,
Rose had told her the story, though without embellish-
ments. Jesse's father had been a noted highwaymen
who had met his end on the gallows at Red Hill near
Leicester. Neither then, in the telling, or later did Rose
shed any tears or bewail her fate. Cheerfully she had
reminded Corinna that Sir James and Lady Webster
had been goodness itself to her, and now Jesse was
wed and settled, and she installed in amity with her
daughter-in-law, she was quite content.

As they sat together in the kitchen, redolent of
Nance's baking, Corinna told her nurse what she had

learned of her parentage and of her fears for the safety of Jules and Oliver.

'Oliver is so hurt and angry,' she said softly, 'that I'm afraid he will be doubly reckless, and Jules with him.'

The older woman glanced up at the horn casement which had been thrown open to the air for coolness. Outside they could hear Nance clucking encouragingly to the hens as she fed them with scraps. Jesse was still at work in the barley field.

'Aye, in nature I fear young Master Oliver resembles his mother. Master Saul might be in sympathy with his views, but he was never one to lack care for his own welfare.'

Corinna was silent for a moment, then she asked, 'I saw my true father only once that I can remember when he visited Manor Court and brought me that doll. What was he truly like, Rose? Mother—I mean Lady Webster, of course; I shall never really consider Tabitha my mother—says he was very handsome and full of laughter.'

Rose nodded. 'He was that, but he sobered up later when he got involved in some political troubles in London. I never heard the whole of it, but it was thought sensible for him to leave the country. He'd made some money earlier at sea and was able to buy a plantation in Barbados. He was a kindly man, like Sir James. I remember he tried to help my mother when she was attacked by the villagers once. She was a wise woman with herbs, and some of the village louts set about her with staves and stones one afternoon. Someone's cow had died suddenly—you know how it is— and that superstitious lot are prone to believe the worst, specially of her for her gypsy blood. Master Edward drove them off and ordered them to their homes and took her on his horse to our cottage. He was no weakling, your father, and would have stood by Mistress Tabitha and seen her right had things not fallen out as they had. You've the look of him, the reason why some as thought you were Sir James's get, right enough. I think he never minded that. He and Mistress Dorcas have loved you well, and never you forget that or blame them for aught.'

Corinna squeezed Rose's hand tightly, and the older woman patted her shoulder as she bustled to her feet. 'There, there, lass, I know this has come to you badly, but you mustn't fret. When my man, Mat, was took I had to set to and pick up the pieces. Look to this Sir Lionel. Though you can't see it now, he may well prove a fine man for you. As for the boys, they'll have to fend for themselves. I'll always think of them as boys, but they're men grown and must take their own risks. Keep your own counsel when your father takes you to town, and if the Lord is kind the two of them will come home safe and sound.'

At mention of Lionel Summers' name Corinna gave a great shudder and sat pensively watching Rose as she began to reach out Nance's honey cakes from the oven.

It was near the end of the month when Jesse came back from the village inn one night with the news which made Corinna's heart race with fear.

'It's being said in Coventry that Monmouth landed at Lyme on the eleventh. The King be in a rare taking and 'as put Feversham in command of his troops to march into the West Country. I can't see as 'ow it'll be much of a rising, though they do say many of the West Countrymen have joined the Duke already.'

Corinna dropped a pewter jug of buttermilk and muttered a hasty apology to Nance, who rose to clean up the mess.

'Tell me everything you've heard, Jesse,' Corinna pleaded.

Jesse looked enquiringly at his mother, who nodded. It was likely Rose had confided to her son the tidings that Master Julian Webster and Master Oliver Hunt had expressed an intention to join the planned rising. He passed a hand over his good-humoured, sweating face and frowned in concentration.

'Well, not much more. He's come from Holland, in some ship called the Heldenburgh or something of the sort. It's rumoured he's gaining men fast as he goes through the towns, be making for Bristol, I reckon, to march on London, but the whole affair'll fizzle out long before then. One of the carters come from Bristol had heard tell that the Duke was well received in Taunton, the house doorways and inns all decorated with green boughs and herbs and flowers.' He laughed joyously. 'The carter chap said some schoolgirls from a nearby school and one of their teachers had made him some flags for his army. Young girls do be prone to such nonsense, but there'll be trouble for them, like as not, when the rising fails.'

Corinna felt the old, familiar stab of pain. Yes, everyone assumed the rebellion would fail but Oliver — and Julian. Knowing her own inheritance as she did now, she could sympathise with the bastard Duke's ambitions. His cause had somehow become hers, as it was Julian's and Oliver's. She, too, was illegitimate and the knowledge had hurt, despite the care and affection she had received from her foster-parents. Apparently the ill starred accident of her birth had not prevented Lionel Summers from wishing to wed her. Was that to his credit or was her sizeable dowry the main motive for his proposal?

Yet her brother and Oliver were now in mortal

danger and both men further excited by the unfortunate happenings at Manor Court. Were they, even
now, in the rag-tail army the carter had so graphically
described to Jesse? Could she prevent them from
further committing themselves to this doomed cause?
Should she send messages to her father, warning him
what was afoot? Surely if he knew he would make
every effort to return his son and nephew to
Leicestershire before they were involved irretrievably.
Even now it might be too late. She blamed herself for
listening to Oliver's pleading and not informing her
parents of their intention. If she could reach her
brother, surely he would agree to escort her back to
the Midlands before danger was too grave for travellers
on the roads.

'Rose,' she said briskly, 'would it be possible to get
word to my father at Barrow and——' she hesitated,
then eyed Jesse determinedly, '—hire a conveyance to
take me to the West Country?'

Jesse opened his mouth to argue, but his mother
imperiously waved him to be silent.

'Corinna, your father would be extremely angry, you
know that.'

Corinna's blue eyes were misted with tears, but
regarded her old nurse steadily.

'Yes, I know it, but only I might be able to turn
Julian from his purpose, and—and Julian would be
able to turn Oliver too, particularly if they both knew
they would endanger me by going on with this folly.'

Rose considered, while Jesse and Nance watched her
uneasily.

'Well,' Rose said at last, 'I've known you too long to
think I can change your mind when it's made up. Jesse,
do what she says. Find out if that carter be headed for
Leicester and will carry a note to Sir James, and—then

go into Coventry and hire us a carriage.' Before he could object further she added, 'I shall go with Mistress Corinna, of course. I would like you to escort us, but you must consult your wife here and do what you both think best.'

She took Corinna's arm and led her towards the stair. 'Come and write your message, my dear. Jesse will decide what he'll do by the time we have done that and put together some necessities for the journey. We'll make for Bath first, along the old Roman Way, and head towards Bristol or Bridgwater when we hear more about the movements of troops.'

'But Mother,' Jesse growled, 'how can Mistress Corinna hope to get near her brother if he's in Monmouth's army? They'll never allow us close to any of the officers.'

Rose's gypsy-black eyes sparkled with a trace of sardonic amusement. 'If schoolgirls can approach this Duke, surely a personable young girl like Mistress Corinna can? In all events, if we can get near enough to the armies, a message might be sent to Master Julian. The officers will be quartered at inns along the way. We must use our good sense and do the best we can.'

'And if the battle be already joined?' Stolidly Jesse's dark eyes glared back at his mother's. Her lips twitched in answer.

'Then, my son, we might well be more use to Master Julian than ever.'

Jesse's lips parted incredulously, then he nodded and moved to the door.

'Nance, my lass, I'm going back to the inn to delay that carter and get him to call here for Mistress Corinna's letter.' He did not need to add that he would drive his mother and former mistress. Nance knew that

only too well, and sighed heavily in acceptance of his
decision, while her mind went to the packing up of
food the travellers could carry with them.

Dorcas Webster frantically scanned her daughter's
message for the fifth time. Where could James be? It
was well past the hour when she expected him home.
He had left early this morning to inspect some barn
roofs on the border of the estate lands near Rothley
and had not returned, and it was now almost three of
the clock.

The carter had been able to tell her little more than
James had heard in Leicester on his visit there two
days ago. The Duke had landed, and it was expected
that he would be confronted by Royalist troops under
Feversham and Churchill in the vicinity of Bristol.
Though Julian had spoken several times of his admiration for Monmouth and the Protestant Cause, Dorcas
had never suspected that her son's enthusiasm would
lead him and his cousin to such foolhardy steps. Why,
oh, why had she paid him so little attention when he
was last down from Oxford? She and James had been
so taken up with Corinna's betrothal and the sub-
sequent revelation that they had ignored the very
obvious signs. She had dismissed the carter after
requesting that he take a verbal message to Nance
Grimsley on his way back west. Corinna's note had
been received, and all would be done as she had
requested. And if James had returned for dinner as she
had expected doubtless he would have been on his way
to Coventry by now. She gritted her teeth importently.
Julian must be prevented from throwing away his life
and Corinna from riding recklessly into danger.

Dorcas looked up when she heard sounds of arrival
from the courtyard, and hastened to the window. A

horse was being ridden in, but so slowly. Her heart misgave her when she saw the reason. A young farmer she recognised as Will Bailey from Rothley was pulling a hastily constructed litter of boughs and blankets, by the side of which two of his labourers walked and clumsily steadied its occupant.

'James,' Dorcas breathed, horrified. Dear God, what had happened to James? She lifted her skirts and sped outside. Grooms had already congregated and were preparing to carry the injured man into the house when she reached the door.

Will Bailey scratched his thatch of reddish hair and gave her what he hoped was a reassuring grin.

'I don't think it's as bad as it looks, my lady. His horse threw him and his leg's hurt. It's bad swollen and anyways the horse had bolted so we had to make the litter and bring him home as best we could.'

Dorcas knelt by her husband's side and took his hand. Fortunately he was fully conscious and able to smile at her.

'Don't worry, Dorcas. If my leg's broken, I'm sure it's a clean break, but it seems more swollen and sprained. The stupid beast was frightened by a pheasant, threw me, and dashed off into that little copse by the road. No one came for a bit and I couldn't stand, let alone walk. If you send for the surgeon in Birstall he'll soon know how bad the injury is, but thanks to these good fellows I wasn't lying for too long.'

'Did you hit your head?'

He shook his head. 'Never lost consciousness for a single moment. The leg's damned painful, though.'

Lady Webster smiled her gratitude at her tenants and stood back while Sir James was conveyed indoors and put to bed and a groom dispatched to the nearby village of Birstall for the surgeon. Bailey and his labourers were treated to ale and cold meats in the kitchen, and left with the fervent expressions of her gratitude still ringing in their ears. Dorcas set about making James as comfortable as possible while she waited for the surgeon. She put on a cold herbal poultice and provided him with wine and food, and finally dismissed her helpers to sit by the bed, her brows drawn together in concern.

'You mustn't stir in case the bone is broken. Thank God Bailey had the wit to hold the limb straight with boards while he brought you home.'

'That was his good wife's notion. She tried to pour some nauseous concoction down my throat, said it would ease the pain. I managed to keep down some of it, but I shall be damned glad when that surgeon fellow has done his work.' James winced as he moved slightly in the bed, and Dorcas's hand tightened on his.

Suddenly he was aware of her mood, sensing it was more than mere concern for him.

'What is it, my dear love? I'm sure I'm in no danger of losing the limb. Stevens is a good fellow and——'

'While I am certainly concerned for you, I have graver tidings, and now I don't know what is best to be done about it. Had you been fit, you. . .' She broke off and handed him Corinna's hurriedly scrawled letter.

He read it quickly and looked up at her, his own brows now pulling together in a sharp line over the bridge of his nose.

'Here's a pretty coil. God's wounds, Jules is like to die for this at Tyburn.'

Her face crumpled, and she gave way to helpless tears. He patted her bent head awkwardly.

'There, lass, no harm done yet, and Corinna's warning has given us time to mend matters. I could wish she had had the sense to stay where she was at Brinklow until I reached her. God knows what dangers she might run into on the road west with armies and, worse, masterless men on the march.'

'But you cannot reach her now, James, and who else could we trust to ride in pursuit?'

He winced again as he eased himself into a more comfortable position.

'No difficulty there, my love. I'd trust Dick's son with my life and, more, my children's lives. He's gone ahead of us to his London lodgings. Send Riley post-haste with a letter I'll write immediately if you bring me paper and quill. Tell the boy not to spare horseflesh and pay well for changes of mounts along the way. Corinna will make for Bath, so she'll go by way of Stow. Lionel can search for her in the inns in Bath and Wells, then in Bridgwater. Trust him. He'll have her and the lads back with us in no time.'

Dorcas looked doubtful. 'What if Corinna refuses to go with him? She can be very obstinate. As for Julian. . .'

Sir James gave a yelped laugh. 'Lionel will find his own method of persuasion with Corinna, and with Oliver and Julian he will use his unique brand of authority. They'll listen to him. In the end they will recognise his greater experience and maturity.' His face grew sober. 'I think, by now, they'll be glad of his assistance.'

Dorcas was glad to have a comforting report from the surgeon.

'It is fortunate, Lady Webster, that no bones are broken, but the limb is badly sprained and swollen. Sir James should not attempt to rise from his bed for a few days and certainly he should not ride for a week at least.'

He took his leave, promising to call back in a couple

of days to make sure there were no further complications. Knowing that a badly broken limb could result in amputation, Dorcas was thankful that she had now only the one great problem of her recalcitrant children. She was by no means as sure as her husband was that she could trust Lionel Summers with the task of finding them and returning them to Barrow. Find them, yes, he was probably capable of that, though Julian and his cousin might even now be enrolled in the Duke's army and subject to army discipline, but to persuade any or all of the three to return tamely with him back to their home — that was a decidedly different matter. She sighed. Corinna had been persuaded to accept him, and James trusted the man utterly, but he was so young, scarcely a couple of years older than Corinna. He had an innate air of authority, but had he the experience to deal with three strong-minded young people, two of whom detested him soundly?

Riley, their most reliable young groom, was dispatched south with Sir James's letter. Dorcas prayed fervently that he would find Sir Lionel at his lodgings and that he would be prepared to ride immediately after his betrothed.

CHAPTER FIVE

RILEY was fortunate to find Sir Lionel Summers at home in his London town house in Golden Square when he arrived late in the afternoon of the next day. He had followed Sir James's orders to the letter and not stopped for anything but the briefest of rest and refreshment on the way. He had spared no expense in the changes of mount, and his last was blowing hard when he rode into the stinking, crowded streets of the capital. Riley had accompanied Sir James and Lady Webster twice on their visits to London and was not unacquainted with the city.

His fears that he might be kept waiting or that Sir Lionel would be from home — at court, perhaps — were dispelled when the wizened little French servant, whom he remembered from Sir Lionel's stay at Manor Court, took a quick glance at him, then left immediately to inform his master, and Riley was instantly summoned into the parlour, where Sir Lionel rose from his indolent position on the day bed, indicating that his man-servant should stay in the room.

'You may very well be needed, Pierre. Come, man, what is it? Barbizet says you've come from Leicestershire, and in a hurry, by the looks of you. Is Mistress Corinna ill?'

Riley shook his head. He was exhausted and still breathing hard.

'No, sir, but Sir James has been hurt in a riding accident. It is not too serious, but he is unable to leave his bed and sends me with this urgent message.'

Lionel took the sealed letter and waved his hand towards a high-backed chair. 'Sit, man, before you fall down. You say Mistress Corinna and Lady Webster are well?'

'Mistress Corinna was still at Brinklow near Coventry, sir, when last I heard. My lady is well, but——' he hesitated '—but anxious, sir. I was told to ride here at all speed.'

'This was written yesterday?'

'Yes, sir.'

'Then you have done well.' Lionel scanned Sir James's letter while Pierre Barbizet watched him closely. When he lowered the paper his expression was inscrutable, but the Frenchman was not unaware of the glint in those tawny eyes and the slight and sudden hardening of the lips.

Lionel said steadily, 'We must leave for the West Country at once, Pierre. Will you pack necessities? But first arrange for this man to be lodged here for the night and well fed before he faces the journey north. I shall write an immediate answer to Sir James, which you will carry for me.' He smiled encouragingly at Riley. 'But take your time, man; the need for mad haste is past. I shall take over from you here.'

The arrangements were made and Lionel and Barbizet on the road to Bath by early evening. Lionel had stayed only to write to a friend at court, pleading the ill health of a relative and the need to absent himself from London for a short time. The man knew him well and could not misunderstand his need to leave town.

'Nowadays any gentleman who is missing from court or his own home is bound to be suspect,' Lionel remarked to his manservant.

Whitehall was in chaos. The King had known of his

nephew's landing at Lyme by June the thirteenth. He had immediately placed almost the whole of the regular army with the exception of the third regiment of the guards — a Scottish establishment, and still on the Border, but with the instruction to come immediately south — under the command of Lord Feversham. The third regiment of foot, some cavalry units and the Admiral's regiment were also kept in reserve. The court seethed with conflicting reports. Monmouth's forces, it was alleged, would vastly outnumber the King's, yet would be mostly ill equipped. By every messenger news came of men joining the Protestant army, and the King was becoming more and more short-tempered and alarmed for the eventual safety of the capital. Lionel knew Feversham, with Churchill as second in command, was already ensconced in a defensive position in the West Country, more than likely quartered in Bath, and his fears for Corinna were very strong.

James had enclosed Corinna's letter with his own as further information, and he knew she was well escorted with Rose and Jesse Grimsley, but the foolish wench was headed for the Royalist camp. Soldiers on the march were not renowned for disciplined behaviour, and the royalist commanders, furious with the malcontents, would be likely to give their men their heads and allow them to prey on the local villagers, with dire results. On his travels Lionel had seen what roistering soldiery could do, and the very thoughts of his betrothed at the mercy of such men caused him to grate his teeth in impotent fury. Corinna was travelling in a hired coach, so he had no need to slow himself down with so cumbersome a vehicle and was able to ride fast.

Pierre was generally silent until asked for an opinion.

Lionel flashed him a grim smile as they mounted up.
Pierre Barbizet had been in his employment for almost
two years now. Lionel had saved his life in a skirmish
overseas, and the man had served him devotedly since
that day. Despite his determination to behave as a
subservient attendant, Lionel considered Pierre more
as a companion, especially now that his soldierly skills
and experience would prove indispensable on their
journey and later.

'Feversham's men will probably be settled in Bath.
It is to be hoped Mistress Webster has either given up
this foolish quest or turned further east, out of harm's
way.'

Pierre's raised eyebrow indicated that he, like his
master, entertained no such optimism. He had watched
the young lady closely during their last visit to
Leicestershire and, while admiring her spirit and
beauty, considered Sir Lionel would have no light task
in enforcing his dominance over her, both now, during
this crisis, and later, when she became his wife.

Lionel went over James's letter in his thoughts.
Corinna was concerned not only for her brother, but
for Oliver Hunt. If the man was now imbued with a
heroic image it would be more difficult than ever to
overturn him in Corinna's affections.

He set spurs to his mount. Even riding flat out, it
would be late tomorrow before he could have hope of
hearing any word of Corinna. There was Reading
ahead of him, then Marlborough, Calne and finally
Bath. He prayed fervently that the city would not
prove to be the armed camp he feared to find it.

Corinna found it almost impossible to possess herself
in patience during the first days of the journey. Fortunately she had no shortage of coin, and they were able

to bespeak private rooms for herself and Rose while
Jesse found relatively comfortable quarters above stables where he could oversee the safety of his vehicle
and horses. They progressed along the ancient Roman
way to Moreton-in-Marsh and the rolling, prosperous
country of the Cotswolds. They stayed at Moreton the
night, then on to Stow-on-the-Wold, where they took
refreshment before turning towards Cirencester. Here
they spent the second night. Jesse, listening avidly in
the tap-room for news, told them later there had been
much talk of a battle at a village called Philips Norton
on June the twenty-seventh. It had proved inconclu-
sive, but Jesse added, after hesitating and being
prompted by Corinna, 'They do say there were casualties on both sides. The Royal army has gone to lick
its wounds at Bradford-on-Avon and the Duke's army
has headed for Frome. He'll be wanting to establish
himself in Bristol, like enough, but the bridge at
Keynsham had to be repaired first, and it was here that
Monmouth's men were set upon and had to retire. The
Duke of Beaufort holds the city for the King. One old
man said a carter told him the Duke had threatened to
burn the city rather than let Monmouth pass. It was to
spare the people that Monmouth bypassed the city and
turned towards Warminster. Then he were caught at
Philips Norton.'

'Jesse, where do you think he will make for now?'

'The road towards London be blocked for him now
by the King's forces, and I reckon he'll fall back on
Bridgwater to rest his men and have a council of war
with his commanders.' Jesse turned a reproachful eye
on his mother. 'With news of the Royalist army in the
district ahead, don't you think as how we should turn
north again? Since battle be joined, any chance of
dissuading Master Julian from taking any more part in

it seems pointless. He be already committed and has burnt his bridges.'

Rose shook her head slightly, but Corinna said stoutly, 'I shall understand if you should decide to return home, Jesse, and take your mother to safety, but I must go on. Surely there must be a way for me to approach Bridgwater and have words with my brother? Perhaps it might be possible to hire a coachman here.'

Rose's inscrutable black eyes challenged those of her son, and he gave her a rueful shrug. 'Well, if'n you be determined, mistress, why then we must go on, but, I warn you, things are going to get much harder the further westwards we go.'

During the following day's journey they saw signs of people fleeing eastwards from Tetbury. Corinna leaned from the coach window to call and enquire for news from an old man driving a heavily laden wagon piled with household goods, with his wife perched precariously atop the lot.

'Good sir, is there trouble ahead, movements of troops or interference to travellers?'

'Mistress, King's men be pouring into Bath and there's the usual unrest in the streets at such times. I'm taking my wife for a while to my daughter's house near Cirencester. Best if you don't go on any further, unless your need be urgent.'

She thanked him courteously. 'Yes, I do need to proceed. Are travellers being prevented or delayed?'

'No, mistress, I saw no evidence of that, but the roads west are no place for ladies of quality. There'll be more blood spilt in plenty before many days be passed, you can be sure of it.'

The cart rumbled on, and Corinna turned troubled eyes to Rose.

'We cannot be far from Julian now. King's officers would not challenge us, surely?'

Rose sniffed, but forbore to comment. 'We have still sufficient coin to have some effect on innkeepers — and soldiery, come to that,' she said drily. 'If you're set on this, why, let's get on, but if there's trouble in Bridgwater, or the men are undisciplined, promise me you will leave at once.'

Corinna swallowed hard and nodded. Her hand reached out to grasp her nurse's, then Rose leaned forward to call to Jesse and urge him to drive on.

Their pace became slower now, due to the increase in travellers using the road, and Corinna fretted until they were in the outskirts of Bath. As the old man had said, she now had her first glimpse of Royalist soldiers marching through the streets in formation, shouldering pikes, drinking disconsolately outside inns, sometimes shouting bawdy comments to the buxom inn girls, but so far there was little evidence of disruptive behaviour. Their party was not challenged and Jesse drove straight through, thinking it best not to linger in the town to partake of refreshment. He stopped at a small village near Wells for dinner and to rest their horses. Corinna was anxious to press on then, and they made it safely through Wells and Glastonbury to arrive in Bridgwater before sunset. Here again, as at Bath, they found the town packed with troops, apparently as well disciplined but considerably less well equipped. Corinna's heart beat somewhat faster as she realised that at last she had reached Monmouth's armed camp and was within a stone's throw of finding Julian.

At first it seemed they would not be able to find accommodation for the night, but good coin spoke more eloquently than words, and Jesse managed to obtain a room for the two women at the White Hart.

'If I were you, Mother, I would bar your door to all but the inn wench and myself. I'll get them to serve you a meal in your chamber,' he said, as raised voices could be heard from the kitchen. Clearly the proprietress was being harassed by some importunate officer who wished the sole attention of one of her serving wenches.

'I've told ye, I'm much too busy to be sparing Bess,' she snapped. 'You'll have to be waiting till I've settled my guests for the night. After that. . .' Her voice was lost then to the newly arrived visitors, and Rose's lips twitched as she ushered her charge hurriedly up the stairs.

'We'll stay to hear no more of that.' There was a trace of laughter in her voice then she bent to whisper in Jesse's ear, 'Get you out and about after you've eaten and stabled the horses. Try to get word to Master Julian that his sister is here and anxious to speak with him.'

'Aye, I'll do that, Master Julian or Master Hunt.'

Rose hesitated, glancing uncertainly at Corinna's back as she reached the head of the stair.

'As to Master Hunt, tell him. . .oh, well, yes, tell him we are here and need news of Master Julian.'

The bed chamber was small and somewhat cramped, but a truckle-bed could be accommodated and the sheets looked clean and well aired. Rose thrust open the casement and leaned out. The noise was surprising for what was habitually a small market town: trundling of wheels, carts, coaches, heavily laden wagons and even two mounted cannon. It was stifling in the room, but once it was aired they would be best to keep the casements closed against the sounds of raucous laughter and drunken shouting.

Corinna joined her at the window. She scanned the

busy street thoughtfully, and there were lines of strain round her eyes and mouth.

'We shall be safe here, don't you think?'

'Aye, safe enough, so long as we keep to the inn. I'll not have you walking the streets in search of that brother of yours. Promise me. Leave the searching to Jesse.'

Despite the noise below throughout the night, the women slept well. Both were exhausted. Jesse had slipped up to inform them that all was well in the stables, but that he had, as yet, heard no news of the whereabouts of either Julian or Oliver.

'The army only began to enter the town this morning and most have been given leave to visit families in the area. The Duke intends to stay here only a couple of days before making for Gloucester. The men seemed to have got a bit out of hand in Wells and stole some lead off the cathedral roof, were about to loot the church itself until Lord Grey stood directly before the altar to protect the chalices and rood cross, so it's probably to build up goodwill again that the Duke has granted leave. I'll see what I can discover in the morning.'

Corinna woke before Rose and washed quietly before waking her. The water, remaining from the previous evening, was cold on her flesh, for it had been close in the night and she felt still sweaty. The streets were quiet now, the men sleeping off the excesses of yesterday, and she sat by the window, revelling in the faint breeze which stirred the curtains. There was a flurry of movement below, an imperious call, as two riders drew up before the inn entrance archway. Corinna drew back, unwilling to be seen, wondering if some news of troop movements brought the riders so early on to the streets.

Rose stirred and sat up.

'Something wrong? Was that Jesse calling?'

'No, some newcomers arriving. They seemed in haste. I got the impression they had ridden through the night. I hope it is not ill news for the rebel army.'

Rose grunted and stood up to dress. 'If so, we'd best breakfast and be ready. Experience has taught me that in dangerous circumstances it's always best to eat well. There may not be opportunity later, and if Royalist troops are on the move we'd best be safer out of the city.'

'Rose, I won't leave Bridgwater till I've found and spoken with Julian.'

'Indeed you will, mistress.' Abruptly the stout door was flung open. The newcomer had, without ceremony, put his shoulder hard against it, pushing clear the bar Rose had set in place last night, and a tall figure strode into the chamber. Corinna gave a frightened cry. Her blue eyes met the furious tawny ones of her betrothed as Sir Lionel Summers walked past her to the window, looked briefly below, then turned back to the two women. Pierre Barbizet hovered in the open doorway behind him.

'Both of you, complete your dressing. We must breakfast outside the town. We leave at once.'

Astonishment gave way to anger, and Corinna stared back at him defiantly. 'I do not know how or why you are here, Sir Lionel, but I intend to stay until my business is concluded. I take it my father informed you of —'

'He did indeed — has fallen from his horse and is too ill to ride. He charged me with the task of returning you to Leicestershire, and I will do so, mistress, if it means carrying you every inch of the way bound.'

Corinna's face had paled at the mention of her father's accident.

'How dare you declare authority over me? Father would never have countenanced such behaviour——'

'Are you not interested in his condition?'

'Of course I am, but——'

'There is no danger, but his leg may be broken and he cannot travel. Naturally he gave me authority over you. He is alarmed for your safety as I am.'

Frostily she returned, 'Then I am duly grateful, sir, but I am in no way threatened here, at this time, in spite of your fears. No one has offered me insult on the journey nor spoken to me so discourteously as you have done. I shall remain here. If you are alarmed for your safety, I suggest you leave Bridgwater at once.'

Her calculated insult caused his features to darken with rage, and he advanced on her and caught her arms in a hard grip.

'I do not intend to bandy words with you, Corinna. It is highly likely battle will commence today or tomorrow. Monmouth will try to leave the town, and his way to Gloucester is barred by enemy troops. He will fall back on the town and be pursued like as not. Have you any idea what will then happen here?'

She drew a hard breath. His words had alarmed her, but she would not give in now she was so close to the two men she loved so dearly.

'You cannot know that, and no man of honour would harm a woman.'

He released her arm and folded his own arms. 'You have much to learn, Corinna, about so-called men of honour. Suffice it to say that I have had more experience of such circumstances. Listen to me, woman. You could be taken by Royalist soldiery, accused of complicity. Oh, yes, anyone who aids or associates with rebels could be so indicted. Do you know what happens to women found guilty of treason, Corinna? They burn at the stake. Men die horribly mutilated at Tyburn, and women burn. Think about it, but don't delay long. I want you ready to leave within the hour.' He turned to Rose. 'I understand your son drove you both here?'

'Yes, sir.'

'Then send word to the stables for him to prepare the coach. I'll order some food to take with us. I'm famished, have ridden through the night.'

He withdrew with a slam of the door, and Corinna flew into Rose's comforting arms.

'I won't go,' she stormed. 'I will not. He is not my husband yet and ——'

'Corinna, child, he is right. We must not be caught here if hostilities begin. What chance would Jesse have if he were arrested?'

Rose's words jolted Corinna to awareness of their danger. She must think of the others. She shuddered as she recalled Lionel's words. 'Men die horribly mutilated at Tyburn'. Was she too late to save Julian and Oliver from such a fate? Her hands were trembling as she drew her small travelling chest to her and began to fold up her night rail.

Rose had not seen Lionel Summers recently, and she was startled by the changes in his personality. The quiet, reserved boy had suddenly become this arrogant, capable man and, though she accepted the wisdom of his orders, she began to understand why Corinna feared for her future happiness as his wife. She finished dressing and descended to the kitchen, where she discovered the pot boy, who proved very willing to abandon his duties and go in search of Master Grimsley.

Jesse knocked on their chamber door well within the

hour to find Sir Lionel and his man impatiently waiting
while the women completed their packing.

'All is ready, sir.' He turned respectfully to Sir
Lionel, who was tapping his riding whip against his
thigh boot. 'The horses are harnessed.' He turned to
Corinna. 'I managed to get some news at last. Both
Master Julian and Master Oliver, as well as their friend,
Master Spicer, are in the Duke's green regiment. All
are in attendance on their commanding officers at
present. I left word with the pot boy, who seems
trustworthy, to get word to one of them, if he could,
before the march began, also that word could reach us
if left at the White Hart. If things work out perhaps I
could ride back here later and see if a message has
been left.'

Sir Lionel nodded curtly and turned hurriedly on
Corinna.

'Can we leave now?'

She nodded and shouldered her way by him to the
head of the stair. She had offered no more objection
to his orders, though Rose recognised that glitter in
her mistress's blue eyes, which boded no easy journey
for her betrothed.

Corinna sank into her place in the coach while Rose
saw to the loading of their travelling chest and baggage.
Barbizet handed in to Corinna a basket of provisions
for the journey, and Rose seated herself opposite,
Jesse climbed to the driving seat and Sir Lionel and
Barbizet prepared to mount up and ride each side of
the coach.

'We may be stopped in the outskirts or on the road
by Churchill's men,' Lionel said coldly to Corinna. 'If
so, leave all the talking to me.'

She nodded sulkily, and Jesse whipped up the horses

as the vehicle lumbered off towards the Glastonbury road.

As she peered through the window Corinna could see no evidence of men preparing for combat or for a march. Most still stood in groups, talking or yawning, before entering inns to seek ale and food. One officer, pistols thrust through his sash, saluted Corinna as they drove past, and then they were out on the open road.

Lionel obtained rooms for them at the Green Man, and, truth to say, they were considerably more comfortable than their accommodation in Bridgwater. Corinna retired to her chamber, unwilling to talk with him, and insisted that breakfast should be served there. He merely bowed in acknowledgement. Corinna felt Rose's disapproval of her conduct, though she said nothing, and at last Corinna laid down her napkin with a distinct slap.

'Well, do say what you are thinking — that I have been uncommonly rude to the man.'

'He is anxious only to ensure your safety as your father asked,' Rose said mildly.

'He has no right to command me so brusquely.'

'And would you have come away if he had requested you to quietly?'

Corinna made a small moué and shifted awkwardly in her seat.

'He angers me constantly,' she admitted at last. 'Father must see that we cannot have any hope of happiness together.'

'Your father knows you need a firm hand,' Rose commented drily. 'I am not so sure this is not the man to ensure that, too.'

'You think I should apologise?'

'If you think the situation requires it.'

Again Corinna shifted uncomfortably. 'Will you go and find him, Rose, and ask him to come to me here?'

Her nurse rose at once, smiling. 'That's my sensible girl.'

Corinna waited miserably until the knock sounded on her door and Sir Lionel paused in the doorway.

'You requested my presence, mistress?'

She avoided his eyes and pleated the silken folds of her skirt in her embarrassment.

'I believe an apology is due, sir. I behaved abominably. Please accept that my rudeness was partly due to my concern for my brother's welfare.'

A faint smile twitched his long lips. 'And my unpardonable arrogance due to mine for yours. Shall we cry truce, Corinna?'

She nodded shyly, and he advanced into the room to bow over her hand in that courtly manner she found vaguely unnerving.

She said anxiously, 'You indicated that you think things will go very badly with the rebels.'

He shrugged slightly. 'The country as a whole is not with the Duke. The people want no more disturbances, and the rebels are, for the most part, inexperienced and poorly equipped.'

'Yet at Philips Norton both sides withdrew without a victory and left many casualties.'

'Yes, but Churchill is a fine soldier and Feversham will be guided by him. Even if Monmouth were to achieve partial victory here, it cannot last. The people will not accept him. I believe he is beginning to know that himself.'

'Then why doesn't he call off this madness?' Corinna's voice rose in agitation as she moved to the window.

'He knows what will happen if he surrenders, though

it is possible he has already put forward an intended plan for flight. His followers will not want him to desert them. How would they stand then? They cannot all take ship from the country, abandon their wives and families. It was to try to protect them that Monmouth had himself proclaimed King.'

'I don't understand.'

'Technically no man can be charged with treason for supporting the man he holds to be his rightful king.'

'Then, even should they lose this battle, the rebels would be safe?' Corinna's heart lifted at this crumb of comfort.

Sir Lionel quickly disillusioned her. 'The King will take no notice of that view. No man or woman who aids Monmouth will be safe after this débâcle. We should do well to get you clear of the whole district and safely on the way home.'

She shook her head. 'I will not leave until I have definite news of my brother's fate.'

'And that of Master Oliver Hunt?'

Crimson flooded her cheeks. 'Yes,' she said quietly, lifting her chin in defiance, 'of Oliver too. We have always been——' she hesitated '—close. Oliver is like a—brother to me.'

'Yet your attitude towards him is hardly—sisterly.' The dry note of condemnation had crept into his voice again, and tears glistened in her eyes.

'No, my feelings have recently been more than sisterly, but all that is over. My father has made plain to me that he would not accept my choice, and—and I must be obedient to his wishes.'

He bowed and moved to the door again. 'Well, it seems I must be patient. Two days, Mistress Corinna, I shall wait before I insist on resuming our journey north. Naturally I shall do all in my power to extricate my future brother-in-law from this unfortunate coil.'

She gave a quick sigh of relief. She had not expected him to concur so easily. The next hours would be unbearable while they waited for news.

Once outside the door Sir Lionel too sighed heavily. This delay was against his own better judgement. James would have had him carry her kicking and screaming if necessary from Somerset, yet how would James face the loss and disgrace of his son? For his friend's sake, as well as his betrothed, he would wait out these next crucial hours until he and Pierre could get decisive news and venture into Bridgwater again.

CHAPTER SIX

IT WAS the middle of the following afternoon before the news they were waiting for came. Corinna had been kept in a state of frantic suspense within her chamber.

'It is not advisable for you to be seen too openly in Glastonbury,' Sir Lionel informed her. 'As I said yesterday, anyone suspected of helping rebels could be charged with treason and, since you are related to Julian Webster, that could place you in peril. I want your promise that you will stay within your room.'

Reluctantly Corinna gave it. Sir Lionel came up to their chamber rarely, apparently realising that his presence was unwelcome. Jesse occupied himself making sure the coach and horses were ready to proceed within a moment's notice, and Rose and Corinna were forced to sit idly by the window most of the time, hoping to see some messenger or even a stranger heading away from Bridgwater ride into the town.

It was Jesse who ushered up the pot boy from the White Hart. The boy looked round anxiously and was clearly uncomfortable about his errand.

'Your message, mistress, wot you sent out to Master Webster to send word to the inn. . .'

'Yes?' Corinna jumped up at once and gestured for Rose to pour wine for the boy. He took the cup doubtfully and downed the contents, still looking round, as if for some suitable person to entrust with his message.

'Well,' Corinna snapped impatiently, 'have you heard from my brother? Where is he? Is he safe?'

The boy's round, dark eyes viewed her cautiously. 'Master Webster be your brother?'

'I have said as much, boy. Tell me what you know of him.'

Before the lad could answer, Sir Lionel entered hurriedly. The boy looked relieved, and turned to face the man so obviously a gentleman and one in authority. Corinna's temper was rising, but she saw the wisdom of allowing the boy to proceed without further interruption.

'You need to know about Master Webster, sir?'

Sir Lionel nodded, frowning.

'He be at our inn, sir. He bade me get word to your party.'

'He is in hiding? The battle is over?'

The boy nodded solemnly. 'Early this morning. The King's men pursued the rebels right into the town, and the Duke, they say as he's flown.'

Corinna gave a little cry, and Lionel let out a sigh. 'Go on. Tell us of Master Webster.'

'Well, the town be all upset, sir, soldiers everywhere, Kirke's dragoons. They do be dragging off prisoners, and some they 'ung on inn signs and posts — not on ours, praise the Lord. They searched the inn though, frightened all our wenches — '

'What happened, do you know?'

The lad shook his head. 'Some say as how the Duke marched out in the night for Gloucester, but the King's men be between him and the road so he tries to make a surprise attack on the enemy camp in the night.' He gave a nerous snigger. 'Course, you do need to know our country, though they did have a guide. They was all told to keep quiet, but somebody fired a musket and warned the enemy. Stumbled into one of the dikes, they did, and them royal soldiers fought hard.' He shook his head. 'Who knows the truth of it? There be rumours all over town, but truth is the battle is lost for King Monmouth, and there be a price on his head and on the heads of all fugitives.'

Lionel lifted a hand to stem Corinna's urgent questions.

'Yet Master Webster came to the inn—after the search?'

'Yes, sir. He stumbles in with a man to 'elp him 'bout an hour after. I sees him and hides him in the stable. He gives me a gold piece,' he explained, looking from one to the other of them, 'said as 'ow you'd give me another.'

'You shall have it,' Lionel said curtly. 'Is he badly hurt?'

'He took a musket ball in the thigh. He can walk— with 'elp—but he daresn't go out on the street, not how he is.'

'Is he well hidden? Does your innkeeper know— does anyone know where he is?'

'No, sir. I be alone in the yard when he come in. The master, he be shouting about the damage the soliders did, and inspecting the barrels in the cellar——'

'Good, so there be two fugitives?'

'No, sir, the other man, he took to his heels and was off the minute we got Master Webster settled above the stable in the hay rack.'

Corinna's heart missed a beat. Could the second man have been Oliver and, if so, how was he faring with a full-scale hunt in progress?

'Right, lad,' Lionel was saying briskly, 'I want you to go back to the inn alone. Tell no one—no one at all—about this. If you do, you yourself could be in danger. Can you meet me in the yard soon after midnight when the inn has settled for the night?'

Corinna said sharply, 'We must go at once.'

'You are going nowhere,' Lionel snapped. 'Leave this to me. Julian must be brought clear after dark. As the boy says, to be seen on the street wounded would mean instant arrest. He is safe enough at present, particularly since the inn has already been searched. Pierre and I — no, better still, Master Grimsley and I — will ride into Bridgwater and bring him out. Grimsley is known and trusted by Julian even better than I am.'

'You will take the coach?'

Lionel gave a short bark of laughter. 'Trundle a coach through Bridgwater at such an hour? No, Julian must ride, and, even then, he must walk a way to the horses. They must be kept well clear of the main street.'

'But he is hurt, his leg. . .'

'He will be worse hurt if he does not manage to obey me,' Lionel said brutally. 'He must be brought here and conveyed by coach tomorrow morning.'

'A doctor — '

'No doctor. We must tend him as best we can until we are well clear of the district. Now, mistress, occupy yourself in tearing up shifts or suchlike for bandaging. I will see to it that Pierre is given instructions. Then we will take supper together in the private room below. Yes,' he said grimly, 'I know you have no appetite for food, but you will eat with supposed enjoyment. I shall have no need to pretend. My appetite is always sharp before a game is actually in progress.'

He moved the boy before him to the door, reaching within his capacious pocket for the promised coin. As Corinna heard them descend the stair she let out a pent-up breath of frustration. For the first time in their acquaintance, she was glad of his presence here. She was seeing him in a new light. Gone was the dandified courtier; here was the man of decisive action. She recognised, bleakly, that in his hands lay Julian's slim chance of survival.

Lionel found Pierre Barbizet in the inn tap-room. Quickly he gave him the news.

'Pierre, I want you to stay here with my betrothed and Mistress Grimsley. Jesse Grimsley was well nigh brought up with Julian Webster and seems the best choice to go with me. We'll need two more horses. Best buy them away from here if you can.'

Barbizet nodded in understanding.

'That might prove difficult since most in the area will have been commandeered for one of the armies. Do your best. Grimsley has seen to it that the coach is in good repair and ready for travelling immediately.' He paused while the Frenchman's bright, dark eyes regarded him steadily. 'If I am not back by daybreak, you should arrange an early breakfast for Mistress Corinna and Rose Grimsley, harness up as early as you can, and start for Leicestershire.' As Barbizet made no comment he added, 'I shall join you the moment I can — if I can.'

Again Barbizet made no objection other than a heavy sigh.

'Do you know how bad the young man's injuries are, milord?'

'A ball in the thigh, I understand, but I dare not risk summoning a surgeon.'

Barbizet pursed his lips. 'Once we are free of this district, I will do my best for him, milord.'

The Frenchman rose and went off about his errand, and Lionel took himself upstairs again. He signalled by one raised brow to Rose that he wished to be alone with her charge, and she instantly obeyed him, murmuring something about ordering supper for all of them early.

Corinna faced Lionel anxiously. He crossed to her chair and, leaning down, took both her shoulders in his grasp, his face very close to hers.

'Things have happened as I feared, and it is time for you to be both brave and practical.'

She swallowed hard, not flinching under the strength of his fingers.

'I swear I will not be a trial to you, sir.'

'Good. I have instructed Pierre to harness up and travel soon after daybreak — if I haven't returned by then.'

Again she swallowed, and he continued, 'The hunt for fugitives will continue for several days. You must not be involved. You understand? It will not help Julian or, indeed, any of us if you are to tarry here and be harassed or, worse, be arrested by a company of the militia. The news from Bridgwater is not pleasant. Kirke, whose regiment appears to be in control of the searches and arrests here, is sparing no one indignity. Old and young, rich and poor, are being questioned, and their properties searched. Sooner or later the hunt will reach Glastonbury and, with or without Julian, you must be away from here by then.'

'Oliver — my cousin,' she whispered. 'We do not know what has happened to him. My aunt will be frantic for news.'

His lips tightened and his brows twitched together in the black scowl she knew well. 'It may be that Julian will be able to tell us more. If not. . .' His voice trailed off as he straightened up, releasing her. 'I have your word that you will obey Pierre Barbizet in my absence as you would myself or your father?'

She was trembling, but she nodded.

As he moved to the door again she murmured, 'Sir —
Lionel, I want you to know how grateful I am that you
are ready to — to risk yourself for my brother.'

His hazel eyes narrowed as he looked full at her, so
intently that she flushed under the scrutiny. 'You are
my betrothed. Naturally I am anxious to render you
any service within my power.'

'If — ' she moistened her dry lips nervously ' — if —
there is any way you could help Ol — my cousin. . .'

'That too,' he returned, more coldly this time.

Supper was taken in the inn's private room, and little
was said by any of them. The innkeeper had served an
excellent meal, but it tasted as sawdust in Corinna's
mouth. She forced down the food while Lionel's eyes
were on her. Pierre tapped on the door later to report
that the new horses were ready for milord's inspection.

Lionel dabbed at his lips with his napkin and rose to
his feet.

'Right, I will be down in moments. Have you and
Grimsley eaten yet? And Pierre, how many times have
I explained to you that I am not my lord and never will
be?'

Pierre's wizened face lit up in a grin as he bowed
elaborately in the direction of Corinna and Rose.

'Milord knows well that all gentlemen in England
are milords to a Frenchman. I cannot know count from
marquis nor earl from duke.'

Lionel waved him away, smiling, and Corinna
realised that there was genuine affection between
master and man. It surprised her. She wondered what
happenings the two had shared had brought about this
trust and closeness of purpose.

Her eyes met Lionel's as he bent to kiss her fingers.

'I shall not see you again tonight. Pray for us and

keep up your heart. If fortune is with us we shall all be safely on the road north together by noon tomorrow.'

She dreaded to see him go, suddenly, to call him back, offer more than conventional words of leave-taking. There had been bad blood between them from the moment she had ridden into the yard at Manor Court and he had told her he had seen her with Oliver. She knew he judged both Oliver and Julian feckless, yet for her sake and for his friendship with her father, he was going soon into danger, possible disgrace, even death. It would not be a simple matter to convey a wounded man secretly from his hiding-place in a town riddled with Royalist troops. As he left she experienced a sudden and unexpected surge of emotional fear for him.

Lionel and Jesse Grimsley drew in their horses about half a mile short of Bridgwater. It was well past eleven o'clock but Lionel was aware that Kirke's dreaded 'Lambs', nicknamed for their regimental badge and their ferocious behaviour on the field and off, were likely to be carousing still in the streets of the town long after all decent folk had taken to their beds. He looked round for some likely place where the horses could be left, near enough for them to return to them with a wounded man, yet far enough away to arouse no suspicion.

Jesse breathed quietly, at his elbow, 'I noticed, when I drove Mistress Corinna into town, a copse about a quarter-mile further on this road, where our mounts could stay hidden, sir.'

Lionel's eyes gleamed in the silvery light from the waning moon.

'It seems as good a plan as any. We could ride in, of course, though at this hour we might well be questioned concerning our business, and we cannot take in a spare mount for Master Julian.'

'Aye, sir. Since he knows me well, should I go in alone?'

'No, you would be more suspect than I am. As my man you should prove safe enough, though. . .' He shrugged.

'I understand the risks, sir. Most fugitives hereabouts are not gentle-born but simple countrymen. And I know I have not the West Country dialect.'

Lionel gave his customary short laugh. 'It's to be hoped neither of us will be seen at all, except by the pot boy, and we must pray he keeps his tryst. The lad is honest enough and means well, I'm sure, but he must be frightened. There may have been further searches — and summary hangings.'

Lionel blessed Jesse's gift for observation when the copse hove in sight and they drew in their mounts well enough in to prevent their trampling or nervous whickering from being heard from the road.

As they made their way back to it, Lionel considered.

'It may be wiser if you stayed with the horses.'

'Sir, you will need my help with Master Julian if he's sore hurt.'

'If he's as badly hurt as that, I doubt if we'll be able to move him at all,' grated Lionel.

They lingered some while near the road until Lionel considered the coast might be clear.

'It must be close to midnight now. We'll go on in. If we should be questioned, leave the talking to me. I am in pursuit of some wealthy tradesman's wife, whose husband is said to be away. It should not prove necessary to name names. Discretion is all in these affairs.'

He saw Jesse grin at him, and thought the man judged him experienced in such encounters. They stepped out briskly until the first flaring torches showed them they were approaching the entrance to the town. Windows were well shuttered and doors barred, showing the inhabitants' fear of the dragoons, and Jesse stopped abruptly as they neared an inn sign with its dangling fruit of two pathetic bodies, black against the faint moonglow.

Lionel cursed softly beneath his breath and put a firm hand on the other's arm.

'I think we shall see more evidence of summary justice before we are clear of the West Country, man. Keep up your spirits.'

They were in sight of the White Hart now, and Lionel halted on the far side of the road.

'I'll go into the stableyard alone and whistle if the coast is clear. If you don't get my signal, don't come in. Get back to Glastonbury as fast as you can.'

'Sir, I couldn't leave the young master——'

'It's to Mistress Corinna we must give your first considerations.'

'Aye, sir. I'll do as you say,' Jesse grudgingly admitted.

The yard appeared to be deserted as Lionel stepped through the entrance archway. A horse trampled restlessly in its stall and he paused, warily glancing around him. Approaching the stable, he heard a slight sound within, and the pot boy's voice came softly out of the gloom.

'It's safe to come in, sir. I'm here, behind the door.'

Lionel stepped inside, and the boy reached out to grasp his sleeve.

'Just stay still a moment, sir, till you get used to the dimness. I daresn't kindle a light near the door. I can when we get up into the hay store if we be careful and quick.'

Lionel waited until the boy moved in front of him and led him to a short rickety ladder placed from the stable floor to the hay store above. From this fodder could be forked into the mangers below.

'I'll go up first, sir, so's Master Webster won't be alarmed.'

'Is he expecting me?'

'Oh, aye, sir, and a mort of others, folk he's less anxious to meet.'

The boy climbed hastily and leaned down a hand to Lionel, who mounted after him.

They were forced to keep a bent position, as the hay occupied most of the room. Lionel's eyes had become adjusted to the dim light now, which came from a narrow grill high up, almost near the stable roof. By its faint light he saw the hay had been piled high at the front, and behind it lay a huddled form which immediately stirred at the sound of their approach.

'Is that you, Dan?'

'Aye, sir, it be and, never fear, it's your friend wi' me.'

Julian's youthful voice sounded higher and more tremulous than Lionel remembered it.

'Jesse? Jesse Grimsley?'

'I left him in the street, Julian. It is I, Lionel Summers.'

The pot boy had withdrawn a dark lanthorn from its cover and kindled it, so that Lionel was able to glimpse Julian's drawn and pallid features by its feeble glow.

'Dear God, Summers, I am thankful to see you. Is Corinna safe? I feared when I got her message that she might have become embroiled in this wretched affair.'

'She's safe in Glastonbury, where we must take you

tonight. I take it you can manage to walk. I'll tell you now, Julian, you young fool, you must, or this could prove the undoing of us all.'

Julian grimaced with pain as he moved his right leg into Lionel's view. The breeches were blood-soaked near the hip, and Lionel could see how badly the wound pained him.

'As you say, I must, but you should get clear before I make the attempt. I just hoped you or Jesse could provide me with a mount near by.'

'About a quarter of a mile away in a copse on the Glastonbury road, and you must ride. All coaches moving in and out of town are likely to be stopped and searched. We must hope that the same problem does not occur further afield. Now let me see the wound. I can do nothing here, but my man, Barbizet, has some skill with a knife and can probably get the ball out for you when we are clear of this business.' He waited till Julian awkwardly undid his breeches and allowed him to view the blood-soaked clout someone had placed over the wound in an effort to check the bleeding. Lionel thought it advisable not to rip up the breeches at this stage, since such a tear would immediately give the truth away if they were seen. With luck, in the darkness the blood stains might not be so noticeable.

He ripped up two linen kerchiefs he'd brought with him, removed the stained rag, and padded the wound as best he could.

'That should hold for an hour or so. Drink this.' He handed Julian a metal flask of brandy and watched as colour seeped again into the pale face after the man took a hard pull from it.

Julian wiped his mouth gratefully as he replaced the stopper. 'That is better, sir. I — I think I can manage now if someone helps me down that damned ladder.'

'Good. First, your sister is concerned for your cousin. Do you know anything of his fate?'

A shadow passed over Julian's face. 'Oliver brought me here, he and Bart Spicer. Oliver wanted to stay with me, but he and Bart argued, and I persuaded Noll it was best if they made off on their own. My own chance looked very slim. Bart stayed in cover while Noll helped me here, and this boy, Dan, did the rest. He'd brought me Corinna's message earlier, just before we started on that last, fatal march. Dear God, Summers, you can't imagine how worried I was when I first heard she was here, in Bridgwater, and how grateful for that mercy when I had need to get word to Jesse or even Father of what had happened, finally.'

'So Hunt and Spicer are still on the run?'

'Yes.' Julian gritted his teeth against a sudden movement. 'What odds do you place on their escaping, Summers?'

'Very slight. Already the first fruits of the rebellion are rotting on the inn signs along their escape route, and it will go ill with anyone giving assistance to rebels, the reason why I hustled Corinna clear of the town.'

'You must leave me. I know where the horse is hidden. . .'

'You'd never make it without help. Now let's get you down the ladder. You, lad, go down first and I'll lower Master Webster down to you, so you can steady him as he reaches the floor.'

'Aye, sir.' The boy scrambled down and Lionel helped Julian up into the crouching posture he himself was forced to assume, positioning him near the ladder.

'Now sit down with your legs dangling, then you can lower yourself till the boy can help you from below.'

Awkwardly Julian obeyed him, holding back a wince of pain, then gave a sharp cry as his body slithered forward in sudden momentum and the injured thigh was badly jarred. Lionel cursed beneath his breath, and they all stayed still, as if they feared the sound of that cry might have carried to the inn itself.

'Sorry,' Julian murmured, gritting his teeth again.

'Now, sir, just let yeself slither a bit further and you'll be on the floor. That's right.'

Lionel leaned down and saw that, despite the pain, Julian was standing upright and managing to limp towards the stable door. He slipped down the ladder and hurried to help him.

He handed the pot boy a small leather purse which clinked invitingly. 'You extinguish the lantern and get to your bed. Your part is done and you have our grateful thanks.'

He cautiously pushed wide the door, and gestured to Julian to join him. 'All seems clear. Try to manage without my help till we get across the road, then Jesse and I can help support you along the street. We must pray no one is abroad.'

He looked back once to see that the stable was again in darkness, and knew the boy was moving back to the inn. The quarter-moon lit the deserted street fitfully. Julian limped manfully at his side, though Lionel was sure every step was agony. They were almost to the shadowed lintel of a barred shop front where Jesse awaited them when disaster struck.

A house door was flung wide abruptly and a burly form in soldier's uniform issued forth, letting out a bellow of raucous laughter. Glancing back, Lionel saw the man was accompanied by a woman, who hurriedly put out a hand to support him, for the solider was weaving uncertainly across the path and waving what appeared to be a jug of ale or wine. He stopped and regarded the three of them owlishly.

'Here,' he demanded truculently, 'what are you three about at this time of night?'

Lionel opened his mouth to reply when the woman suddenly flung herself into his arms, almost knocking him off balance.

'There you are, at last,' she shouted. 'I've been waiting for you half the night.' She stood back from him, arms akimbo, at the sight of his companions. 'I see you 'ad to bring them along and as near pickled as you be, by the look of them. You best all come in.' Turning to her erstwhile soldier companion, she said, 'I told you, Sergeant, I was expecting me gentleman friend. Now he's here, and you'd best be back at your post before your captain catches you drinking on watch.'

The man gave a drunken laugh and put a huge hand on Lionel's shoulder. His breath stank of sour wine. He leaned forward, his face too close to Lionel's, in a travesty of a confidential gesture.

'I wish you luck with her, comrade. She's got a tongue on her when roused. Still, there's three of you to share the cost of her services, and she's worth it. I tell you straight she is, and I should know. I've had my pick of lasses hereabouts.'

Again he gave a great gust of laughter, pushed Julian out of his way, and continued along the street, lurching from wall to kerb as he proceeded.

'Inside, all of you.' The woman ushered them into the house. 'You'll need to wait here awhile, till he's well clear of the street. I take it you are the gentleman our Dan was to watch for? He's my lad,' she explained. 'Let's get your friend on to a bench. He looks like he's ready to fall down.'

She led them into a small, frowsty room which obviously served as a bedchamber for herself as well as kitchen, for there was a rumpled bed which gave evidence of her recent activities with their military acquaintance, as well as a rough, stained table, several stools and a bench near the wall. Julian sank down on it thankfully and she poured out wine for him from a flask on the table, glancing apologetically at Lionel and Jesse.

'I can't offer a drink to you two. That pig has nigh near emptied the bottle—two or three bottles, if the truth's known. I knew about Dan's business with you tonight, and when that fellow appeared in the street I thought as 'ow he'd be best locked in here with me than prowling about to spy on his betters.'

She was tall and very thin and had once been handsome, Lionel decided, but the poverty which had necessitated her way of life and the unyielding harshness of her existence had done its worst. He could not determine her age, but judged she was much younger than she looked. Her unwashed brown hair was straggling free of her cap, and her bodice still gaped from the pawing of her over-eager and clumsy latest client. He also recognised in her raddled features some surviving remnant of the enthusiasm he'd glimpsed in the eyes of her son. Both burned to serve the cause for which Julian had suffered, but both were too frightened to act, though willing now to help the injured man who had done so.

'Dan, he wanted to go join the Duke,' she said in answer to Lionel's unspoken thought. 'I begged him to stay clear. We cannot afford that sort of trouble. He's all I have, you see, and now that he's found work at the inn. . .' Her voice trailed off uncertainly, and Lionel smiled and nodded.

'You must not risk yourself. One moment and we shall be gone, but Julian here will not forget what you and the boy did for us this night. He has what he was promised.'

The woman avoided his gaze and awkwardly began to do up the front of her bodice.

She went to the street door and beckoned them to join her.

'God go with you. Be off now. I'll pray you get clear of the town, for the militia'll be back in tomorrow and there'll be more slaughter. You can bet on that.'

Lionel reached for her grubby hand and kissed her fingers. She stared at him incredulously, and in an instinctively coy movement attempted to smooth her disarranged hair. The street was clear now, and he and Jesse, each with an arm round Julian, went out into the darkness, moving as silently and quickly as they could to the place where the horses were hidden.

Corinna did not sleep that night. Mindful of the need to behave normally and not raise suspicion in the minds of any of the inn servants, she and Rose retired to their chamber and sat in the darkness, for Rose thought it best not to leave a rush dip burning. Some hours after midnight Rose fell asleep, fully clothed on the bed, but Corinna sat on, her ears straining for any sounds of arrival from below. Very early she heard the inn servants stirring and stood up to stretch her cramped limbs. Rose woke instantly, as she always had when Corinna had been a child and needed her.

'Any sign of them?'

Corinna shook her head. 'No, nothing. It should not have taken all night to ride from Bridgwater, but I imagine Lionel thought it best for them to stay hidden until the inn was ready for business.'

'Aye, likely so.' Rose busied herself tidying her

appearance. 'I'll go below and order water for you to wash, and see if I can see that Frenchman around.'

She was soon back, followed by a wench with a ewer of warm water.

'Breakfast will be brought up very soon now, mistress.' The girl curtsied and left.

'Well?'

'I found that Pierre in the stables. He knows nothing as yet, but thinks as you do. He has instructions to prepare the coach for the road, and says you must be ready to leave within the hour.'

'Without Sir Lionel and Jesse? Rose, we cannot.'

Rose pursed her lips. Clearly she was deeply concerned for her son's safety, but she shrugged philosophically.

'We can do no good making things hard for the Frenchman. If those were his master's orders we'd best obey. They'll catch us up on the road.' She avoided Corinna's anxious gaze, as if she feared the girl would question such unreasoning optimism.

Corinna was about to send down to order breakfast when she froze in her chair as a knock sounded on the door. Several people had already ridden into the inn, and she dared not hope it could be Lionel and Jesse this time.

She forced herself to answer normally. 'Come in.'

Lionel stood in the doorway. 'We met a friend of ours on the road, Mistress Webster. It is my hope that you will have no objections to his travelling with us back to the Midlands.'

She opened her mouth to expostulate when the man behind him entered the chamber. He was wearing one of Sir Lionel's light travelling cloaks, and Corinna saw now that it had begun to rain, for the drops glistened on the shoulders. She stared upwards into Julian's

drawn face and, leaving her chair, raced to throw
herself into her brother's arms. He tried to fend her
off, but she almost bore him backwards, off balance,
and he gave a sudden groan of pain. Terrified, she
watched as he lurched awkwardly, and Lionel quickly
threw a supporting arm round his shoulders and drew
him towards Corinna's bed.

'Close and bar the door,' he hissed through his teeth
at Rose, who hastened to obey.

Now Corinna saw that beneath the cloak Julian's
clothes were torn and ominously stained. She put up a
frightened hand to her lips. Lionel looked back at
Rose. 'See if you can find Pierre and bring him up. Tell
him he will need his tools. Corinna, bar the door after
her. No one must enter the chamber until we have
made Julian presentable again.'

Rose left, and Corinna shut and latched the door
from the inside after listening anxiously for a moment
on the landing. All was bustle below, but no one came
to look upwards, curious about the new arrival. When
she moved back to Julian Lionel had already divested
him of his cloak and coat. Julian's face was as chalk-
white as the pillows against which his head rested. His
teeth were biting hard on to his bottom lip. Horrified,
Corinna saw the blood welling in a large patch on the
soaked cloth of the breeches.

'How — how bad is it?'

'Bad enough,' Lionel commented briefly, 'but we
cannot summon a doctor, not here. We should put
both Julian and the man in peril. The bleeding has
begun again because Julian was forced to ride, dis-
mount without assistance, and walk normally into the
inn. We dared not excite comment.'

Barbizet scratched at the door, announcing himself
quietly. 'I am here, milord, with Rose.'

Corinna admitted them both and noted that Lionel's manservant carried two bags, one which she thought was a valise containing Sir Lionel's travelling clothes, and a smaller one resembling those she had seen carpenters carry, or masons, to hold their tools.

'It will be necessary, *monsieur*, to dispense with your blood-stained clothing,' the Frenchman explained, 'and it is to be hoped that milord's garments will fit you. *Tiens*, we must make the best of it, as you English say.'

Cheerfully he approached the bed with his tool bag, smiling at Corinna's obviously apprehensive expression.

'*Mademoiselle* must not be alarmed. It is not our intention to cut off *monsieur*'s leg. A ship's carpenter is often the doctor aboard many a vessel, and I have some surgical instruments with me as well as other tools. We must cut out the ball, milord?' His bright black eyes appealed to Lionel for agreement.

'Yes, there will be risk of infection if the ball is left. Do your best for him, Pierre. We can consult a physician later, if it should prove necessary. Here, Julian, take another pull of brandy.' He thrust the flask against Julian's lips again. 'Pierre, have you a block of wood Master Julian can bite on? It would be fatal for him to cry out.'

Rose was busying herself tearing up linen from Corinna's travelling chest, and Corinna went to help her at a warning glance from Lionel.

'Stay near the door, see it's well barred, and put off any servant who might try to enter with a breakfast tray.'

He gave a backward glance at Rose, who came to the bed with a bowl of water and bandages. 'Your son is safe in the stables, caring for the horses, Mistress

Grimsley. He will take breakfast below and be ready
to drive you very soon now.'

Corinna said softly, 'Cannot Julian be allowed to rest
for a while here?'

He shook his head. 'Out of the question. A man sick
in his room would instantly be called to account for
himself when Kirke's dragoons come, and they
assuredly will, probably before noon.'

The Frenchman was attending to his task. He had
thrust a piece of smooth-planed wood between Julian's
teeth while he skilfully extracted the ball. Julian
writhed under Lionel's hold on his shoulders, shuddered, and lay still. Rose came to wash the wound
clean, and the Frenchman applied some salve from a
small pot he withdrew from his bag. He clucked his
satisfaction as he rose and began to wash his bloodied
hands in the ewer brought up for Corinna's washing
earlier.

Julian spat out the improvised gag and tried to sit
up, but Lionel thrust him back again.

'Rest while you can, then you must change into some
of my clothes and be ready to leave.'

Rose said calmly, 'I will go and bring up some food
to this chamber. We must all eat while we can.'

Lionel nodded. 'That is very true. Once on the road
I would prefer it if we made good speed and stopped
only to rest and water the horses. Julian, at least,
should not enter any other inns in this state. Pierre,
will you eat with Jesse?'

'If you can manage the changing of Monsieur
Webster. . .'

'Of course I can. In the tap-room you may hear
something further about the battle and the pursuit.'

Julian murmured with effort, 'Try to hear word of
the Duke. And — thank you for your work on me.'

Pierre gave a mirthless grin. '*Monsieur* is kind and so brave to take such grim treatment without so much as a gasp.'

Julian's answering grin was ghastly. 'I had little chance to be cowardly, *monsieur*. All of you risk yourselves for me, and I feel now that you have helped me so far I should try to manage alone.'

'Nonsense,' Lionel said tartly, 'you're as weak as a kitten and must be guided by us as to what is best to be done. Now lie back again and rest.'

Rose and Pierre left the chamber, and Lionel drew Corinna to the door.

'This journey is going to be hard for him. You must try your utmost not to show too much concern. You understand?'

She glanced round at the bed, where Julian had fallen back against the pillows again, his eyes closed.

'He will—live?' The whisper was agonised.

'I pray he will. He has lost a deal of blood, but infection is our biggest dread. If we can get him quickly to Leicestershire we can have him under your father's physician before we arrange passage for him abroad.'

She gave an anguished gasp. 'He must leave England? But——'

'Certainly. The safety of your parents will depend on it. It is well known he was from home, and it will become evident that he and your cousin were absent from college. Questions will be asked. His only hope is to fly the country. I understand you have an uncle in the Indies.'

She nodded absently. Barbados might well be the safest place for Julian now, but his loss would bring deep unhappiness to Sir James and Lady Webster.

'My cousin?' she asked, colouring hotly, knowing his

feelings about Oliver Hunt. 'Did you — did you hear anything concerning him?'

'Julian says Hunt and that fellow Spicer helped him to the White Hart and made good their escape. It's to be hoped they make it safely to the coast.'

'You think the hunt for fugitives will be so thorough now that it is all over?'

He shrugged. 'Since all who offer help to rebels will be judged like guilty, there can be little hope for most of them. The King will want to make examples of those captured.'

'And it is likely the Duke will be taken?'

'There will be a high price on his head. He is too well known to escape detection.'

She reached out and put a hand on his velvet sleeve.

'Sir — Lionel, I want you to know how much I am in your debt.' Her eyes filled with sudden tears. 'Without your capable handling of this matter Julian would have had no hope at all.' She swallowed. 'And I know how little patience you have for his views.'

His golden eyes gazed deep into her blue ones, bright with her tears.

'You are to be my wife, Corinna. Julian is kin. It was necessary.'

She drew a snatched breath. 'No, many men would have dissociated themselves from such danger, and — and I did not think you. . .' She stumbled for the right words, and he gave a short laugh.

'You thought me too much of a court fop. You know very little about me, Corinna. One day I will tell you how badly you have judged my abilities and how Pierre Barbizet acquired his skills. Not now. There is much to be done before we take to the road. Now here is Rose with breakfast. We must eat quickly, and you can help me get Julian out of those betraying clothes.'

Afterwards Corinna could not have said how they managed to convey Julian safely to the coach. Lionel's clothes fitted passably, and Rose bundled up the torn and stained ones and carried them to the coach to be disposed of later.

Descending the stair unaided must have been pure purgatory for Julian, but the landlord was waiting for them at its foot, and his cunning little eyes rested curiously on the new arrival.

Lionel explained how Julian had come to join their party. 'My betrothed's brother, Master Julian Webster. He has been overseeing some business for me on Watchet harbour. We arranged to meet here. Unfortunately he was benighted on the road and came in very early.'

The landlord nodded as the bills were paid, and with generous amounts for the staff.

He said, as they were ready to go, 'I should make some speed out of the district if I were you, Sir Lionel. These parts will not be healthy for those without strong stomachs, and your friend appears to be over-wearied for his journey.'

Lionel's eyes met the other man's directly, and he inclined his chin.

He knows, Corinna thought, her limbs turning to ice. He knows and could betray us. Suppose there is a pursuit?

She and Rose took their seats in the coach, with Julian opposite. Jesse mounted to the box, and Lionel and Barbizet rode, one on each side of the vehicle, as they lumbered out of the inn yard.

It was clear that the jolting of the coach did not improve Julian's condition. Corinna longed to question him about the battle and the campaign, but saw that he was too weakened to talk. At length he appeared to

fall into an uneasy doze, and she was thankful he was
spared further pain and discomfort.

They were stopped only once, by a small detachment
of militia some miles short of Wells. Julian started,
fearfully awake, and Corinna cautioned him to silence
by a raised hand, as she could hear Lionel talking with
the officer. Eventually the man came to the window
and bowed to her courteously.

'Sir Lionel here tells me you are heading for the
Midlands. There should be little trouble now. We are
mopping up all fleeing fugitives and dealing with them
as they deserve. You may see some military activity
near Bristol, but I have furnished your escort with a
safe conduct. Have a pleasant journey, mistress, and
you, sir.' He bowed again in Julian's direction, and
Corinna's nails dug into the palm of her other hand as
she forced an agreeable smile in answer, then the man
had left the window and Jesse whipped up the horses
again.

In Wells they stopped to rest the horses and took a
frugal meal of ale and cold meats outside the inn, for
the rain had stopped now, and the sun, though watery
still, was warming up the landscape once more.

Lionel said quietly, 'The captain of militia had news
to impart, which you, Julian, will not find welcome.
The Duke has been taken.'

Julian gave a hurt gasp.

'He, with Grey and Buyse in attendance, set out for
Downside near Shepton Mallet, and managed to cross
into Dorset near Gillingham, where, apparently, they
picked up a guide. At Berwick St John the Duke
assumed a disguise and attempted to proceed on foot.
He had gone only three miles where he separated from
Grey, but an old woman saw them disappear into a
nearby thicket. Here the Duke lay in a ditch and

covered himself with leaves, because they had already almost run into bands of militia searching the area. Buyse was found early the same morning and, probably guided by the old woman's tale, Monmouth was found later in the ditch and identified by his George badge of the Garter and a personal pocket book.'

Julian swallowed. All of them thought silently how foolish it had been to change clothes yet still keep such betraying articles in his possession.

Lionel continued, 'The captain says he was taken before a magistrate at Holt Lodge near by and will probably be conveyed to Ringwood, the nearest town. He is unlikely to be given any further chance of escape and will, likely, soon be taken to London for trial.'

Julian nodded and turned away, his eyes brimming with tears. Corinna reached out and took his hand within her own.

So it was all over, this ill advised adventure which had been doomed from the beginning, as she had feared it would be. But for Lionel's assistance, Julian too would be facing a magistrate. And what of Oliver? Was he lying concealed in some ditch somewhere, or was he too already imprisoned and awaiting summary trial and execution?

They ate quickly and resumed their journey. Corinna felt the familiar ache in her throat from the weight of suppressed tears. When Lionel rode to her side of the coach she could only summon up a weak smile. He saluted her gravely and then fell back a trifle. They could only pray that they would not encounter other soldiers less suspicious than the young captain had been and would manage to arrive safely in Leicestershire.

CHAPTER SEVEN

CORINNA sat with her mother and father in the parlour and listened to Joel Briggs' tale of disaster. Julian was lying on the cane day-bed, still pale and strained-looking, but considerably improved from the day he had arrived home almost two weeks ago. Fortunately he had not succumbed to the fever which might have followed a severe infection. Barbizet had done his work well and, though Julian had obviously been in severe pain throughout the journey home, he had taken no great harm from the wound. The doctor had been summoned to examine him, but had declared himself satisfied by the treatment his patient had received.

'You're an extremely lucky young man, Master Webster,' he had said, standing up and wiping his hands on a towel. 'You might well have lost the leg if someone had not been knowledgeable about removing balls from wounds.' He raised his hands in a deprecatory gesture in Sir James's direction. 'I have no wish to know how your son came about his wound, sir. Better I should not. I suggest he keeps to his room for at least a week and it is given out that he has suffered a tertian fever. That should suffice.'

Gratefully Sir James had seen him to the door, relieved that no embarrassing excuses had been necessary. To Lionel he almost wept in his gratitude. He himself was still not fully recovered from the accident and was continuing to limp round the house with the aid of a stout cane.

'Fortunately I was at hand to be of service to you,'

Lionel said suavely. 'I advise that Julian takes time to recover here while arrangements are made for him to take a sea voyage, equally beneficial for his health.' His eyes met Sir James's, and he gave a slight nod. 'There will be enquiries and repercussions. I have an interest in a vessel in harbour at Whitby. The captain will be only too pleased to carry passengers on his next voyage to the Antilles.'

Sir James sighed heavily and laid an arm round his wife's bowed shoulders. Dorcas Webster was weeping copiously at thought of losing her son so soon.

'There, lass, it will not be for long. The King will be amenable to grant pardons — for a price, I'm thinking.'

'But not yet awhile,' Lionel agreed.

Barbizet was sent north to make arrangments, and the family settled to await news from the south-west. It soon became evident that Oliver was not about to return. Tabitha visited Manor Court and confessed to her sister and Corinna, in a bout of weeping, that she feared for his life.

'Saul is determined to believe all is well. He thinks prayers will aid him,' she said bitterly. 'I have never noticed that prayers helped me in desperate circumstances. We have had no news and Julian knows nothing. . . Dear God, what shall we do?'

Corinna's own eyes were filled with tears. The days of waiting stretched to eternity. Rose had agreed to come home with her. Jesse was now reunited with his wife at Brinklow. The farm needed his attention, and he could do no more, but Corinna was thankful for Rose's presence at Barrow.

Lionel, visiting Leicester, brought back the news of Monmouth's fate for which Julian was anxiously waiting.

'He was taken from Winchester first to Farnham

Castle, then lodged in the tower of Archbishop's Abbots Hospital, then from Lambeth to Whitehall. He had requested an audience with the King, which was granted. It's rumoured he begged for his life on his knees, but it was useless. The King was in no mood to grant mercy and, indeed, would have been foolish to do so. His mistake, in my estimation, was in granting an audience at all, knowing he could not excuse such treachery.'

Julian said through stiffened lips, 'Has — has he been executed?'

'On Tower Green on July fifteenth. He was imprisoned for two days in the Tower, where he was able to see his wife and children. They had been lodged there since July ninth. It was Archbishop Turner who informed him he was to be executed the next day. I heard he died very courageously, considering that the executioner botched the job badly, needing five blows of the axe to dispatch him.'

Corinna covered her eyes and turned away with a little cry of pity and distress. How terrible that so handsome and high-born a young man should come to so terrible an end!

'There is no news from Glebe?' Julian questioned, his face white. Corinna could see that his lips were trembling. His Duke's fate had finally brought home to him what disaster his behaviour had brought on the whole family, and made his fears for his friends more acute.

'Nothing. The talk in Leicester is that it is a mercy that the rising did not affect this part of the country at all, but questions could still be asked about why you students absented yourselves from university, and the trials in the West Country have scarcely begun yet,' Lionel forecast grimly.

They were to wait and pray, until Joel Briggs arrived to confirm their worst fears.

He arrived from Glebe one wonderful summer morning when the sun shone gloriously, as if to mock their despair.

'I studied with Oliver, Bart Spicer and your son, sir,' he explained to Sir James when requesting his permission to see Julian. 'I have come from Glebe Farm, where I was able to give Master and Mistress Hunt news of their son, and they told me to come on here and see Julian.'

He was conveyed to the parlour where Sir James, Corinna and her mother stayed too, sitting close together, their hands clasped so tightly that the flesh showed white against their knuckles.

Julian pushed himself further up against his cushions and welcomed his visitor with a glad cry.

'Joel, you made it this far? Thank God.' His expression changed as he became aware of the grimness of his fellow student's countenance. 'You have news of Oliver and Bart?'

'Aye, I have. Both taken and condemned already, confined in Taunton gaol. I dared not risk attempting to see them in their cell, and I can't be sure whether either of them glimpsed me in the court. They were all chained together in a line and brought before the Lord Chief Justice, God condemn his foul soul to the flames of hell.' He turned apologetically to Lady Webster, who let out a little plaintive cry of 'Hush' then relapsed into silence again.

'Aye, milady, my curse seems harsh to your delicate ears, but if you had seen that fiend incarnate, sitting there enthroned in his scarlet robes, sniffing at his nosegay, the specific against the jail fever which has caused the deaths of many of my companions-in-arms,

you'd have said the same. They had no chance at all.
Some of them had done no fighting, simply given aid
out of the goodness of their hearts to stricken men they
found hiding in barns or abandoned near their doors.
He was not only merciless, but scornful and cruel with
his tongue. Oliver and Bart pleaded guilty, as indeed
they were, and they tried to stand up proudly, borne
down as they were with neck irons. Jeffreys subjected
them all to a biting tirade, then condemned them all
out of hand. They were in the court scarcely half an
hour, and most of that was taken up by the pitiful
shuffling they all made when they were brought in and
conveyed out again. I'd had no speech with either of
them since the battle itself, so I've no notion of how
they came to be taken. It's well known many of the
prisoners were betrayed for paltry amounts put on the
heads of fugitives.'

'How did they look?' Julian said huskily. 'I mean,
when sentence was pronounced.'

'I was at the back. It was a grave risk to be there at
all, so I couldn't see their faces, but they both spoke
up well when giving their pleas and, as I said, they held
their heads high then and when they were hustled out.'

'Is there no hope?' Corinna breathed softly. 'Can
there be no pleas of mercy to the King, no bribes. . .?'

Joel Briggs looked near to tears himself, as he turned
from her. 'I doubt it, mistress. Jeffreys is adamant, and
it's said the King sent him to the West Country
specifically to see to it that none of the rebels escaped
the extreme penalty of the law. Those young lasses,
schoolgirls who gave Monmouth that embroidered
banner, were arraigned with their teacher. They only
escaped death by the pleading of their parents and the
payments of heavy fines, and they were guilty only of
encouragement to the cause. 'Tis unlikely that any of

the men who actually fought will escape the death penalty, let alone the officers. It was being said that some of the farm workers—the strong, labouring folk—might be sentenced to transportation. They could be sold into slave labour on the plantations and would bring in a healthy profit, but gentlemen do not come into that category. I fear they will be made examples of. I wish I could offer you more comfort.'

Corinna forced herself to ask, 'How long—how long have they got?'

Briggs shrugged. 'It's hard to tell. Many rebels were hanged on the spot, as you know, but now it's taking longer. Some of them'll not make it to the scaffold, by the looks of them. The jails are full to overflowing, and jail fever must be rife, as well as many succumbing to lack of care for their wounds.'

Julian said, 'How did you manage to leave the district, Joel?'

'I hid in ditches and slept under hedges, managed to discard my buff coat and pistol holster as well as my sword belt.' He grinned ruefully. 'I stole a shirt and frieze breeches from some goodwife's washing line and dirtied my face. For a while I didn't try to leave the district. The roads were all ringed with Kirke's cursed dragoons; that's why I was near Taunton when the first trials started. After that the roads weren't so well watched. Knowing I could do nothing for Oliver or Bart, I made good my escape across fields, and by falling into those damned drainage ditches the county abounds in.'

Sir James offered hospitality. 'We can give you dinner, Master Briggs, and see you safe in one of our rooms for a while.'

'Thank you kindly, sir, but my father has given me a sound horse and I'm off to Lynn to take ship for

Holland before my luck runs out. I stayed only to bring you all the news, sad though it is. Noll would have wanted that.'

Sir James escorted him downstairs and made sure he was provided with food and wine for the beginning of his journey. Lady Webster went and stood by the window, tears falling, unrestrained, down her cheeks.

'How will Tabitha bear it?' she whispered huskily. Corinna felt a deadly chill within her. Surprisingly, now that she knew the worst she could find no tears to shed. Julian sat silent, wrapped in his own misery, with no word of comfort for his mother, whom he knew loved Oliver almost as dearly as she did her own children.

Abruptly Corinna rose to her feet. There was one hope only, one thing to be tried, and she the only person who might be able to make it possible.

Ben, the head groom, informed her that Sir Lionel was within the stable. She found him fondling his sorrel hack. His hand moved soothingly down the animal's nose as he blew gently into its nostrils. Corinna was touched by the affectionate gesture. As usual, Clytie, Corinna's spaniel, was frolicking about his booted legs.

She felt suddenly constrained and tongue-tied. After these last days she had felt considerably more at ease in the presence of her betrothed. She had been genuinely grateful and impressed by his competent handling of Julian's escape from Somerset, and had been glad when he had decided not to go immediately to London but to stay at Barrow until Pierre Barbizet returned from Whitby. Somehow his very nearness gave them all confidence, as if he could prevent any further dangers touching them. Now she was afraid that what she had to say would shatter the comradeship which had developed between them.

She said softly, as he turned to greet her with his habitual courteous bow, which she no longer found mocking, 'Ben said I would find you here. There has been a man come, a student, with news of Oliver.'

He moved closer, his eyes glinting in the dimness of the stable, but he did not speak.

'He — Oliver — has been caught and tried and — ' she fought back the weak tears which threatened to close her throat ' — condemned to death.'

His head was lowered as he wiped his hands on a towel. At length he gave a little sigh. 'Ah. I'm sorry.'

'Are you?' Her question was very low.

He looked up at once. 'Certainly I am. I would see no man lose his life when there was all of it and a wealth of promise before him.'

'Joel, the man who came, was a friend from the university. He too was a fugitive, but he went into the court and saw them. Oliver's friend, Bart Spicer, was with him.' She turned away again. 'Joel says — they were both very brave.'

Again he gave a little sigh.

'Sir Lionel?'

'Yes?'

'Is there nothing to be done? Is it possible that the judge might be — bribed, or that someone with influence at court. . .?' Her voice trailed off. 'My father is still not fit. He might not accomplish the journey in time.'

He waited gravely for her to continue.

Suddenly she said in a rush, 'I would be so grateful — you have already done so much. It may be that you know this man, Jeffreys. . .'

'I have met him at court, yes.'

'Joel said he was so ruthless and spoke so cruelly, but he was said to be venal. . .'

'George Jeffreys suffers agonies with the stone, which makes him drink excessively to attempt to dull the pain.' Lionel shrugged. 'I doubt he is more venal than the next man, but it might be possible to sway his decision by a suitable inducement. Such is the way at Whitehall.'

She turned back to him, her face suddenly alight with hope. 'Then you would go, try to save Oliver? My father would willingly pay a considerable sum, and I have jewels beside those you gave me. . .'

'It will not be necessary for you to part with them.' His tone was flat now, emotionless, but she was hastening on.

'If. . .if you will do this for me I will—I will marry you instantly, whenever you please. I know you did not want to wait until I was—ready, but now. . .' She stared back at him imploringly.

His expression was inscrutable, and she waited in an agony for him to answer.

At last he said, 'It shall be as you wish, Mistress Corinna. I will ride south today, the moment preparations can be made. If you inform your father of your willingness to marry me more quickly than we intended, doubtless he will make arrangements for the ceremony to take place soon after I return. Of course,' he added suavely, 'you realise that I might not be successful. George Jeffreys has been sent to the West Country to see that this rebellion is well and truly destroyed. He may well refuse to listen to my pleas.'

She whispered, 'I know that—Lionel and—and I trust you to do your best. Whatever the result, I—I will be prepared to pay the price.'

He nodded and reached out to take her hand, squeezing it as he would a male companion's. 'Good. Then it is a bargain between us. I am not a patient man, Mistress Corinna, as I am sure you have discovered. Your agreement to the consummation of our betrothal is welcomed by me, as I am sure it will be by your parents.'

She met his smiling answer uncertainly. There had been a note in his voice which she found vaguely disquieting. She bit her lip thoughtfully, and he released her hand.

'Perhaps if you were to return to the house and explain to your parents I will order my horse saddled and then go up and change for the journey,' he prompted as she still stood watching him anxiously.

She had thought he might kiss her as he had done that first day in the arbour, but he made no move to capture any more than her hand. He had not done so once in Bridgwater, nor in Glastonbury, nor throughout their journey home, not even when they had been alone together. She felt somehow at a loss, unsure whether she had angered him by her request. He did not appear disturbed, but there had been a subtle change in his manner towards her. He had greeted her as a friend. Now she had the uncomfortable feeling that she was no longer that, simply a pawn in a business arrangement between them.

She curtsied formally and withdrew. Once out of the stable she turned and ran for the house, arriving breathless and panting. She had achieved her end. He would go, and she knew instinctively that no man would be more likely to meet with success on this errand, yet she knew she had widened the chasm between them and a bridge must be made to cross that on his return, otherwise her life with this man would be hellish indeed.

* * *

The days which followed seemed long and painful. Sir James appeared surprised by Corinna's stated intention of marrying her betrothed much sooner than she had formerly intended. However, he made no objection, indeed, was considerably relieved. Corinna was twenty, ripe for marriage, and previously she had seemed so unwilling to consider matrimony that he had feared she might withhold her final consent to the ceremony. The nuptial arrangements occupied his mind, turning it from his grinding anxiety concerning the welfare of his only son and his agonising sorrow as he faced the shameful death of his nephew.

Corinna spent much of her time now in her chamber, preparing her clothing for her coming marriage and the move to London or Yorkshire which would follow quickly on Lionel's return. She was unwilling to spend time with Julian, who constantly upset them all by voicing his anguish about Oliver and his friend, Bart Spicer. Julian felt, in some indefinable way, that he had failed them both, deserted them in his own successful escape, though he knew well enough that his capture would have served no purpose.

Pierre Barbizet arrived two days after his master's departure for Somerset to inform them that arrangments had been finalised for Julian to sail to the Indies from Whitby within the week. From then on Julian, too, had some preparations to occupy himself, and the family was thankful that his constant and tearful denunciations of his own behaviour were stilled at last.

Corinna found her mother, Tabitha, weeping desperately in a corner of their garden, and gathered her into an unaccustomed embrace.

'You must not break your heart so,' she chided gently.

'I had to come here. Though Saul suffers as deeply

as I, his faith keeps him resolute, and he will not allow himself to give way, nor would he wish me to do so.'

'Sir Lionel is well thought of at court, and he knows what he is doing. I feel confident that he will do everything possible to save Oliver. You must have faith in him, as I have.'

Despite his warning that the outcome was doubtful, Corinna believed fervently that Lionel would accomplish his purpose. She could not analyse the source of her confidence, but only knew that, since he had promised her his best endeavours on Oliver's behalf, he would come soon with good news for them all.

Her optimism proved correct, though she was not entirely satisfied by the result of his plea.

Lionel arrived back in Barrow two days after Pierre Barbizet's arrival, and he came alone. Corinna hastened down the stair when one of the servant girls informed her their guest was back. She had hoped, against every indication to the contrary, that Oliver might be with him. Sir James and Dorcas were greeting Lionel in the withdrawing-room, and Corinna saw that his elegant riding coat was powdered with dust, and knew he had ridden hard with his news.

When he turned to face her, she strove to read the result of his mission in his expression, but he looked neither exultant nor entirely cast down.

Sir James quickly gave orders for refreshment to be provided, and pulled forward a chair.

'I can see you have not spared your horse, Lionel. Will you eat first? You must be exhausted.'

Lionel pulled off his riding gauntlets. 'No, no, my news first. I have managed to save your nephew's life, but could not win his freedom. The best I could manage was to have his name and that of his companion in misfortune added to the lists of those sentenced to transportation to the Indies. Both are indentured for ten years and then permanently exiled, forbidden to return to England.' He shrugged. 'Who knows what will have happened here by then? We must hope that the climate of opinion will have changed and that he will not be entirely lost to you.'

'Oh, thank God he is out of immediate peril,' Lady Webster murmured fervently. 'I did not believe we could possibly save him. His mother will pray for you every day of her life, Lionel.'

Julian came dashing in, his face white, his eyes pleading. A servant brought food and wine, and Lionel downed a glass of Madeira while Sir James informed Julian of what had occurred. He sank down in a chair, as if his limbs had lost their power to support him. 'Dear God, I've not been able to sleep nights, believing him already swinging from some scaffold. We shall always be in your debt, sir.'

Corinna stood frozen to the spot, and her eyes met Lionel's at Julian's words. She must pay the price, and she would, willingly, but she had to know more details of Oliver's fate.

'What will happen, Sir Lionel?' she asked quietly. 'I do not know quite what indentured labour means. Does this mean that he will remain a prisoner for all of that time?'

'I'm afraid it does. The fugitives will be shipped out on some prison ship, then exhibited on the auction block in Port Royal, Kingston or Bridgetown. The planters will bid for their services and, most likely, the men will then be set to labour in the sugar-cane fields. The King has been advised that there is considerable profit to be got from these transactions. It will not be pleasant, but Master Hunt and Master Spicer are young and strong and should survive the discomforts.'

Corinna closed her eyes. She had a mind picture of
Oliver standing, chained on a rough wooden platform,
being pawed by some red-faced, portly planter. She
saw, in imagination, the filthy, confined conditions of
the ship's hold, which would be his prison for the long
weeks of the journey. Oliver, a slave; the indignity of
it! He who cherished his freedom to ride and hunt and
fish. She gulped back her tears and tried to meet her
parents' gaze with optimism.

'Yes, they are both strong, but——' her voice faltered '—Joel spoke of the overcrowding in the jails
and of the fever which is so prevalent.' Tears brimmed
her lashes. 'However strong a man is, his stamina can
fail and his courage desert him in despair.'

'Yes, I grant you that, Mistress Corinna, but there is
hope now where there was none before.'

Corinna saw Lionel's golden-brown eyes intent on
hers, and she went to him and took his hand.

'Certainly there is, sir, and you have my devout
gratitude.'

'I have done enough?' he questioned so softly that
her parents could not overhear.

She blushed hotly, her eyes avoiding his. 'You have,
sir, and—while you have been away I have been at
pains to do my part. My father has arranged the
wedding ceremony for noon tomorrow. A special
licence was necessary, but that has been obtained
and—and I am packed and ready to go wherever you
wish.'

He bent and kissed her chilled little fingers. 'Then I
am well content.'

Lionel took himself off to his chamber, where
Barbizet was dispatched to give his report. Sir James
sent Ben, the head groom, whom he knew he could
trust, over to Glebe to give the welcome news to Saul

and Tabitha Hunt, and Lady Webster hastened to give instructions concerning Sir Lionel's accommodation and comfort. Julian sat silent and thoughtful. Corinna watched him anxiously. His leg still pained him, and today he looked as pale and depressed as he had done during the earlier days following his arrival home. She sat beside him on a stool.

'You are not happy about Oliver? His enslavement will be hard for him to bear, but he will live, Julian; surely that is much to thank God for?'

He nodded gloomily. 'I feel so responsible. Here I am, soon to travel to the Indies in relative comfort, to escape the very fate which he and Bart must endure for ten long years.'

'You cannot be blamed that you were more fortunate,' she said gently. 'Oliver would be glad you escaped that terrible time in Taunton gaol. He was never one to envy any man good fortune, except. . .' Her voice trailed off, and Julian squeezed her fingers hard.

'You are thinking your marriage tomorrow is a betrayal of the love he has for you?'

'My early marriage is the price I offered to pay for Lionel's good offices on Oliver's behalf, but you are never to speak of the matter to Father or Mother or — if ever an opportunity should arise — to Oliver himself.'

His eyes widened in shocked astonishment. 'Corinna, you have sold yourself — I thought you had come to prefer Lionel Summers and, God knows, I have good reason to wish him well, but I always had high hopes for Oliver —'

'That can never be, Julian,' she said hastily, rising to her feet. 'I do not want to talk about my reasons for accepting Lionel. I have —' she hesitated '— deep affection for Oliver, but, even were things otherwise, I could not marry him. Father is anxious for this match and I saw no reason to delay it further. It seemed a good bargain to make with Lionel. He—he might not have agreed to go to Somerset, and I was ready to make any sacrifice to save Oliver.' Julian's horrified expression deepened, and he struggled to rise from his chair, which movement still was not easy for him. Quickly she added, 'Sacrifice is a foolish word. I had hoped for more time, it is true, but I am sure Lionel Summers will make me an excellent husband. We have both seen he is not the useless fop we imagined him to be. He is capable and influential and—and he loves me, I am sure of it. You must not regret any of your part in this. Put it from your mind, Julian. I am—content.'

He shook his head at her in bewilderment, but she hastened from the room before he could say more.

That night Corinna sat for long hours at her window, unwilling to attempt to sleep. She wondered how Oliver was faring at this moment. Was he still immured in Taunton gaol or was he already within the cramped confines of the prison ship hold? At least he had Bart for company. What would Oliver think if he knew that within a few hours she would be Lionel Summers' wife? Her breathing quickened at the thought. Even now she could not quite accept the idea. Willingly she had agreed to go through with the ceremony, yet now she knew she was icily afraid. Oliver was her brother. Weeks ago she had come to terms with that knowledge, and was aware that from the moment she had known it her feelings towards him had changed. She no longer loved him as a prospective suitor. Her longing to have him safe was still strong, but as a dearly loved brother, like Julian. Perhaps she had never really loved him as she had thought. Certainly his nearness had never thrilled her as closeness to Lionel Summers did. Had

this really been the night before her marriage with
Oliver she would not have been afraid—for she *was*
afraid, terribly afraid, so much so that she was biting
her lip until it bled.

Why was she afraid? Recently he had shown her
nothing but courtesy and consideration. That fierce
possessiveness which had terrified her in the arbour
had totally disappeared. Only the explosive short scene
after their betrothal when he had found her again with
Oliver had reminded her that those feelings slumbered
still below the surface of the bland, affable outward
appearance he revealed to the world.

Now she was aware that he was a man to be reckoned
with. Over the last days, while she had waited for him
to return from Taunton, she had wondered why he had
consented to go, since he affected to despise Oliver so
thoroughly. Certainly she had offered herself blatantly,
and he professed to be wild with desire for her. Yet
desire was not love. She was well aware of that. He
wanted her, possibly because she had at first so vehemently denied him. That was his character. Lionel
Summers must have what he wanted. He had said as
much. He had been led to believe that she was to be
his, and he would not lose her to another. She stared
at herself in the mirror of her travelling chest. Was she
truly beautiful? Men had said as much—Oliver had,
but teasingly, as her cousin. . .and brother, though he
knew it not. Her complexion was good, certainly, and
her eyes, dark blue, and shadowed now with heart-
searching and distress for Oliver's fate, were large and
luminous. She ran a hand through the thick, luxuriant
tresses of her golden hair. Yes, most men would
consider her fair, yet she was vaguely dissatisfied with
her own appearance. The bone-structure was tolerable,
her figure good, but she could discern nothing unusual

in the pale reflection which swam back at her, wavering slightly in the candlelight, nothing to distinguish her from other pretty girls in the district. Surely Lionel must have seen and known many more remarkable beauties?

Fortunately she was not entirely ignorant concerning her marital duties. Both her adopted mother and Rose had seen to it that she was fully instructed. It was not the giving of herself she feared, but the man himself. Lionel Summers remained an enigma.

Impatiently she pinched out the candle flame and turned to the bed. Tonight was the last night she would have the luxury of sleeping alone, at least until such time as her husband tired of her and decreed that she should be dispatched northwards while he turned south to the court and more sophisticated pleasures.

There had been no time to have fashioned a special wedding-dress. The one in which she had been betrothed must suffice. Rose woke her early with a tray of breakfast and afterwards summoned the maids to pull into the bedchamber the wooden tub in which she could bathe. From the bed Corinna watched sombrely as the maids hastened in with jugs of steaming and cold water, while Rose laid out the dish of perfumed soft soap made in the house still-room. She sat docilely while Rose soaped her, and stood equally quietly while her old nurse rubbed her dry and enveloped her in a large, soft towel. Her hair had been washed and rinsed in a rose-water and rosemary wash. It fell to her waist in a burnished cloud as Rose combed out the tangles, arranging soft, curling wisps on to her brow.

'There, Sir Lionel would find no lovelier bride if he went to the world's end,' she murmured with motherly pride, 'and you would go as far to find a husband so bonny.'

Corinna grimaced. 'So you find him handsome, do you? I always understood you had a rare taste in menfolk, Rose.'

Her former nurse chuckled. 'Aye, I was never bound by your grandfather's puritanical notions of what a woman should or should not want. Thanks be to God, your father has no such ideas, nor, I'll warrant, has your husband-to-be. He will teach you the delights of love, or I'm not the judge of manflesh I'm reputed to be.'

'Rose, you are no true guardian of my morals. Look, already your words are dyeing my cheeks red. Mother would be horrified by such shameless talk.'

'Not she; she knows me too well,' Rose confidently replied.

She bent and peered into Corinna's eyes. 'You are not afraid? Nay, lass, I've taught you too well for that.'

'I'm — naturally somewhat apprehensive.'

'Well, that's to be expected; 'twill give spice to the occasion.'

Despite herself Corinna laughed again.

'I thought you eager for the ceremony, understood it was you yourself brought it forward.'

'Yes,' Corinna countered breathlessly. 'Yes, well, since Julian must leave England so soon, it seemed sensible for him to know me already wed. I wish,' she added wistfully, 'he could be present in the church, but Father thinks it wiser he should not attend, since he is believed to be still suffering from the effects of the tertian fever. He will be here for the celebratory meal afterwards.'

After Rose had dressed her she withdrew, and Lady Webster hurried in. She nodded her approval of Rose's handiwork. The white and gold gown still bore its pristine splendour, and Corinna wore the sapphires given her by Lionel. Her hair hung uncovered to the waist. She would go to church, as custom decreed, proclaiming to the world her virgin state. Corinna smiled a trifle grimly as her mother lovingly smoothed back a long, curling tendril. The ceremony had been arranged in such haste that many of the local gentry would be eyeing her slender waist intently, in hope of seeing some sign there that such unseemly hurry was necessary.

'You are not regretting anything?' Lady Webster enquired, her brows raised. 'Even now, and despite everything, you do not have to go through with this if your heart fails you.'

Corinna surrendered her chilled fingers to her mother's grasp.

'Oh, but I do. My word is given.'

'But even so. . .'

'Now—now Oliver is lost to me there is no man I would rather wish to give myself to than Lionel Summers. He has proved himself a loyal friend to us all.'

'I believe you are gaining a true man today, but I, more than any of us, know how things are with you.'

Corinna forced a smile. 'See, the sun is shining. Now that Julian and Oliver have escaped the worst consequences of this sorry rising, we shall all find some measure of happiness, I am sure of it. I know how you will miss us both, Julian and me, but we shall be in good hands, I in the care of my husband and Julian in Uncle's——' she hesitated then corrected herself '—in my father's hands. Lionel thinks the King will relent in time and Julian will soon be free to come home again.'

And her heart bled for Oliver, who would not return to Barrow at all.

There had been no time for the usual marital cus-

toms. No young page went before the bride, bearing
the traditional pot of decorated rosemary. There were
no bridesmaidens either, nor decorated arches of
flowers, but the church was blessedly cool and quiet,
and Corinna saw the glory of the sun light up the
medieval colours of the window above the altar. By
some miracle it had escaped the depredations of the
Civil War, the one remaining splash of colour in the
grey little building. Before it Lionel waited with
Barbizet beside him. He turned once as her father led
her towards him, and the light caught those strange
amber eyes of his. Corinna's fingers trembled in her
father's hold and she broke step just once, almost
causing her to stumble over the exquisite silk of her
gown's hem, then she steadied herself and went forward confidently.

There were few in the congregation—her parents,
Saul and Tabitha Hunt, Rose, of course, most of the
Manor Court servants and men from the quarry with
their wives, but no members of the gentry and no
Julian. She forced herself to concentrate on the words
which made her wife to Lionel Summers—Lady
Summers, she thought wryly, as she recalled Julian's
shouted accusation of her desire for a title on their ride
to Brinklow. She made her responses clearly, so that
Lionel turned towards her, his expression triumphant.
He looked elegant as ever in a coat of mulberry silk,
trimmed with gilt braiding over an embroidered waistcoat and white silk breeches. His long periwig was
elaborately curled. Corinna thought she could not
remember seeing him with a hair of it out of place, not
even during the hectic days following Sedgemoor.
Letting her mind wander irreverently from the parson's
strictures for a while, she wondered how he had
managed to achieve such splendour in so short a time,

for she had seen him in none of these garments before. Had he brought his wedding clothes with him, or were they just another addition to his extensive wardrobe, bought in France or in London before he set eyes on her this visit? She was jolted back to awareness as he took her nerveless hand and the wedding-ring was placed on her finger. It felt unfamiliar, heavy, and she glanced down at it, faintly astonished by the emotive rush of feeling it aroused in her. As they knelt together for the final blessing she prayed, desperately, that she would make Lionel a dutiful and loving wife. The latter thought caused her to turn surreptitiously towards him, as if she could read his feelings in that dignified, grave expression and bearing.

Then they were out in the bright sunshine again and villagers had gathered, surprised by the suddenness of the colourful occasion. Girls called to her, wishing her well, and young boys and labourers murmured together laughingly, offering their own bawdy good wishes to the bridegroom.

As they moved towards the carriage, her aunt Tabitha checked Lionel as he was about to hand her in.

'One moment, sir,' she said shakily. 'Give me one private moment with my niece.'

He stepped away from them with a courteous bow.

'Oh, my dear,' Tabitha said brokenly, 'tell me you are truly happy.'

Again Corinna forced a confident smile. 'Of course I am. Who would not be, married to so handsome and influential a bridegroom?'

Her mother understood instantly the underlying meaning of her words. Lionel's influence alone had saved her son's life.

She searched Corinna's face beseechingly for any

signs of distress and gave a little heartfelt sigh at finding
none. Leaning forward, she kissed her daughter's
cheek soundly, and Corinna was left with the soft
wetness of her mother's tears there as she silently
squeezed her hand and stepped back from her. Lionel
took her place by Corinna's side and, with the help of
his strong arm, she stepped up into the carriage, and
waved to the village well-wishers, then Lionel joined
her on the leather seat, his body pressing intimately
against hers, and they were driven back to Manor
Court, the first to return and be greeted by an eager
Julian waiting within the hall.

Corinna found herself hugged close and, during the
meal which followed, tried to avoid her brother's
searching gaze. She would be glad to withdraw to the
privacy of her own chamber, for it seemed that everyone was anxious to question her decision, save Rose,
who appeared overwhelmingly confident of her
charge's future happiness. Corinna's heart leaped
wildly as she realised that withdrawal would no longer
give her the privacy she had always prized. Lionel
would join her very shortly, and she must make every
endeavour to grant him the reward she had promised.

She stood by the window of her chamber, gazing out
over the gardens. The sun was westering, and she had
always loved this hour of the twilight, but tonight the
pinkish glow dyeing the landscape gave her the
impression that her familiar and loved landmarks were
tinged with blood. She gave a shiver, despite the
warmth of the evening, and hugged herself for warmth.
She knew this chill was the onset of fear. Rose and
Lady Webster had left her only moments ago. She
wore a night shift of finest white lawn, and her hair was
caught back with a silken white ribbon. This quickened

breathing and heightened awareness of the body must be common to all young brides. Not all of them were fortunate as she was, to be waiting for a handsome man who had proved his own courage, a man who made her senses swim whenever he came near her. The minutes lengthened unbearably until she heard his hand on the door-latch and turned to greet him. She had meant to go towards him, not remain like a frightened child determined to leave the width of the room between them, but her treacherous limbs let her down and she was forced to put out a hand to a high chair back to steady herself.

He was clad in an elaborate bed gown of brocaded green and gold silk, and for the first time in her presence he had abandoned his fashionable, high periwig, and she saw that his hair was dark auburn, close-cut and curling into his neckline. Without that cumbersome wig he appeared suddenly much younger and more vulnerable. She smiled a little tremulously as he strode across to her side.

'It is a fine night,' she said, half turning back to the window, as if to explain her presence there so far from the bed.

He did not answer as he stopped an arm's length from her, his head slightly tilted as he surveyed her slender form. Her breath now seemed very shallow, almost painful. Hesitantly she put down her arms by her side and waited. Still he said nothing, but she could see the pulse racing just above that tendril of curling hair in his neck.

Abruptly he came close and put both hands flat on her shoulders.

'You are cold?'

'No, no, the night is still warm.'

He nodded.

'They — they are still feasting below?'

He laughed softly. 'Julian is very drunk. Your father
had to keep him forcefully from insisting on
accompanying me upstairs.'

She gave a little grimace. One advantage of this
marriage arranged in haste was that there was not a
crowd of bawdy guests in the house to demand the
ceremony of seeing the bridal couple bedded.

She was so lovely that Lionel found it hard to
breathe. He had waited over a year for this moment,
and weeks ago had feared he might have to postpone
his conquest for some time. His betrothed was reluctant, and he knew better than to force the issue with
her doting parents. Yet fate had intervened and she
herself had consented, however unwillingly. The man
she would have preferred to bed this night was miles
away in a less comfortable couch.

He gave a slight bark of triumphant laughter and,
swinging her into his arms, carried her to the bed. She
made no remonstrance when he feverishly undid the
ribbon strings of her shift, thrusting the flimsy cloth
down her shoulders, baring the perfection of throat
and upper arms. One hand possessively over her soft
breast, he lifted the other hand to untie her hair so that
it cascaded free in a golden shower round her shoulders
and throat. He bent and buried his face in its perfumed
silkiness.

She gave a little gasp of surprise, but again made no
move to gainsay him.

'It is warm enough to dispense with your shift,' he
said thickly.

He was standing back a little now, regarding her
intently again, and she sat up on the bed, then obediently pulled the shift over her head and thrust it from
her. She was sitting supported by one arm, and her

blue eyes were half hidden from his gaze, but he could see the agitated rise and fall of her breasts and could not tell if this was the result of fear or aroused excitement.

She turned her head, a little perplexed. She had not known quite how this was to be, but this hesitation on his part had certainly played no part in her imagination. Yet he was a gentleman, had always treated her courteously, so she expected patience and consideration from him now. Then it was that a little flicker of terror crossed her mind. What was it he had said that time in the arbour when he had declared himself? That she would be his, whatever she said or did to prevent it, and he would not need to treat her with gentleness?

As if he read her thoughts, he smiled almost mischievously and, leaning forward, cupped her chin in his hands. At the same moment she heard the whirr of stiffened silk as he let fall his bed gown, and he was beside her now in the bed, thrusting her gently but inexorably back against the pillows.

Obviously, like her, he had bathed with his usual fastidiousness before the wedding ceremony, and his body smelt fresh and clean, his breath warm and wine-fumed. Now his lips were pressing hard down on hers, and she found herself struggling vainly in sudden panic. It seemed that he was demanding her very soul, crushing her physical being beneath his weight and drawing the life force itself from between her lips as he forced them apart. Excitement rose within her. She was expecting pain, but had been promised that it would be merely momentary. She must be brave and docile and then she would know delight never before experienced. Rose's words flashed before her mind as she tried to relax in his arms and surrender herself. But his sudden assault on her body was horrifying. He was holding her pinned down while he rained fierce kisses upon her throat, her breasts, her belly. She was terrified, yet she longed to respond, and her body arched towards his. When he entered her there was searing pain, yet a fulfilment she had never known before. She gave a great cry of combined fear and ecstasy. Now she was his at last, and all the struggles she had made against the inevitable had been foolish and useless. Tears lay wet on her cheeks, pricked at her eyelids.

The pain she had endured was past, and now she would know only the pleasure.

Suddenly he released her, and leaned down over her, his weight supported by both arms.

'Dear God,' he murmured. 'Dear God. What have I done?'

Her closed eyes flickered open and she stared up at him beseechingly.

He rolled clear and put up a hand to trace the progress of one tear.

'My pardon,' he said at last, stiffly. 'I thought you an experienced and willing partner in this sport. I have hurt you, and I had no such intention.'

Her blue eyes widened, first in astonishment, then in dawning horror.

'You thought — you thought. . .' She choked back furious tears and hit out at him, catching him a blow upon his cheek, grazing it with the edge of the heavy bridal ring. He did not flinch, nor did he move from her.

'How dare you?' she spat. 'Did you think I would come to you as a virgin bride, hair unbound, present a living lie before God? I told you there has been no intimacy between Oliver and —'

'Hush, hush.' He put a restraining hand upon her mouth. 'I deserve the full force of your anger. I should have recognised an honourable and truthful woman when I saw one, but such qualities are rare at either the French or English courts. When I saw you both running eagerly towards the copse near the quarry I thought the inevitable had taken place, despite your words to the contrary. I know better now. Words cannot express my sorrow for what has taken place. Nothing can change the situation. What should have been for you a pleasurable occasion has been a frightening ordeal. I can only promise you that it will never happen again.'

She blinked back further tears. She would not react like a spoilt child, she told herself. At least he had offered her an apology for his unworthy suspicions. Yet she remained bewildered. If he had truly thought the worst of her, why had he been so insistent on the match?

He said drily, 'You cannot deny you have given me every indication that you continue to love your cousin. You offered yourself as the final sacrifice when all other efforts to save him failed.' In the dim light she saw the sudden curl to his lips. 'Surely you realised that you had only to ask me to go and I would have done so immediately?'

Numbly she thought back to their conversation in the stable. She had been puzzled by his change of attitude. Now she understood. Her desperate offer of herself had seemed proof to him of her love for his rival. No wonder he had reacted stiffly to her pleading. There had been no need for any of this. He would have gone, had always been at the service of her family, and she had misjudged him. She jutted her chin aggressively. Well, if she had done so, he had scandalously misjudged her. It still rankled that he had thought her

so loose in behaviour that she would have given herself
to any man before marriage, even Oliver.

She had been about to refute his claim that her
feelings for Oliver still ran deep. Yes, she loved him
still, would always love him, but not romantically, as
she had first believed. That secret must be kept from
Lionel Summers. Her pride would not allow her to try
to explain, and she could never reveal the truth that
could so damage Tabitha's happiness. Her mother had
suffered enough, and was continuing to suffer now that
her remaining child had been taken from her. His life
was no longer forfeit, but could Tabitha and Saul Hunt
ever hope to see their son again in the flesh?

Lionel was lying beside her and pulling her head
down to his shoulder while he stroked her sweat-
dampened hair.

'Rest now and try to sleep. I must be up at dawn.'

Her brow wrinkled in doubt. 'Up early? You are
leaving Manor Court so soon?'

'I sail with Julian for Barbados.'

The shock was so great that she jerked herself once
more from his grasp and sat up in the bed, turning
agitatedly towards him.

'Do you doubt his promise to remain in the Indies,
or is it that you fear he is still not safe from arrest?'

Again she saw that mocking curl of Lionel's lips. 'My
fears are not for Julian. He has learned his lesson and
will do what he is told. No, I go to see if I can extricate
that dearly loved cousin of yours from the web he is
enmeshed in.'

She let out a little frightened cry.

'You mean you intend to try to—to free Oliver?'

'Isn't that what you most desire?'

'Yes, yes, of course. But how can it be done? Won't

it be dangerous for those involved? You have already risked your life for Julian. . .'

'And didn't that please you?' His whisper was provocative.

'Yes,' she murmured a trifle hoarsely. 'That pleased me. It revealed something of your nature I did not know, sir, but——' she hesitated '—I would not have you harm yourself or your prospects further. You have done all I could have asked to prove your—regard for me.'

'Regard? Do you still fail to recognise my obsessive desire for you?'

She gave a little frightened laugh. 'Those are strange and alarming words, sir.'

'Then let me prove it.'

She was silent, then she said softly, 'I—I would like to sail with you.'

His own bitter laugh rang out loud and clear in the silent room.

'Certainly, my dear, you may accompany me. I thought you would wish to do so. If I were to deny you, who knows what foolishness you would get into attempting to follow me—or should I say follow Oliver? Now lie down again and sleep. It seems we must both rise very early.'

She lay beside him docilely, and suffered his possessive arm firmly clasped round her waist, while her mind was in turmoil.

Once again he had misjudged the situation, and she could find no way of disabusing him of her reasons for sailing with him to the Indies. Perhaps on the ship there would be moments alone together when she might make him understand her growing desire for his presence. For the present she must rejoice in his decision. In Barbados she would see her true father, and maybe she would be able to understand what had brought him and Tabitha Hunt into the desperate situation which had brought about her own agonising plight. There, too, she might come to terms with the depth of her emotional bondage to both her husband and her cousin. There, God willing, she could satisfactorily end the doubts and fears which could destroy her marriage. If Oliver were free, she would no longer feel responsible for his fate. Yet, knowing his wife so anxious to ensure the future happiness of another man, could Lionel be brought to understand the bewildering nature of her need for him?

CHAPTER EIGHT

'SAIL to the Indies, today?' Lady Webster's voice sounded unduly high in her incredulity.

Corinna stood her ground while she faced her adopted mother and her real one. Tabitha and Saul Hunt had remained at Manor Court overnight, following the wedding festivities, and Tabitha sat now at Lady Webster's side, biting her inner cheek nervously. Sir James, with Saul and Julian, was overseeing the loading of the boxes on to the two carriages which were to convey the travellers to Whitby. Corinna had seen little of Lionel after they had taken a hurried breakfast in their chamber. He had then dressed and left her to Rose.

Lying on the disordered bed, Corinna had watched as Rose began to lay out the clothes for the day.

She had said softly, to avoid later questioning, 'Yes, I am a true wife, Rose. You can inform my mother of that, and yes, my husband treated me with due consideration.' She knew her cheeks had been dyed crimson, and felt the fast beat of her heart as she tilted her chin, a trifle aggressively. The whole family and the household servants would be considering the matter, she knew. There would be sidelong glances from the wenches and possibly some bawdy talk in stables and outbuildings. Well, best they all knew. That should settle the matter. Her marriage was duly consummated and she would now be addressed as Lady Summers.

When Rose had approached the bed and curtsied, calling her milady, she had been startled. She must get used to the mode of address. She had no desire for grooms and inn wenches to think her so newly wed that they too would speculate upon her happiness.

She hoped Rose would not ask directly how she had fared, or even show too obvious curiosity in her manner. She loved Rose dearly, as she did both her adopted mother and Tabitha Hunt, but she had not understood her own emotional response to the events of the night.

That her husband had apologised for his own too hasty passion had vaguely disturbed her. Certainly he had spent little time in wooing her, or preparing her body for the moment of taking, as Rose had informed her would likely be the case. She had been afraid, startled by his fierce desire, but now she was left with a feeling of disappointment. This she was prepared to discuss with no one. Lionel believed she was still deeply in love with Oliver. He had made that patently clear, and she had added to that by her declared wish to sail with him to Barbados. Now her own mother and aunt were questioning her intention. She would not be denied. She *must* accompany Lionel. She would see Oliver, and know him safe and happy, and — after that — she would be able to surrender herself totally to her husband.

She said mildly, avoiding eye contact with the two older women, 'Surely you would not wish me to be parted from my husband so soon after our marriage? I shall have an opportunity to see my Uncle Edward again. The last time was when I was still a child.'

She felt, rather than saw, Tabitha Hunt give a great start of combined surprise and dismay, and she swept on with her explanations. 'I shall be sure of Julian's position on the plantation, which will set all our minds at rest. I am packed, having expected to leave with

Lionel for London or Yorkshire. There can be no bar to our immediate departure. I shall not be delaying him in the slightest.'

Lady Webster sighed. 'And whom can we send with you to attend you? I had expected you would acquire an experienced lady's maid in London. Our girls are willing, but hardly suited to the work, and I do not know how they would face the prospect of a long sea voyage.'

'Rose has agreed to accompany us, if Father will send a message to Jesse at Brinklow. I shall be well chaperoned with Rose, who will prove a companion rather than a maid, and who better than Rose to face any contingency that could arise?'

Lady Webster's eyebrows rose as she considered the matter, but she did appear more agreeable at that news. Rose Grimsley had proved a stalwart helper to them all during the terrible days of the plague year, and she could trust her daughter to no one more qualified.

'So be it,' she said quietly. She gave her sister a meaning glance, and Tabitha rose and embraced Corinna.

'God go with you and grant you happiness, child,' she said huskily. 'I—pray you might see Oliver. . .just once, and be able to convey to him our love and our prayers that he might find some measure of ease in his suffering.'

Corinna heard the rustle of her stiff silk gown as she departed to search out her husband.

'It *is* Oliver, isn't it? You are hoping to see him?' Lady Webster's voice was grimly condemning.

Corinna fiddled absently with a ribbon at her waist. 'Yes.' Her voice was oddly muffled, defiant. 'Lionel has promised to try to free Oliver.'

This time Lady Webster's gasp was distinctly audible.

Corinna continued. 'I have no idea how it can be accomplished, but——' she hesitated '—if it can be done I know Lionel is the man to do it.' Her tone changed to one of eagerness. 'I swear to you he will have no cause to be distrustful of me. When I agreed to wed him I put all thoughts of my—my association with Oliver from my mind. He is now—to me—the brother I cannot acknowledge. I want to see him happy, return with that news for you all, and—and settle to the rest of my life trying to please my husband.'

Lady Webster gathered her very close, and Corinna could feel the hot tears wetting the silk at her shoulder.

'Oh, my very dear child, I shall pray for your happiness every night of my life. Yes, it is right that you go. On the journey you and Lionel will have a chance to come to some understanding possibly denied you had you been immediately absorbed in the hectic life of court. He is a fine man, Corinna. Do not sell him short. He loves you deeply.'

'Does he?' Corinna murmured almost audibly. 'Yes, I think perhaps he does, though I cannot understand why.'

Lady Webster dried her eyes on her kerchief. 'It will be hard to part with both my children, but you know that you go with our blessing, as Julian does. God grant that you all return safely to us and soon.'

Corinna travelled with Lionel and Julian in the first carriage while Barbizet and Rose followed in the second, which carried the bulk of the baggage. Julian had appeared somewhat bemused when his sister had announced her intention of accompanying him, but made no comment. The morning was bright and sunny without being unduly warm, so that Corinna did not find the journey too uncomfortable. Indeed, she found the road north interesting.

Lionel smiled at her eager desire to note the small towns and villages as they passed.

'As we shall be journeying through Yorkshire, shall we pass close to your estates, sir?' she enquired.

'No, our land lies too far west in the Dales. We shall take the Great North Road for a goodly part of the journey and will need to stay one night in Lincoln, but we should be in Whitby and on board the *Curlew* by tomorrow night unless we suffer some mishap.' His mobile mouth curled slightly. 'And, since I gave careful instruction about the readiness of our vehicles, I shall have a great deal to say to our coachman if that should happen. We need no more delays. Julian should be clear of the country as soon as possible now.'

Corinna shot him an anxious glance. 'What have you heard? Is there more danger?'

Julian, who had been slouched in a corner facing them, sat up abruptly.

Lionel shrugged. 'Barbizet tells me he heard in Leicester yesterday that there had been more hangings.' He added grimly, 'Some of the bodies have been quartered and the remains sent to several towns to be exhibited as a sharp reminder of what is to be expected should further risings follow. The harassment of fugitives seems to be continuing, though I had hoped for a respite by now.'

Corinna's pleasure in the beauty of the countryside was abruptly shattered. She realised, with stark horror, that, should the reason for his absence from Oxford cause comment, Julian could now be in more peril than either Oliver or Bart Spicer.

'You must not allow me to delay you,' she said hurriedly. 'If you would prefer to abandon the carriages and ride I am perfectly capable of riding all day if necessary.'

Lionel shook his head. 'There should be no need for that. Indeed, undue haste could cause notice. We should do well enough as we are.'

The inn in Lincoln, near the castle wall and in the shadow of the great Minster, was comfortable and well patronised. Only one room was available, and Lionel suavely agreed to sleep with Julian and Barbizet in the common-room while Rose kept Corinna company.

Supper was served to them in Corinna's private chamber, and Rose left her alone for some moments with her husband before she retired.

'I'm sorry, my dear, that we must be separated so soon, but it appears today is market day, which I had overlooked, so extra accommodation for Rose was simply not available. It would have been unthinkable for her to sleep in the women's common-room. I'm sure you will agree.'

Corinna felt her heart fluttering as he bowed over her hand. 'Yes, of course,' she managed to stammer.

His lips quirked once and he drew her into his arms, his lips closing possessively upon hers.

'I had not expected to spend the early days of our marriage in a hectic race halfway across the world,' he said regretfully, 'but there should be time on board the ship for us to become closer acquainted.' His amber eyes were dancing now as he noted the crimson flush which mounted from her throat to her cheeks. How enchanting she looked in her simple lawn shift beneath the bed gown, which fell tantalisingly half open. His lips slid down to the swell of her breasts and she closed her eyes, almost stumbling in the sudden rush of tenderness which swept over her. Then he was gone and, trembling, she sank down on the bed as Rose re-entered.

'Now there's a pity,' her nurse remarked. 'That husband of yours is just too considerate. I assured him I'd no objection to sleeping with the farmers' wives, but he'd not have it.' She glanced shrewdly in her nursling's direction. 'You have not quarrelled already, I trust.'

'No, Rose, certainly not,' Corinna snapped. 'How could we have done, since we've had scarcely a few minutes together since we rose this morning?'

'Sits the wind in that quarter, does it?' Rose laughed, as she moved to turn down the bed on her side. 'It's a good sign, resentment at separation from your husband. I've heard of some silly misses who would have welcomed such a respite.'

Corinna promptly burst into tears. Instantly she was enfolded in her nurse's arms and hugged to her breast.

'Tell me,' Rose demanded grimly.

Hesitatingly,' Corinna told what had occurred. Rose listened, her dark eyes glistening strangely.

'You say he hurt you unduly?'

'Yes — no.' Corinna gulped unhappily. 'I didn't know how to take it. One moment he was. . .' She broke off, her cheeks hot with embarrassment again. 'Then he withdrew, as if I had failed to please him. He thought. . .he thought Oliver and I had — that I was experienced. . . Oh, Rose, I am so unhappy. I wanted to prove a good wife to him and now ——'

'Hush, my lovely. He knows the truth now, that nothing of an intimate nature happened between you and your cousin. Happen he's angry with himself and fears he has afrighted you. There,' she soothed, 'everything will be well again when you are alone together on board ship.'

'But Rose, will it? Was I wrong to ask to come with him? He thinks I am hot to see Oliver again.'

'And are you?' Rose's question was as blunt as Lady Webster's had been.

Hastily Corinna looked away. 'I shall always love Oliver, but — differently. Now I know something of my husband's nature, I think. . .' She paused and looked briefly down at the heavy gold of her wedding-ring. 'I know I am very fortunate, but — but if I cannot please him in bed. . .'

Rose chuckled. 'Don't run before your pigs to market. You will learn and he will find pleasure in teaching you. This need for separation is forced on him. Now come to bed and sleep. There are still many miles before us tomorrow, and you will not wish to appear washed out and exhausted from journeying when you are alone with him at last tomorrow night.'

Affectionately she touched Corinna's bright curls and watched as she climbed into bed, bent and kissed her, then tucked her in as she had done over so many years of her nursling's babyood. As she settled to sleep herself she sighed, frowning in the darkness. This was a pretty state of affairs, set into motion so many years ago. Sir Lionel Summers was a fine man and highly suitable for her lady, but he would need to be convinced of her love for him before his pride allowed him to confess the depth of his feelings for Corinna. Rose was aware that Corinna would be unable to reveal her own emotional needs until she was surer of her own feelings for Oliver Hunt. Pray God, all would soon be settled and that young man freed, for Corinna still considered herself partly responsible for his plight.

Corinna was somewhat disappointed that her very first sight of the sea was by night. Even so, the port of

Whitby, lit by torchlight, with the great dark bulk of the ruined abbey above the town, was fascinating. Their journey from Lincoln proved as uneventful as Lionel had hoped, and Corinna revelled in the views of the great sweeping moors with their vast expanses of heather and broom. They reached the port well past suppertime, and Lionel was anxious for his party to board the *Curlew* quickly, so Captain Greenwood could sail on the midnight tide. Cramped and stiff, Corinna was glad to descend from their carriage on the harbour front. Lionel took her arm and urged her immediately towards the gangplank.

The size of the ship astonished and overawed her, viewed, as it was, in the gathering gloom. She was still able to see the great projecting beakhead, the low forecastle and the dominating mass of the high sterncastle as she was helped aboard and welcomed by the captain. Jack Greenwood was a bluff-mannered giant of a man in his middle forties, Corinna thought. Though his manner towards Lionel, as owner, was deferential, it still bordered on friendliness, and Corinna realised the two knew one another well and had possibly sailed together before. She took a great gulp of sea-laden air with the indefinable and unfamiliar traces of tar and bilge and hot, tangy scents of spices which made her wrinkle her nose in doubt before she was escorted down the main companionway to the master cabin in the sterncastle.

She stopped in the doorway and stared, amazed, at the solid comfort of the place. There was a huge bed as elaborately carved as Sir James's own in the master bedroom at Manor Court. The cabin was lit by swinging lanthorns, and she stepped hesitatingly forward to touch the silk of the bed coverings and turn admiringly

to the padded chairs and carved chests, one of which
bore a fine Venetian mirror.

Lionel smiled at her childlike bewilderment. 'What
had you expected, a hammock slung between bulk-
heads? Jack has put his cabin at our disposal and we
should be very comfortable here, unless,' he added
with a glint of mockery in his hazel eyes, 'you suffer
badly from *mal de mer*.'

She gave a litle shiver of alarm. 'Does everyone?'

'No, but if you do it is nothing to be ashamed of.
Many fine seamen have fought to overcome the discomfort, some even have never entirely managed it,
and suffer for the first few hours of every voyage.'

'And you?'

He shrugged. 'So far I have been fortunate, but
when crossing Biscay one can never tell. Excuse me
while I see to it that Julian is suitably accommodated
and that Greenwood has made arrangements for Rose.'

Rose was staring round-eyed at the luxurious
appointments of the cabin, and needed to be
shouldered gently aside by a burly young seaman who
arrived with Corinna's baggage, followed by a second
man bearing Lionel's huge sea chest on his shoulder.

'Well,' Rose said, 'I never did imagine the like. The
ship is so big. I didn't think there would be so many
passages and rooms, and did you hear the grunting and
squawking of livestock as we came up the gangplank?'

Corinna nodded. She moved hurriedly to the great
stern window to peer out over the harbour. Lights
bordered the shore and she could glimpse nothing
below them but darkness, yet already she could feel
the swell of the sea beneath the planking of the 'tween-
deck like a terrible monster heaving and thrusting at
their feet. Surprisingly she felt no fear. This was a great
adventure, and surely now Julian would be safe, while

this floating receptacle of tarred timber and sailcloth carried her nearer and nearer to the man she scarcely knew, yet who was her father, and to the man who would be sold like an animal to toil in the sweltering heat of the cane fields unless Lionel could save him.

She turned shining eyes on her nurse. 'Oh, this is wonderful, Rose. I never thought to leave Leicestershire, yet now I welcome this voyage. Is it not strange? I was doubtful about going to London; now I shall see foreign lands and tropical islands, exotic plants and birds and——'

'Oliver,' Rose finished drily, and turned hastily, as if she feared Sir Lionel would be right behind her.

'Yes, Oliver—and—and my father.'

Rose shot her a hasty glance and nodded thoughtfully.

Supper was served at the great carved oak table in their cabin, and they were joined by Captain Greenwood, his sailing master, Rose, Julian and Pierre Barbizet. Corinna noted the snowy drapery, the silver and glass appointments of the table, and the food was well cooked and silently and deftly served by two young seamen she thought would be termed cabin boys. The captain talked with Lionel about the voyage and assured the ladies he expected no unfortunate changes in the weather, rose soon afterwards, and excused himself to take his place on the poop deck and oversee their sailing on the midnight tide.

After the others had gone, Julian to his cabin and the ship's sailing master to his duties on the poop deck, Lionel turned smilingly to Rose.

'I will leave you to unpack necessities and get your mistress to bed. I trust you have all you need?'

'Yes, indeed, sir. My cabin is small but comfortable. Don't you fret yourself about me. I'll be no trouble and I'm very near. You'll only have to call and I'll be here at once to attend my lady.'

'Good.' Lionel bent and kissed the top of Corinna's head. 'I shall be on deck with Jack Greenwood. I like to see the ship slip anchor and leave the harbour.'

The cabin boys cleared the table and left with their silent efficiency. Rose quickly unpacked Corinna's night shift and bed gown and laid out a fresh gown for the following day.

'There, that will do it for now. We'll see to the rest tomorrow.'

She came to help Corinna undress as bidden. 'You look very tired.'

'Do I? I don't feel it at all.'

Rose clucked her tongue. 'Ah, I see. Perhaps nervousness is painting a frown between your brows.'

Divested of her heavy gown and stays, Corinna sank thankfully upon the bed. 'Perhaps,' she echoed softly.

Rose also kissed the top of her head and bade her goodnight.

Alone in the great carved bed, Corinna looked ruefully round the cabin. So Lionel wished to observe the raising of the anchor and the passage of the ship from the harbour. Was he again to make excuses and stay clear of her tonight? She bit her lip in doubt. Rose was so sure that things would improve between them when they were alone together, yet were they so? The ship was huge, but everyone was packed close, and Lionel might well feel it expedient to join Julian for the continuance of the voyage. Were his thoughts, too, on Oliver, as he gazed at the waters which lay between them and Barbados?

She need not have worried. He arrived soon after the slapping of bare feet on the boards of the upper deck, the rattling of chains from the anchor locker and the hoarse, shouted commands told her that the ship was nosing into position for the harbour wall. She let out a little excited breath and sat up against the pillows, her eyes shining in the lanthorn light.

'So we are on our way at last?'

'Aye, you can set your heart at ease about Julian's safety now.'

'How long will the voyage take?'

He shrugged. 'About four or five weeks, depending on winds and currents. We shall sail south to Madeira, take on fresh water and supplies, pick up the North Equatorial current and the north-east trade winds. The journey home is faster, by the Gulf Stream, the Westerlies and the North Atlantic Drift.'

'You sound very knowledgeable,' she said wonderingly. 'Have you sailed this way way more than once?'

His smile was enigmatic. 'I told you, you know very little about me.'

She watched as he began to undress.

'I suppose you will miss the services of your valet.'

He laughed. 'I can manage to undress without assistance. You must think me a mere fop, and weak-minded as well.'

She flushed hotly. 'No, of course not, but—you always set such store by your apparel. . .'

His smile broadened. 'I do like to preen myself in fine feathers. It is a weakness I confess to.'

He rummaged within his opened sea chest for a bed gown and came to sit on the side of the bed.

'Alone together at last.'

'Ye-es.'

His smile faded and he put out a hand to lift one of the long tresses of her hair that draped the pillow. 'You are not afraid of me?'

She sounded indignant. 'No, of course not.'

He gave a little sigh. 'I thought perhaps I had spoiled things. . .'

She turned from him towards the faint light glowing from the great stern window. 'No, I. . .that is — I was afraid I had disappointed you.'

He turned her chin so that she was forced to look deep into his eyes. 'No, my lovely one, you will never disappoint me. I can teach you the art of love. Will you trust me?'

She inclined her head briefly, and tears smarted to her fine blue eyes.

'I impose just one condition. There shall be no mention of the plights of Julian or Oliver for the remainder of the night. Agreed?'

Again she nodded tremulously.

She did indeed discover that lovemaking could be extreme delight. He wooed her gently, caressing her body until she was ready, so that she responded eagerly. Afterwards he lay beside her, having extinguished the lanthorn, quietly content. Presently he fell asleep, but she remained wakeful by his side. She could feel the movement of the great ship beneath them now, and, so far, she acknowledged no stirring of discomfort. Perhaps they had not yet embarked upon open or rough waters. She hoped and prayed she would be a fair sailor. She had no wish to be seen by him to disadvantage, sick and weakly.

His lovemaking had been considerate and experienced, but there had been no sign of the ruthless passion he had exhibited on the night of their marriage. Even before that, in the harbour at Barrow, when he had fallen into that wild rage on her announcement of her intention to wed her cousin, he had revealed that arrogant determination to possess her which had both frightened and angered her. Now, though she believed he wanted her still, she was sure he was holding himself under rigid control. He had wanted no reference to Oliver. Corinna sighed in the darkness. It was obvious that he believed her to be deep in love with her imprisoned cousin, and, while Oliver and Tabitha could be hurt by her revelation of the true state of affairs, she must keep silent.

She must have fallen asleep at last, for the next thing she remembered was light falling on her face and her husband laughing down at her.

'Sleepyhead, I thought you would be impatient to go on deck and view the sea. I understand it will be your first sight of it in daylight.'

She scrambled up into a sitting position.

'Oh, I'm sorry, I hadn't realised how late it was.'

'I'm going on deck myself. I'll send Rose to you. Join me when you've had breakfast.'

She heard him speak to someone outside the door, and guessed it was Julian.

When Rose arrived, it became very clear that her nurse was in a sorry state. She looked positively green. Corinna rose at once.

'Oh, my dear, you look quite ill. You must go to your cabin and lie down. Let me dress, and I'll come and tend you.'

'Sweet Virgin, I have been so ill in the night.' Rose shuddered. 'I couldn't believe I would succumb, I who survived the ravages of the plague! How can you manage without me?' she wailed.

'Of course I will, and I am adequately chaperoned with my husband and brother on board. You taught me to be self-sufficient. Rose, you have always tended me; now it is my turn. Lionel says seasickness rarely lasts long. Once you get your sea legs you will enjoy the voyage.'

Rose groaned and shuddered again.

Corinna dressed and helped her nurse back to her own cabin. The small place still stank frowsty and of vomit, though the bowl Rose had used had been emptied and the place tidied. One of the cabin boys had evidently opened one of the portholes, for already fresh salt-laden air was filling the cabin, and Rose sank down thankfully on her bunk again. Corinna left her resting, a bowl at hand in case she felt sick again, biting her lip at Rose's hasty rejection of food. Outside the cabin she encountered Pierre Barbizet.

'Oh, Monsieur Barbizet, I'm afraid Mistress Grimsley feels decidedly unwell. I've settled her to rest, but could you get one of the cabin boys to bring me some breakfast in my own cabin?'

The Frenchman's eyes twinkled. 'Then milady is finding herself an excellent seafarer. That is good; Sir Lionel will be relieved. Your brother appears to be enjoying life at sea, so far, at least.'

Corinna smiled in answer. 'Rose is usually the strong one who never ails. I'm afraid she will take this weakness badly. It will affect her pride.'

'There are several herbal remedies that are sometimes beneficial. I will go and search out one and visit Madame Grimsley. Please to return to your cabin, milady, and I will arrange for food to be served.'

Corinna re-entered her own cabin and found, to her relief, that it had already been tidied, and the young boy who bowed deferentially withdrew, promising to serve her breakfast immediately.

She ate ravenously, revelling in the strange sea air. The light from the stern window cast a greenish-grey glow, as if she sat in some underground cavern, and, for moments, she remained afterwards, watching the spray part in the ship's wake. The boy who came to clear the remains of the meal escorted her to the poop deck, advising her to don a cloak, since the air on deck would be keen.

Lionel turned from his conversation with Captain Greenwood near the huge steering-wheel. The steersman gave her a fleeting glance as her husband and the captain both doffed their beavers as she approached and Lionel came to take her arm. She was glad of it, for the heaving and plunging of the deck beneath her feet was unnerving and somewhat embarrassing as she gave a little frightened cry and reached out for the polished taffrail for support.

'You'll soon acquire your sea legs. Why is Rose not with you?'

Corinna grimaced. 'I'm afraid Rose will take even longer than I to get her bearings. She has been dreadfully sick. Monsieur Barbizet offered to find her a tisane which he assured me would give her some relief, otherwise I would have stayed at her side.'

'Pierre knows his business. Best leave him to it and allow Rose to rest. She must eat soon or she will feel even worse. Fortunately she's a sensible woman who will do what she's bid.'

He drew her to the rail, and she looked up to see the wheeling sea birds who swooped above the mizzen mast. The boy was right; the wind was very strong. Corinna pulled her hood up as the sides of her cloak bellied up like wings around her.

'it is—very bracing,' she gulped as the wind snatched her voice away.

'You are cold? Do you wish to go below?'

'No, no, certainly not. The air is like wine. Where is Julian?'

'With the sailing master. He is apparently finding navigation fascinating, which is good, since he will not

fret with boredom during the voyage.' Lionel watched
her animated features as her gaze was everywhere,
above to the rigging, below to the swell of the waves,
forward to the lower forecastle where men were
engaged in washing down the decks.

'The ship seems so huge and powerful. What cargo
does she carry, sir? She is truly a merchant ship?'

He laughed throatily. 'Certainly the *Curlew* is a
merchantman. We carry fine furnishings and ornaments
for the houses of the planters who have a fancy to
imitate the comforts of the homes they have left. There
is jet from Whitby for the ladies and amber beads,
mirrors, and gewgaws of all kinds, rapiers and pistols
for the gentlemen of Barbados, imported from France
and Spain, silks, brocades and wool. We shall take on
wine in Madeira and travel back from the Indies with
our holds stuffed with sugar and tobacco.'

Her face clouded. 'Sugar from the cane fields where
the rebels must toil. Does my uncle employ black
slaves, sir, and indentured labour?'

He was leaning forward over the rail, not looking at
her, but she saw a pulse race at his throat.

'All planters employ slave labour, my dear — it would
be unprofitable to work the cane fields or the crushing
sheds without — but not all slave owners are cruel. I
have visited your uncle on several occasions and assure
you he is well loved and served.'

She swallowed in distaste. Monmouth's cause, which
had been Oliver's cause, and was, in some indefinable
way, *her* cause, had championed man's right to freedom, freedom of religion and way of worship; ironical
that those who had espoused it were doomed to
indentured labour, little better than slavery, for the ten
long years of hard service would mean early death for

many, and, for those who were left, even then they were refused the right to return home.

Lionel insisted on going with her later to visit Rose, and they were both relieved to find her feeling much better.

'That Frenchman, whatever he gave me, I can't imagine, it smelt and tasted so bad, but it did the trick. I shall be up and about again tomorrow, I'm sure.'

Lionel grinned. 'Pierre's a fine doctor when no other is at hand. He'll put you right, but you must start to eat as soon as you feel you can. An empty stomach can only make things worse.'

Rose wrinkled her nose disdainfully, and Lionel laughed outright. 'Take my word for it. I've suffered from *mal de mer* in the past, so I know how you feel.'

'Truth to tell, I prayed to die last night,' Rose confided. 'And I feel so foolish. I rarely ail and I agreed to come on this voyage because I thought the serving girls would fall prey to some trifling disorder, then I goes and suffers myself.'

'But it will make you more understanding.' Lionel dimpled at her and, squeezing her hand comfortingly, withdrew with Corinna.

At dinner Corinna ate well and looked up, blushing, to find the eyes of the ship's officers full on her. She hastily held her napkin to her mouth to hide her amusement. Obviously they had expected Sir Lionel's wife to be laid low, and were astonished that it should be her lady companion who was absent from table. Lionel excused himself after the meal, and Corinna was left to herself for most of the afternoon, for Julian was off somewhere about the ship. She could not imagine what should hold Lionel's attention. She bit her lip in perplexity. He, like Julian, appeared to find the shipboard life wholly absorbing.

She was determined not to complain, however, and was glad that evening to take supper alone with him in their cabin, the others presumably eating in the captain's cabin for once.

'Have you been very bored? I should have sent for you on deck, but I thought you might find it a trifle too breezy now. The wind has sprung up to almost gale force.'

'Had you business to discuss with Captain Greenwood?'

He hesitated and eyed her thoughtfully over the rim of his wine glass.

'Yes, I had. Greenwood is probably in a position to help us over the matter of — the indentured fugitives.'

Her hand trembled on her own glass, and he reached out to steady it.

'You mean he — he would help them escape? Would not that be dangerous for him?'

Lionel shrugged. 'Jack Greenwood is no stranger to danger, though no, I would not ask him to carry escaped fugitives aboard this vessel, but doubtless he is knowledgeable about other seamen who would be prepared to serve us — for a price.'

She gave a little nervous swallow. 'I have been thinking about it most of the afternoon. They cannot return to England. What will they do?'

His lips twitched as if he were laughing at her. 'I assure you there are many things landless men can do, my dear, none of them quite — lawful, shall we say? — but profitable.'

She opened her mouth as if to question him, then thought better of it. More and more she was beginning to suspect that Lionel had lived somewhat adventurously and not always honourably during his time from England. Though curious, she was unwilling to press him to divulge his own source of profit. If his knowledge could aid Oliver and Bart Spicer she would be glad it had been so.

She knew so little about him. She was acquainted with his mother, though only briefly, and her father had spoken glowingly about his friend, Sir Richard, Lionel's father. They had been so close in exile, but Lionel must have been born, as she had been, after the restoration, so surely he must have spent most of his life in Yorkshire.

She said suddenly, 'Will your mother be very angry that we were wed so precipitately, and could not invite her to the ceremony? It was necessary for us to arrange it all so hurriedly; I confess I did not think too seriously that she might be hurt by my thoughtlessness.'

'Mother is a sensible woman. True, she had hoped for a fashionable marriage in London, where she could have queened it at court with your mother, but she is so anxious to ensure my future that she will be thankful it is all settled. She will love you very much, Corinna. Do not doubt that.'

'I—I am not so sure. Mother says she is a lover of fashionable society, and I fear she will find me too countrified for her taste.'

'Nay,' he said merrily, 'she will be delighted that you possess the skills to take the reins of the household. As for your life in London society, it will give her the greatest pleasure to present you at court, oversee your introduction to society, and proudly revel in your beauty. So many times she has said how she longed and longed for a daughter. I assure you you'll have no problems with my mother. I sent her a message informing her of the situation.'

'Do you prefer life in London? Will you—will you always wish to live there?' There was a wistful note in her voice. Corinna was fond of country pursuits and would sadly miss her life in Leicestershire, yet she would not wish to be apart from Lionel for long, lonely months of the year there or in Yorkshire.

'I can enjoy both modes of life. The manor house is small, but a little grey jewel set in Wensleydale. In summer it is green and lush, sweet with the sound of the river. We are very close to the ruins of Jervaulx. The sheep graze as peacefully there, but without the monks to tend them since the Reformation. Heigh-ho, the glories of the old days are departed.'

'But surely the abbeys and priories had become very lax and corrupt. Do you regret their passing? Are you of the old faith, like the King?'

'No, no, I am Protestant, but many a Yorkshireman clings to the old ways and faith. Time appears to run more slowly in the Dales. I think you will grow to love the house as you do Manor Court, and we will visit and stay there as long and as frequently as you wish, but I, like my mother, am anxious to show you off at court, and I confess I enjoy the cut and thrust of gossip and intrigue as the best of the hangers-on.'

She said a little stiffly, 'I cannot believe that I shall wish to be presented to a man who has treated the rebels so shamefully.'

He sighed. 'Like many a monarch before him, James has become testy as he has been made aware of his own peril. Life can be corrupt and venal at court, but it has its own amusements to offer.'

'You mean the promenading in Whitehall and the dancing and gaming.'

He shot her an amused glance. 'So do I find myself wed to a little puritan? You take no enjoyment in harmless dalliance?'

Her eyes flashed in answer. 'You wrong me, sir. I

am no prude, but I would have a man attend to his own estates and hold to the welfare of the people who depend on him for their livelihoods, not be a heedless gambler to ruin himself and them by such idle pursuits.'

'More and more I see I made the right choice.' His eyes lingered on her breasts rising and falling rapidly now in her agitation. 'Not only beautiful and courageous, but capable and prudent as well.'

'Do not tease me. I know you regard me as a child, but — '

He leaned across the table and caught her wrist in a tight grasp. 'Indeed, it is your turn to wrong *me*. I regard you as a true woman and look forward to having my confidence in the fact compounded very shortly.' He looked pointedly towards the great bed and, again, Corinna felt the hot blood rushing to her face and throat as she looked down at her imprisoned wrist, but she made no futile effort to free herself.

Later, she lay in his arms, content again. This time he had taught her the art of teasing the senses into aroused awareness, and new unexpected delight. She longed to surrender herself completely, but feared too great a desire to please might make herself cheap in his eyes, so she held herself back, though the effort to do so was becoming more and more difficult.

Over the next days they fell into a pleasing comradeship. He no longer neglected her, escorting her on deck whenever the weather was clement and remaining with her in the master cabin at other times. They played cards and chess together and one evening Lionel produced a Spanish lute and revealed a previously concealed talent for music, playing skilfully upon the instrument and singing love-songs in England, French and Spanish. When she wondered aloud about his proficiency in that language he laughed in his usual bantering way and informed her that many of those who had lived in the Indies or sailed the Main had more than a smattering of the Spanish tongue and needed to have to conduct their business affairs. Rose recovered quickly and was soon able to prove a pleasant companion once more, but she had the tact to know when Corinna needed to be alone with her husband and frequently took herself off about her own concerns.

In Madeira Lionel took Corinna ashore and bought her trinkets which filled her with delight. The weather became warmer and one day they were totally becalmed and Corinna waited, fascinated, as the men watched anxiously for a breeze which would free them from the necessity of taking to the boats and attempting to haul the ship into fresh currents. Their prayers were answered, however, and the *Curlew* proceeded, unhindered, on her way.

Corinna was lulled into a quiet period of happy contentment. They were away from all the tribulations and anxieties of land, and each day followed upon each other in a pleasing monotony. Julian also seemed content. Corinna watched him became more mature and knowledgeable concerning the workings of the ship. He was often in Pierre Barbizet's company and talked enthusiastically of the Frenchman's adventurous life, which he wished to emulate. Corinna noted the amused glances her husband cast her brother.

Then, abruptly, she was reminded that she was married to a man whose previous existence was a mystery to her. They were spending a quiet hour in the cabin, Corinna embroidering and Lionel intent on some scholarly volume of classical poetry, when Barbizet broke unceremoniously in on them.

'My apologies, milord, but the captain requests you

join him on the poop deck.' He shot a hasty glance at Corinna, who was sucking at her thumb where her needle had slipped and pricked her at the suddenness of his intrusion. 'The matter is urgent and it would perhaps be wiser if milady were to stay below.'

Corinna swept aside the cambric cloth and rose to her feet immediately to follow Lionel.

'Please,' she begged, 'if there is some danger I wish to know of it.'

Lionel nodded briefly and signed for her to accompany him up the companionstair.

Jack Greenwood stood by the helmsman, his seaman's glass to his eye. As Lionel reached his side he silently handed over the instrument and stood, one hand on hip, the other shading his eyes from the bright glare of the sun. Corinna leaned eagerly forward over the taffrail to follow his gaze. She could only distinguish a black speck in the distance to starboard, which she was sure must be a following ship.

Greenwood said grimly, 'By the lines of her she's a turn of speed to overtake us by morning. I reckon she's French-made or perhaps a Hollander, but she resembles no merchantman I've known, and in these waters. . .' He broke off and chewed his nether lip reflectively.

Lionel lowered the glass and rubbed his chin.

'Aye, you could be right, and we should take no chances with women abroad and burdened with so rich and bulky a cargo. It's best we take all precautions. Can we outsail her?'

Greenwood grimaced. 'We can try, but I doubt it. She's made for speed and war, by the look of her. Do we stay and fight if we have to?'

Lionel raised a quizzical eyebrow. 'It would seem we'd have no choice. We can be by no means sure she'd tamely accept our surrender, seize our cargo, and let us proceed.' His gaze passed to Corinna, who was staring at him incredulously.

'You think that is a private ship?' she gasped, and Rose, behind her, echoed the sound.

'In these waters it's not unlikely. You two should go below. We'll prepare the ship for action, and you're best out of harm's way.'

Rose took Corinna's arm determinedly. 'Come, milady, you'll not wish to hinder the men.'

Reluctantly Corinna allowed herself to be drawn to her cabin. An hour later Lionel appeared and she ran to him. He held her close and kissed her bright hair.

'There is no cause for alarm. We may be worrying unnecessarily. Ships sailing these waters are always on the alert.'

'Captain Greenwood said he thought the ship was French, but. . .'

'Exactly. If it is a privateer, as we think likely, she may be bound for Tortuga. We fly the flag of St George. It's mainly Spanish ships which fall prey to these sea robbers, on their way from the New Spain gold and emerald mines, but it is imperative, should we need to engage them, you stay well below.'

Her heart was thudding uncomfortably as he put her gently aside and bent to rummage within one of his sea chests.

'I'd best get out of this finery, and ready for action.'

Corinna sat numbly on the side of the bed, Rose close by, while he divested himself of his long full-skirted coat, embroidered waistcoat, ruffled shirt and periwig. Instead he donned a plain linen shirt, tucking it hastily into his breeches, and pulled on a leather waistcoat, and over that a baldric and swordbelt. She watched, open-mouthed, at the change in him. The short reddish-brown curls glistened under the light from the swinging lanthorn, for it was already gloomy in the cabin, and the light glimmered wickedly also on the blade of a serviceable cutlass he thrust through his belt; then he stood facing her and checked the priming of a brace of pistols. There was a hard line to the set of his mouth which boded no good for any marauding privateer who threatened his ship.

She forced a smile. Now she knew the source of his suddenly acquired wealth and told herself, grimly, that she had been naïve and foolish not to have realised earlier that she had married a man of action, experienced in warfare and tactics. No wonder he had proved so competent when planning Julian's escape. She gulped back a feeling of panic which threatened to turn her legs to water. She had lain with him, accepted his caresses, and not known that there had often been blood on those hands which had so stirred her to transports of delight.

He checked for a moment as he saw her eyes, wide-stretched and gloriously blue, upon him. His lips twitched slightly, as if he was aware of the tumbled thoughts that raced in her mind.

'I told you there were aspects of my nature you knew nothing of. I'm sorry that so soon you may come to witness that side of my character. I'll send Julian below if there is any cause to fear for his safety.'

She nodded, but could find no words, not even to wish him well, and his lips twisted again in wry acceptance of her misgivings, then he was gone and she could hear his quick, sure steps ascending the companionstair.

Turning, she hid her face against Rose's skirts. 'He has been a privateer, Rose,' she murmured thickly, 'a

murdering pirate, no better than the men they all fear
on that pursuing ship.'

'Yes,' Rose returned, unperturbed, as she sat down
on the bed beside her and gathered her close. 'Let us
be very thankful he knows what he is about, or we
might very well find ourselves in grave circumstances
indeed.'

'Did you — did you always know that?'

'I suspected it might be so. Men take desperate
measures when they need to mend their fortunes. It
was so with your — father.' There was a slight pause
before the final word, and Corinna knew she referred
to Edward Webster. 'He sailed under letters of
marque. It allowed him sufficient coin to set himself up
in the Indies when he was forced to leave England.
Neither the Websters nor the Summerses can be
blamed for needing to repair the damages done to their
coffers by the war. Though the late King had the means
when he came into his own again, he failed to recom-
pense those families for the sacrifices they had suffered
in his name. When your mother married Sir James and
came to Manor Court the house was practically a ruin.
Her dowry provided the means for much of the restoration work. How do you think your maternal grandfather obtained his wealth?'

Corinna lifted her eyes to her nurse's face. Indeed,
the war had given men licence to steal and destroy the
property of those they considered enemies. Lionel now
only sought to restore the balance, as his father and
hers had done, by whatever means open to him.

Dear God, she prayed, let us survive this threat.
Now, when I consider us all safe and the possibility of
freedom for Oliver is within reach, let it not all
come to ruin, and — and let Lionel come safely back to
my side.

When the cabin boy brought food she eagerly questioned him, but the boy could tell her little.

'All I can say, milady, is that the ship's been made ready, canvas sheeting round the gunwales, the one or two guns we carry readied to run out, and all the crew standing by.'

'But this is a merchant ship. Do you always carry guns?'

The boy looked puzzled. 'Can't say, milady, 'aving only sailed on this one, but we carry four swivel guns, two on starboard and two larboard, and a stern chaser being assembled ready now. This is my first time,' he confided, as he sidled towards the cabin door.

Neither Corinna nor Rose felt like eating, but managed to take some food, for, as Rose remarked, 'Ye never know when we have such a good opportunity again.'

Corinna sat near the stern window, peering through the gathering gloom until it was much too black outside to see anything but the swinging stern lanthorn. Above her head she could hear the rumble and thuds as gunports were being opened, and the bare feet of seamen moving into their positions slapping on the boards of the deck. Remorselessly the waves dashed against the sides of the ship, emphasising their danger, since there was no place to escape to for any of them.

Suddenly the noise above increased. Sails flapped and rigging creaked while staccato commands came from the poop deck, all of them incomprehensible to Corinna. Were they putting on speed to outsail their pursuer or were they turning about to meet a possible enemy head-on? A new sound now assailed her ears, the noise of something heavy slithering and grating on deck. Chains? Were they laying down the anchor? Surely not. Impatiently she snatched up her cloak and made for the door. Orders or not, she was determined to see what was going on. Protesting, Rose breathlessly followed. Outside the cabin boy tried to bar their way, but Corinna shouldered the frightened lad aside, and he fell back as she ran up the companionstair, her skirts held high. Another seaman attempted to halt her at the head of the stair, but arrogantly she demanded to be allowed entry to the poop.

Lionel's voice cut across the man's stumbled apologies.

'All right, Green, let Lady Summers come if she wishes.'

Awkwardly Corinna scrambled above deck and stood for a moment, panting, then she turned to the ship's ladder, where a man was in the action of climbing aboard. He was big-made, burly, and clothed entirely in black, save for the white and silver ostrich feather which ornamented his beaver. He stepped on deck and, turning, and seeing her, swept off his hat and made her a courtly bow. His long, curled black periwig almost touched the boards of the deck, so graceful was the movement, then he turned to her husband, who stood, one hand on the hilt of his cutlas, the other on his hip.

'Allow me to present my wife, Marcel,' he said curtly, and the black-clad figure inclined his head again in acknowledgement.

Captain Greenwood came to take her arm and lead her towards the little cluster of officers assembled near the helmsman.

'Captain Lenoir of the *Genevieve* is well known to us, my dear. Fortunately, as his ship came closer, we were able to recognise it and welcome an old comrade aboard.'

Lionel's eyes were coldly glittering in the yellow

lanthorn light as he watched the Frenchman's openly
admiring glance at Corinna. Nervously she tucked away
a stray fair curl beneath her hood and, at Lionel's slight
nod of approval, offered her hand to the newcomer.
He bent and gallantly kissed the tips of her fingers.

'Lionel, *mon ami*, you are fortunate indeed. I should
seriously think myself of returning to Europe if such
prizes were to be found there.'

'Captain,' Corinna murmured somewhat lamely.

Turning to Lionel, she said softly, 'I'm sorry; I could
not stay below. I was afraid—I thought——'

The Frenchman gave a deep-throated laugh.
'*Madame* thought the worst, *naturellement*, when she
could hear that this ship was preparing to blow mine
into the next world, *n'est-ce pas*?'

Corinna swallowed and Lionel said evenly, 'You
know as well as I do, Marcel, that no one sails these
waters without expecting and preparing for trouble. It
was well you hailed me. While you are here there is
some business I would like to discuss with you, if my
wife will excuse us.' He turned pointedly towards Rose,
who came close to urge Corinna towards the head of
the companionstair.

'My dear,' Lionel addressed her, 'as you can see,
Marcel Lenoir and I are old comrades, and we'd like
to take a tot or two of rum together before he rejoins
his ship. Best in your cabin, Jack?' he asked.

Greenwood cleared his throat before answering
gruffly, 'Oh, certainly, Sir Lionel, of course. I'll make
ready. Does your lieutenant accompany you, Captain?'
He glanced pointedly to the man who stood near the
entrance to the ship's ladder, a short, portly barrel of a
man, unlike his captain, clad in typical seaman's garb
of canvas breeches and rough homespun shirt, his hair
concealed in a scarlet cotton handkerchief. Corinna

saw that, like Lionel, the man was keeping his right hand very close to the cutlas hilt he too wore thrust through his swordbelt.

Corinna let her bewildered eyes take in the sight of the watchful, wary crew, the grappling hooks which had been responsible for that strange, slithering sound that had so alarmed her, which held the two vessels close, broadside to broadside.

The French captain made an expansive gesture which took in his fellow officer and flung his arms jovially round Lionel's shoulders.

'*Certainement*, if I have your permission, *mon ami*.'

Now they were close, beneath the lanthorn, Corinna could see that the man was much older than she had first thought, possibly in his late thirties or early forties. He was lithe, sure-footed for such a big man, like some predatory animal, and his face was long and lean, clean-shaven, but for the elegant thin black moustache. The periwig was as black as night, like his clothing, and she could not help thinking he donned such garb to strike terror into the minds of his victims, for she could not doubt that the man was a pirate, likely enough bound, as Lionel had indicated, for the notorious buccaneering stronghold of Tortuga.

Within the cabin she faced Rose's enquiring look with a frown and a premonitory shiver. 'I trust we shall not meet too many more of Sir Lionel's scoundrelly companions,' she said drily.

Rose made to answer, then closed her mouth again and proceeded to prepare Corinna for bed.

She lay for hours, waiting for her husband to join her. At last she heard the scraping as the grappling hooks were withdrawn and the *Curlew* began to get under way again. Lionel came to her side, and she averted her head as she smelt the heavy, cloying scent of rum on his breath. He laughed as she struggled faintly in his arms when he climbed into bed beside her.

'What a pity,' she snapped, 'that the so gallant Captain Lenoir did not stay longer and give you more time for pleasant reminiscences.'

Again he chuckled, low in his throat, as she made to evade his embrace.

'Now, now, my lovely, do not be too hard on Marcel. He could be very useful to us.'

She sat up hastily. 'You are not thinking of joining him on a scavenging voyage?'

He bit the lobe of her ear very gently. 'Certainly not, but you do wish your cousin, Oliver, to be free, do you not?'

'With that — pirate?' Her voice sounded sick with disgust.

'He could do considerably worse.'

'Lionel — '

His voice hardened. 'He cannot remain free on the island, Corinna. He has no future beyond the need to sail from English territory. I have arranged with Lenoir that, on a given message from me, he will rendezvous at some hidden anchorage off Barbardos. Your uncle will know of some secluded spot. If there is need, he can take off Hunt and that other friend of his. From there they can make what arrangements they please with him and sail where they will. I've paid Lenoir in advance. It is the best I can offer.'

He turned from her abruptly and reached to extinguish the bedside candle.

In the darkness she said tentatively, 'He is French, Captain Lenoir; nobly born, do you think, or is his gallant manner assumed?'

She could almost see Lionel's wry smile, despite the

dimness. 'I know very little about him. He is one of the famed captains of the Brotherhood of the Coast. Despite your detestation of him on sight, I have heard nothing to give me the impression that he is any more ruthless or cruel than his fellows, rather the reverse. He is known to be courteous with ransomed captives, especially women. I doubt that Lenoir is his true name, but rather the one he assumes to fit his dark plumage. Likely enough he has been forced to leave France for some political misdemeanour. He and your Oliver will suit well enough.' He yawned and settled himself to sleep.

Corinna was indignant. How harshly he judged Oliver. Yet, as she snuggled down beside him, she pondered on the need for Oliver and the Frenchman to become associated. The idea soured her stomach, yet, as Lionel said, she could see no other future for her half-brother.

CHAPTER NINE

BARBADOS was a blur of brilliant blue, white and green in the morning sunshine, like an illustration in a precious Book of Hours Corinna's foster-father had in his library of rare books. She stood on the deck of the *Curlew* as they nosed gently into Bridgetown harbour. Rose was busied about their baggage and Julian, as usual, was on the poop deck with Captain Greenwood and the sailing master. Lionel descended from the poop deck where he had been in conference with the captain and came to her side.

'Well?' he said, smiling.

'It's beautiful.'

He grinned at her impishly. 'I doubt you will say that when you can get a nearer view of the harbour front. This sun provides the glister, and you know what Master Shakespeare had to say about everything that glisters.'

'Is not gold.' She smiled in answer. 'But he is wrong; you can see he is.'

'Wait till your nose tells you different.'

Wrinkling hers wryly, as their long boat came ashore an hour later, Corinna was forced to agree that he was right. The island sweltered in sticky heat which caused her gown to cling to her ribcage, and the stinks which assailed her nostrils were many and varied: bilge, tar and cordage, damp cloth wrappings from the huge bails which littered the waterfront and more pungent scents she could not identify. The place was a hive of activity. Corinna saw Negro slaves, gleaming ebony-black men,

195

naked to the waist, everywhere, hauling on ropes, carrying seemingly impossible burdens on their shoulders and heads and pushing and pulling the bulky packages she knew were the island's chief products — tobacco and the crop which made the colony one of the richest in the New World: sugar.

The harbour taverns spilled out men from open doors; seamen in canvas drawers and rough holland shirts, planters sweating in Western full-skirted coats and straw hats, some who continued to wear their heavily gilt-trimmed coats and waistcoats and cumbersome periwigs, despite the heat, were followed by young black slaves holding aloft huge umbrellas to shade their masters from the worst of the sun's glare.

All was noise and confusion. Rose fanned herself and Corinna vigorously until they tied up at the waterfront and Lionel stepped from the long boat and turned to help his wife and her companion alight.

Corinna felt a little giddy to be at last on dry land after the weeks at sea, and Julian, who followed her on to the quay, staggered and had to be steadied by Lionel.

'Get your land legs, man, before you make for the nearest tavern,' Lionel laughed.

Almost instantly he was gently shouldered aside as a tall, elegantly dressed man came to greet them. Corinna knew him at once; tall, slim and fair, like his brother, Sir James Webster, he sported a velvet-trimmed blue coat and embroidered waistcoat of blue and silver over white silk breeches.

He bowed over Corinna's hand, kissing her fingertips, and turned to embrace his nephew.

'Here at last. Your message reached me a week ago by fast frigate. I have my carriage waiting to take you instantly to the plantation.' He gripped Lionel's hands, smiling. 'Welcome to Barbados, again, my dear young friend, now my nephew by marriage. I have to say I'm delighted. My niece could not have chosen better.'

Corinna was suddenly tongue-tied as his gaze came to dwell fully on her. His eyes were as blue as her own, and he looked scarcely older than he must have appeared to Tabitha when she first saw him over twenty-one years ago in Barrow church. You had to peer closely to see the deeply etched laughter lines which edged the corners of his eyes, and his erstwhile fair skin had been tanned to a warm brown shade by the island's sun. This, then, was her father, and now that she saw him she could not doubt that parentage. Her mirror told her how much she resembled him. She gave a little nervous laugh as he put both hands on her shoulders and, drawing her close, kissed her gently on the forehead.

'I have been waiting to do that for so many years. How good it is to have you both with me, for a while at least. Delighted as I was by the announcement of Julian's impending visit, I was overjoyed to hear he was to be accompanied by his sister, and she newly become Lady Summers. Come out of this ageing sun, my dear. The carriage has an awning. Once at the house you will wish to bathe and change into a cooler gown.'

The carriage, driven by a Negro coachman, was drawn up on the mole, a young Negro boy holding the horses' heads. Corinna was helped into the welcome shade and sank back against the luxurious leather padding of the cushions. Rose was assisted to sit by her side, and the Negro boy produced lace-trimmed umbrellas for them both, though the tasselled awning would have proved sufficient.

Lionel said quietly, 'Julian and I will take the second

carriage I see you were thoughtful enough to provide. I'm sure you will be glad to squire your niece this first day on the island.'

Corinna took a hasty glance round the harbour, at the bustling, industrious workers, the whitewashed clapboard ramshackle buildings, the busy river mouth with the bridge which gave the port its name, Bridgetown, before Edward Webster seated himself opposite and the coachman whipped up the horses for the drive to the plantation.

Her father sat back in his seat and regarded her smilingly. During the short drive he told her something of the island — its crops, fruits and animals — and of his neighbours, with whom he appeared to be on good terms. The heat was becoming more and more oppressive, and Corinna looked longingly towards the low green hills she could see in the distance.

As the coachman drew in his horses before the plantation house, Corinna stared open-mouthed at the long, two-storeyed stone house, white-painted and surrounded by white painted stoops in the Dutch style where, presumably, the company could sit on cane furniture during the cool of the evenings. Rose dubiously allowed the Negro footman who came to her side of the carriage to help her down and, as Corinna was preparing to follow, her uncle leaned over and caught her wrist in his grasp.

'Tell me, my dear, you are happy with Lionel?'

She gave a little gasp, her blue eyes searching his for signs that he might reveal their true relationship. For a moment he looked almost haggard, then instantly he released her and murmured a quick apology.

Corinna said softly, 'Lionel is very good to me. We are — content.'

His own blue eyes blazed back at her, then he

jumped lightly down and reached out to 'ift her to the ground.

Inside the house was airy and full of light, though the windows were shaded. The entrance hall was spacious and leading up from it was a graceful newel staircase to the upper floor. A buxom Negress in colourful cotton skirt and blouse, her head swathed in a cotton turban, curtsied and led Corinna and Rose to their bedchambers.

Corinna and Lionel had been apportioned two finely furnished rooms with a dressing-room for each on either side. Corinna marvelled that the house resembled a comfortable and fashionable English country house in its tasteful furniture and porcelain, as well as the curtains, tapestries and carpets. She recalled that Lionel had explained that their own ship, the *Curlew*, constantly traded in such commodities so that wealthy planters could feel at home in their colonial surroundings, and recognised, a trifle cynically, the possible source of Edward Webster's wealth which had made all this possible. A tub was wheeled in and house slaves saw to it that Corinna and Rose were able to bathe and make their toilets. Rose was conducted to a chamber near by when Lionel made his appearance and also called for fresh water and a tub so that he might bathe.

'I spoke to your uncle briefly when we arrived. He informs me that the ship bearing the rebel fugitives has not yet arrived but is expected within the next few days.' He slipped on a cool silk bed gown and came to sit on her bed where she was resting. Rain had suddenly begun to lash against the windows and Corinna sat up, alarmed.

'This is the pattern of weather here,' he said. 'Hot, sticky, oppressive heat in the mornings, followed by swampy rainy conditions later. It does produce good quality cane, so planters learn to bear with it.'

She shook back the heavy mane of her hair which was damp with sweat.

Lionel——' her voice was husky '—what if—if Oliver has not survived the voyage? Some indentured workers do die, do they not?'

His lips twisted wryly. 'Unfortunately that is often the case, but Oliver was not wounded, or his comrade would have informed us, and he seemed a sturdy enough young man. You must not allow yourself to become prey to unnecessary fears.'

She was about to speak further, but he got up quickly and hastened to his own dressing-room, and soon Corinna heard him and Pierre talking together. She bit her lip in anger. Why must she always reveal her worries concerning Oliver? It irritated Lionel, and she must learn to keep her anxieties to herself.

Later that evening she faced her uncle, Lionel, Julian and Rose over the long polished oval dining-table for supper. The heat had diminished somewhat and the headache which had plagued her all afternoon and prevented her from dozing had eased. The meal was well cooked and served by the house slaves, and her uncle dismissed them and pushed the port bottle in Lionel's direction.

'Since we are far from home I suggest we dispense with the custom of allowing the ladies to withdraw, since I imagine Corinna is as anxious to hear us discuss our business as we are to conclude it,' he said.

The Negro butler had placed a glass of sweet canary wine before Corinna, and she choked on it and, trembling, put the fine crystal goblet down on the damask tablecloth.

'Oh, please,' she said imploringly, 'you know how impatient I am to hear what plans you might have.'

Julian nodded and poured himself a glass of port, an anxious frown marking his brows.

Lionel said thoughtfully, 'I presume you intend to bid for Master Hunt and his companion on the quay. It will be essential for Julian to be present, since he can identify Master Spicer, though it has occurred to me that, unprepared, either or both of them could reveal something incautious on seeing him there.'

Corinna said eagerly. 'But *I* know Bart Spicer and can point him out equally well as Julian. That would be much safer.'

'But hardly suitable,' Lionel said icily. 'I've no wish for my lady wife to be present at an auction of indentured workmen. It would not be seemly.'

Ned Webster's brows rose slightly, and he looked over the rim of his goblet at his niece. Her breast was rising and falling in agitation, and he turned towards Lionel as the source of her uneasiness. 'It is not unusual here, Lal. Ladies do attend the slave sales without undue comment. In the circumstances Corinna would naturally be distressed——'

'That is quite beside the point,' Corinna put in hastily, before Lionel could proffer further objections, 'I am the only member of our party to be able to point out satisfactorily the men for whom you need to bid. Rose knows only Oliver, and she will be with me. You see, Lionel, my uncle sees no impropriety in my presence there and I shall be most careful not to show any concern for the prisoners — or, at last, no unusual concern.'

Lionel tightened his lips and, meeting Julian's open stare, made no other comment.

As they prepared to separate preparatory to retiring,

he said abruptly, 'Ned, it would be unwise for you to offer too large a bid for either man.'

'I have considered that. If the worst comes to the worst, we must make other provisions. It seems fortuitous that you encountered our scoundrelly friend, Lenoir, on the voyage.'

Julian put a detaining hand on his sister's arm. 'A word with you before you retire, Corin.'

She nodded to Rose, who preceded her up the stairs, and turned in the dimly lit hall to face her brother.

'What is it, Jules?'

'I may not have opportunity later to let you know.' He hesitated. 'I intend to go with Noll and Bart when the time comes.'

She stared at him incredulously. 'But they will remain fugitives, forced to take to the high seas, become — privateers. . .'

'I know.'

'Jules, there is no need for you to live so — ' she sought for a suitable word and failed to find it ' — dishonourably. Surely you can remain here on the plantation with Uncle Ned?'

His youthful lips tightened mutinously as once she had seen Oliver's do at his talk of joining Monmouth's force. 'I do not consider life with the Brotherhood of the Coast any more dishonourable than making a fortune from the anguish and toil of men enslaved. I'm sorry, Corin; I am grateful for all Uncle Ned is prepared to do for us, but it in no way alters my opinion.' His chin lifted defiantly, and she moved closer to kiss him lightly on the cheek.

'I think I understand,' she said softly. 'You are no longer a youth, Jules. All of us have grown up very quickly over the last months. You must do what you think right.'

He touched her arm in a relieved and affectionate gesture, then she mounted the stair and left him.

The next day the *Royal James* sailed into Bridgetown harbour on the evening tide, but it was two days later — days of nail-biting anxiety for Corinna — before the auction notices were posted on the harbour-front walls and Ned Webster informed them all that he intended to be present at the public sales on the following morning.

'Why has it taken so long?' Julian enquired over the supper-table. 'I would have thought the ships's captain anxious to rid himself of his charges.'

'So he is, I'm sure,' his uncle agreed, 'but the ship will need cleansing, and the men themselves will need to be examined for signs of sickness before they can be allowed to spread gaol fever or any other contagious disorder to their fellow slaves. Workers are valuable commodities and must be protected. Here the white indentured servants are not so highly prized as the stronger black field-hands.'

'So you do not think it will be beyond your means to purchase the men we want?' Corinna said, her eyes huge with concern.

Ned Webster smiled reassuringly. 'Lionel has provided me with ample funds to add to what I already had. Oliver's parents were eager to contribute, and James and Dorcas too. Money is not our problem.'

'There could be a problem?' She shifted uneasily on her chair.

Lionel stretched his legs contentedly as he drew on his long clay pipe, a habit he had acquired again since his arrival once more in Barbados. 'One can never tell at an auction. I've seen many strange ones in my time, especially in Tortuga. You can never be sure what some other man will fancy, but we must be present early and hope for the best.' His light brown eyes dwelt on Corinna's face lazily, and she had the uncomfortable feeling he was deliberately torturing her with doubt.

She rose abruptly and announced the onset of a headache and the need to retire to her chamber.

Her uncle called after her as she reached the door. 'Be sure to wear cool clothing and your shady straw hat. The heat will grow intense if we are forced to wait till noon. Sleep well, my dear, and try not to worry.'

How could he say that when fear of failure was tearing her in two?

When Lionel joined her in the great cane-headed bed she continued to use her head pain as an excuse and made to turn from him.

Firmly he took her by the shoulder and turned her back to face him.

'Let us have no megrims, madam,' he said grimly. 'If thoughts of your cousin invade our bed and lie shadowing our lives it might be best if we fail to bid successfully.'

There was an edge to his voice, and she stared up at him, wide-eyed. Dear God, he could not still be jealous. Did he not understand that she was longing to have Oliver safe and free before she could devote herself completely to Lionel's need?

She reached out for him, tears wetting his shoulder. 'You know I no longer care for Oliver in the way you fear, but we all still need to assure ourselves that he is well and as happy as circumstances will allow. When this auction is over we can put all this behind us and face our future together with nothing to intrude.'

He took her fiercely, almost savagely, only remembering at the final moment of taking, and restraining the ugly dominating streak in him from hurting her as he had that first night of their marriage. Afterwards he covered her face with kisses, and she slept, worn out at last with the strain of waiting and worrying about the coming auction.

Despite being dressed as she was in obedience to her uncle's warning, Corinna found the morning heat on the quay at Bridgetown almost unbearable, even before ten of the clock, when they arrived well before that hour scheduled for the start of the public auction. The place stood at the end of the quay, a space roughly square in shape, with the sea on one side, and an area of shaded awning on the facing one, where the planters and their women sheltered from the burning rays of the sun. Corinna stood with Lionel and her uncle, an uncomplaining Rose at her side, both women sweating even under the protection of their lace-trimmed parasols. Corinna strained her eyes towards the low, roughly constructed timber huts on her right, where she was sure the indentured men were kept imprisoned. As her uncle had said, there were several women present, older women, their faces lined prematurely by the unkind sun, together with younger women twittering with excitement at the novel thought of white men soon to be paraded before them. Corinna looked steadfastly at the raised timber platform in the centre of the square and swallowed sharp bile which rose in her throat. How could these people remain so unconcerned at the plight of their fellow Englishmen?

A man appeared in the doorway of the central hut. He was huge, red-faced, clad in typical planters' garb of linen coat and linsey wolsey breeches, his full-brimmed straw hat thrust well back from his sweating brow. He moved to a table on the raised platform and barked out a single word of command. Two subordinates followed, in rough canvas drawers and holland shirts, sleeves rolled up on brawny arms. So alike they seemed in face and figure that it seemed to Corinna they must be brothers, and, since both resembled the auctioneer, possibly both his sons also. One held a bull-hide whip in his right hand while the other carried his thrust through his broad leather belt. Behind came the pathetic line of fugitive prisoners. Corinna caught her breath in a little gasp of pity, and found the cold stare of her female neighbour full on her.

Two other gaolers brought up the rear and herded the men into line with their backs to the huts, and the four stood guard over them; not that there appeared to be the least sign of resistance from any one of their prisoners. They were all dressed in the rags of their regimentals, their hair grown long and unkempt, their faces unshaven. Some attempt must have been made to cleanse them, for none looked as filthy as Corina had expected, despite her uncle's words concerning the need for caution over the newcomers' health. All were shackled still by the wrists and by leg manacles, and shuffled along like old men. Few even bothered to look around them, and they must have been kept in a windowless prison, for, on first emergence from the huts, they all seemed to be blinking in the harsh sunlight. From close confinement in an unlit ship's hold, they had been conveyed to these airless, stifling huts with their shuttered windows.

Lionel put a warning hand on her arm as her eyes searched eagerly for sight of Oliver. The men all looked so haggard and woebegone, so old, that she could not believe he was present in this first batch, then she stiffened as the second man from the end suddenly lifted dull eyes to the platform, and she almost called out his name in the sudden joy of recognition.

He had survived the horrors of the voyage, and the man beside him she now saw was Bart Spicer. He steadfastly continued to eye the ground, but Oliver, once used to the strong light, was eager to view his surroundings. His brown hair straggled to his shoulders, and his features were more pinched, his cheeks more hollow than she remembered, but his eyes had not lost their brightness, and his chin jutted defiantly as he shifted his weight from one leg to the other and stood more upright.

Tears welled in Corinna's eyes and threatened to roll down her cheeks. Resolutely she held them back and deliberately shaded her face with her parasol. Oliver must not see her and betray her interest, not at this stage. She half turned, and saw Lionel watching her closely. His expression was inscrutable, then, turning from her suddenly, he spoke softly in Ned Webster's ear. Her uncle nodded silently, then turned to Corinna, one eyebrow raised in interrogation. Carefully she mouthed the words, To the right of Oliver, that is Spicer, and he nodded again.

The first man in line was hustled to the platform. The man with the whip thrust through his belt tore the prisoner's ragged shirt from top to bottom, revealing the breadth of his chest. Despite the depredations of the battle's aftermath and the prolonged voyage, the man was clearly in his prime and, subject to a period of rehabilitation, would prove a strong and healthy worker in the cane fields. Most probably he was a Somerset farm labourer and used to manual work. Bidding began briskly. Corinna was sickened by the performance. Not only the men near them gave the proceedings careful attention, but the women too, the older women often making pithy comments to their spouses. Edward Webster listened gravely, since the bidding for the first prisoners would give him some idea of what sums he would later be required to proffer if he were to succeed in acquiring Oliver and Bart as his indentured servants. Corinna saw that Lionel's attentions were straying from the auctioneer as his eyes moved thoughtfully along the line of prospective slaves. Was he considering which of them would make good crewmen for privateering ventures? Corinna wondered fleetingly, but her concentration was only on Oliver, and she watched covertly as he continued to stand motionless, his head held high throughout the transactions.

Four men were successfully purchased, and the two guards saw to it that they were once more hustled off, presumably to be freed from their chains. One man stumbled, and the first guard brought his whip down hard across the prisoner's shoulders. The man gave a howl of pain, but no watching spectator took the slightest notice, as if the cry was a normal accompaniment to the event.

Corinna was now clearly impatient for Oliver to be brought to the platform, but dared not show it. She felt Rose move nervously behind her, and knew her former nurse's anxiety was as great as her own. One by one the prisoners were dealt with until only four remained, Oliver and Bart forming two of their number. Without warning the auctioneer signalled for the four to be returned to their hut, snapped shut his heavy account book, and prepared to step down from the platform. Corinna gave a little imperceptible movement, and her uncle half turned and smiled at her, then stepped into the square and put a detaining hand on the auctioneer's elbow. Already the people around her were beginning to disperse. Lionel stood, scowling thoughtfully.

'What is wrong?' Corinna hissed in his ear. 'Why aren't Oliver and Bart being included in the bidding?'

He shrugged and turned back again to follow with

his eyes the two gesticulating men near the platform. 'I have no idea. We must wait and see. It appears that those four men are not available.'

'Not available?' Corinna grated her teeth in impotent fury. 'But they must be. Why not?'

'My dear, I don't know.' Lionel smiled genially at a horsy-faced woman who stared at Corinna curiously. He bowed and gallantly raised his hat. 'Do keep calm. Nothing can be achieved by getting excited.'

Corinna was almost crying with rage and disappointment. This morning was to have seen her hope for Oliver's freedom. Now it was to be postponed, and she could understand no reason for the blow. Edward Webster strolled back to them and indicated that they should all return to their carriage. By now the bidding square was almost deserted.

'What happened?' Corinna clawed at his arm, and he smiled down at her with the same irritatingly calm manner that Lionel displayed.

'We'll talk in the carriage, my dear.'

Swallowing her disappointment, Corinna obediently allowed herself to be led to the waiting carriage. Lionel assisted her to step into it, and soon they were bowling along the dusty road to Ned Webster's plantation.

'Please,' she begged, 'don't keep me in suspense any longer. What went wrong? Why were those four prisoners held back?'

'It seems that the vice-governor has already inspected the goods and marked those four out for his own property. Apparently they were led out in line in error.'

'You mean they will never be available?' Corinna registered the dread news in shocked tones.

'Not by bidding for in open market.' Her uncle shook his head. 'I questioned the auctioneer, as you

saw. He gave no reason for the vice-governor's choice,
but it seems likely that those four were gentlemen and
the deputy governor had need for someone with writing
skills to keep his accounts. White indentured servants
are often acquired for such purposes, but as most of
them are poor debtors from Ireland they rarely meet
the need. The deputy governor undoubtedly thinks he
has a bargain in those four.'

'Then what are we to do?' Corinna whispered
despairingly.

'Certainly not give up hope,' Lionel retorted imper-
turbably, 'but the matter will prove less simple than we
supposed.'

His tone was cool and she saw the old, arrogant
gleam in his golden-brown eyes, and she sat back
against the seat cushioning, before she could reveal to
him her naked desperation.

Julian was as devastated when he was informed.

'What in God's name are we to do?' he asked. 'Can
the deputy governor be bribed?'

They were seated on the low, shaded stoop behind
the house, the men sipping rum, Corinna and Rose
enjoying some of the drinks prepared from the juices
of the many exotic fruits native to the island.

'That would not be impossible, certainly,' Ned
Webster remarked with some cynicism, 'but the man
would prove very curious as to my reason for acquiring
those particular men and it would not suit our purpose,
especially not if the men were to shortly disappear
from my workforce.'

Julian turned instinctively towards Lionel, who gave
his characteristically irritating shrug.

'Petitioning the governor would make Ned's purpose
suspect and will not do. We must free the men without
approaching their new owner.'

'Even if we could arrange for an escape,' Corinna said, almost tearfully, 'we are on an island. Where could they go before being discovered and returned to their owner?'

'Have you forgotten my old friend, Marcel Lenoir?' Lionel smiled broadly. 'I knew that association would have its uses. You will need patience, my dear, until I am able to contact him.'

Corinna's heart sank. Oliver must languish for awhile longer in slavery.

Several times over the next few days Corinna looked up to find Lionel's eyes on hers, searching her expression. Certainly she was finding the extended waiting almost unbearable and the heat very trying. She was not eating, often pushing away the most tempting dishes, and, though he did not comment, she knew he was concerned. Rose was much more direct.

'It's not the slightest use starving yourself. That young idiot got himself into this and, with luck, your uncle and Sir Lionel will manage to extricate him. If you become ill they'll have their hands full and less time to deal with Oliver's predicament.'

'I know,' Corinna said miserably, 'but I can't help it. I feel so sick and the heat makes it almost impossible to sleep.'

Rose looked at her intently, and Corinna flushed and squirmed under her nurse's knowing gaze.

'No, I'm not going to have a child. My monthly course came as usual just a few days ago.' She pushed a restless hand through her sweat-dampened hair. 'I should be able to bear this anxious time if the heat would diminish even a little. I did not seem so affected aboard ship, even when we came in sight of the Indies.'

'Sea breezes give some relief.' Rose shuddered at memory of her early suffering during the first few days

of the voyage. If truth were told she was dreading the
return voyage, but hoped optimistically that she might
not be so ill the second time.

When Edward Webster knocked on Corinna's
chamber door an hour before noon a few days later a
slight breeze had sprung up, and Corinna eagerly
accepted his invitation to accompany him on his morning ride of inspection round the plantation. He had
been somewhat disappointed to find that Julian
appeared to have little or no enthusiasm for life as a
sugar planter.

She changed into a simple, fairly loose-fitting riding
habit in mulberry cloth with a wide-brimmed hat for
shade, and followed her uncle down the stoop steps
into the courtyard, where a Negro groom had their
mounts waiting.

'Lionel is off in Bridgetown, hoping to hear some
news of the Brotherhood of the Coast and a possible
message from Lenoir,' Ned explained to Corinna.
'Gossip concerning the privateers is always circulating
about the harbour-front taverns.'

He cupped his hands for her to step up into the
stirrup, watched her settle into the saddle, nodded to
the boy, and mounted his own horse. Corinna patted
the velvet nose of her mare admiringly. She had ridden
the animal several times and found her spirited but
manageable. Her uncle had commented on her horse-
manship and she had reminded him that life at Manor
Court had always centred itself round country pursuits.
With a sudden pang, she recalled that it was these
interests which had linked her so strongly with Oliver.

They cantered gently out of the courtyard and on to
the dirt road which led towards the cane fields. Unlike
Julian, Corinna had taken a keen interest in the
ripening cane, the fruits and other products of this

fantastic island: the plantains, prickly pear, custard apples, the gaudy, exotic flowers and birds and the rank, luxuriant vegetation. Had it not been for her continual gnawing anxiety, she would have enjoyed her stay here. She had not come to terms with the concept of slavery, but noticed that her uncle's slaves were well fed on delicacies beside the cornmeal mush and sweet potato she had heard was habitually fed to the island slaves. They seemed happy enough as they went about their duties. Certainly the house slaves were cheerful and willing whenever she called upon their services.

The crushing-sheds were, as usual, noisy and overbearingly hot, and she was glad when they emerged again. He lifted her once more into the saddle and they rode to a small bluff overlooking the sea. From here the water looked invitingly cool and blue, and Corinna fanned herself energetically with a palmetto leaf while she rejoiced in the shade of a mature prickly pear tree.

Her uncle turned from his contemplation of the coast and regarded her gravely. 'You seem restless, Corinna. I hope you are not unwell. Oliver will be freed, you know. It will take time, and you must trust the business to Lionel and me. For his mother's sake I would make every sacrifice to see this through.'

Corinna's heart leaped wildly at mention of her real mother's name, and he leaned towards her as if he feared she would fall from the saddle, she appeared so deadly pale.

'You *are* ill.'

'No, but you are right: I am deeply concerned for Oliver. At the sale the other day it seemed such a simple matter; now there are so many complications. We are fortunate, of course, that Oliver was brought to Barbados. He could have been conveyed to Jamaica, and we should have had little chance there.'

Her uncle grinned. 'There was no luck about that. Lionel saw to it that Oliver and his friend were included in the list of men to sail on the *Royal James*.'

Corinna gave a ghost of a smile. Lionel missed nothing when making his plans, left nothing to chance.

'I realise that you are fond of Oliver, but. . .' He broke off, alarmed again as Corinna swayed in the saddle. 'What is it, Corinna? Trust me. I have ──' he hesitated ' ─ your happiness very close to my heart.' It was a husky murmur, and tears sprang to Corinna's eyes, but she dashed them away resolutely. This was her opportunity, and she decided to take full advantage of it. She might not be alone with her father again, and she wanted to make herself known to him, to have him acknowledge her as a daughter, if only once in their lives.

'I know ─ the truth,' she said gently.

He stared at her wonderingly, and she nodded. 'Yes, I know I am your child and Tabitha's.'

He swallowed, then abruptly dismounted, came to her mount's side, and lifted her down, then he turned her face towards his and looked keenly into her eyes. Bending, he kissed her gently upon the forehead.

'Oh,' he said brokenly. 'Oh, my dear, then you know how necessary it is for me to free Tabby's son. It is the one favour I can do her now. Do you know the whole of it?'

She nodded again, and tears rolled down her cheeks as she remembered the agony of hearing her adopted mother's explanation.

'Then you know Oliver is your half-brother. . .' He stood away somewhat and stared at her, as if he realised the source of her grief. He drew a hard breath.

'He does not know? And he ─ loves you?'

She blinked back the foolish tears, biting her lip against unwary words.

'And you——' he paused deliberately ' — unknowing, loved him? And Lionel knows this?'

'He does not know of our relationship; at least I think he does not. Is he aware that I am your daughter?'

'No, I pray to God he isn't.'

'Mother — Aunt Dorcas — swore me to secrecy for Tabitha's sake. Oliver and I. . .' She broke down tearfully '. . .had just realised our love. There had been nothing unseemly between us, you must believe, but Lionel saw us together. I could not tell Oliver the truth, and he rode off, furious and broken-hearted, and as a result. . .'

Ned Webster gathered her to his heart, his fingers smoothing her long golden tresses, for her straw hat had fallen back on her neck.

'My loved child, that you should have suffered so and because of my irresponsibility. Tell me truly, Corinna, do you still feel for Oliver as — as a lover?'

'I think not. We were comrades, brother and sister without knowing it.' She flushed and turned her face from him, her voice coming somewhat breathily. 'Lionel — after we were wed — he showed me — I mean — I know now what it is to be loved by a man like that, a man experienced, knowledgeable, strong — but I cannot think of anything but Oliver's fate and my partial responsibility for it, and until he is free I — I cannot give myself entirely to Lionel, and I know he loves me, but — he is——'

'Jealous,' Ned Webster concluded grimly, 'and not without cause. This is a bad business, Corinna. Lionel is a fine man, as fine as his father. I *know*, I who was a friend to both. Do you not think you should tell him the truth?'

'What good could it do? And — ' Corinna strove to control her tears '— Oliver must not know. It would break his heart to think his mother — '

'Aye, aye, and Saul Hunt must never discover the truth, that is certain.'

He drew her to him again and they clung together, then he sighed and released her.

'I shall pray constantly that you come to find true happiness with Lionel,' he said soberly, then he led her towards her mount and swung her upwards into the saddle.

Lionel appeared in jubilant mood over supper. There was a glint in his eye which made Corinna wonder if he had partaken too freely of the island's favourite product, rum, but when the servants had been dismissed and she rose from table to leave the men to their port he gestured to her to remain.

'She will wish to hear my news, Ned.'

Her uncle nodded, and Julian paused in the action of pouring wine to stare at his brother-in-law, hope dawning in his expression.

Lionel kept them waiting on his words while he held his glass to the candlelight, admired the ruby colour of the port, and drank appreciatively.

'How difficult will it be to have words privately with the deputy governor's newly acquired pair of indentured servants?'

Ned Webster considered. 'Not difficult to *see* them. The white indentured men are not constantly under the overseer's eye during the day, but are kept under lock and key in the stockade with the other slaves at night. To talk with Oliver privately, that could prove more difficult, but I dare say it could be done.'

Lionel nodded. 'Two evenings from now I want Hunt and that friend of his to escape into the jungle and make their way to the northern coast. You know the small inlet there? We visited it together once, fishing.'

'Yes, but no large vessel could approach there——'

Lionel waved a hand dismissively. 'I know that. The shallow draught would allow for the passage of a small ketch. Lenoir wil lie off the coast some three miles out to take Hunt and Spicer on board.' He turned to Julian. 'Has Hunt any experience of sailing?'

Julian shook his head slowly. 'I doubt it, but I could manage,' he said doubtfully. 'At least I think I could handle sail and navigation well enough to reach Lenoir's vessel.'

'That will not be necessary. I have already purchased the craft and hired two men to make the trip.' He shrugged. 'They have been well paid, and I've told them the ketch will be theirs once they have safely delivered their passengers. It will be to their advantage to see that my instructions are obeyed to the letter.'

His eyes caught and held Corinna's, as if he read her anxiety there that she could not entirely trust Oliver's safety to either her husband or the reliability of his hirelings. He smiled thinly. 'Of course, Lenoir is another matter. He cannot be relied on completely. Initially he will do as I ask, but once aboard his ship it will be up to Hunt and Spicer to make themselves sufficiently useful to him to prevent themselves being dumped overside. My message to Lenoir conveyed my desire that he would carry the two of them to Tortuga, from where they might try for a passage to New England or wherever they will. Life will not be easy. They may prefer to continue in service with Lenoir.'

Her uncle was tamping down the tobacco in his long-

stemmed clay pipe. 'I can visit O'Brian's plantation
tomorrow, of course. I'l find some trifling pretext. It
should not seem suspicious. We often visit each other
to exchange gossip and observe progress in the crushing-sheds. I could even show interest in his newly
acquired indentured men. The difficulty will be in
drawing Oliver aside and speaking with him. Also, I
confess, I have see him few times and would not be
sure I had the right man.'

Lionel frowned and again looked challengingly at
Corinna. 'I know Hunt well enough, but I doubt if he
would trust my intentions. There has been some show
of hostility between us.'

Corinna felt her face flame, and fiddled idly with the
ivory handle of her fruit knife.

Julian said eagerly, 'If I could accompany you,
Uncle, I could perhaps talk with him while you kept
the deputy governor's attention. Even if I were seen
doing so, my interest in English rebels could be
explained away, having only recently come out from
England.'

Ned Webster's blue eyes looked into the distance,
then he nodded. 'I see no great problem with that. I
have already spoken of my nephew's arrival and my
hope that he will involve himself in the family business.'

Julian flushed with sudden embarrassment.

Corinna said quickly, 'But how will Oliver know
where to go, and is it possible the two of them will be
left unguarded long enough to make their escape from
the plantation?'

She knew her uncle's slaves moved about with
reasonable freedom on the estate, but the white indentured rebels had only recently arrived in Barbados and
would surely be regarded with suspicion.

Her uncle drew thoughtfully on his pipe. 'Until I've

seen the situation on O'Brian's plantation tomorrow I cannot tell how closely Oliver and his friend will be watched; as to his journey through the undergrowth to the cove, possibly I could arrange for a guide.'

'If I am shown the way I could go to some pre-arranged spot and meet the two,' Julian volunteered, and Corinna's mind winced from the thought that he would take his opportunity to sail with his friends and take to the precarious life of privateering.

Lionel surveyed him blandly. 'That would seem a sensible plan. Hunt trusts you, and he will view anyone he meets with suspicion, considering his present predic-ament. As for the means of escape, I have already arranged for a concentration of interest elsewhere, with the assistance of Marcel, of course.'

Webster's tanned face blanched. 'Lenoir does not intend to attack Bridgetown, by God?'

'Marcel is not so foolhardy, though such a plan is not entirely beyond his powers or his wishes. No, no, between us we have concocted a plan which will enrich Marcel's pockets and, at the same time, with some inconvenience to the deputy governor, assure his pres-ence well away from his own plantation.'

'God's wounds, Lionel, you do not intend to abduct O'Brian?'

Again Lionel smiled reassuringly back at his friend.

'Only for a short time, Ned, sufficiently long for his overseers to be kept busy searching for him, so that their attentions will be occupied, and——' he paused, laughingly '——Marcel will see to it that the man is kept safe and, in return, gain sufficient ransom to repay him for the cost of the ketch.'

Ned Webster exploded into laughter at the sheer audacity of the plan with all its hazards, but he faced

Corinna's horror-stricken expression with some amusement.

'Do not fret, my dear. Ransom-taking is a game well known in these waters, and I know Lenoir well enough to be assured O'Brian will take no harm, provided he behaves himself, and I know O'Brian well enough to be sure he'll not endanger his hide. I've no great liking for the man, but I'd not have him harmed, for all that.'

Corinna was silent. Her world had altered so radically since they had sailed from England that she could hardly believe she was listening to such illegal plans. That such behaviour was not unusual here dumbfounded her, yet, if all this gave hope for Oliver's freedom, she was content to wait and trust. The men's voices droned over her head as her mind shied from the thought that Oliver would soon be utterly lost to her. Somehow she must persuade her uncle and Julian to allow her to visit the neighbouring plantation with them next day, or, if that were not possible, to see Oliver just once, however fleetingly, before he boarded the ketch to sail from the island. Lifting her head, she caught Lionel's golden-hazel eyes observing her closely and knew that somehow she must evade his watchfulness to achieve her purpose.

The party broke up an hour later when one of the overseers came to the house requesting Master Webster's urgent attention. One of the slaves had been injured, falling on a sharpened stake from the stockade fence. Edward Webster excused himself, murmuring crossly that undoubtedly there had been a fight or some such foolishness which had caused the man to stumble so carelessly. Fortunately the overseer was able to inform him that he did not think the hurt serious, but he wanted the master to see the man and judge for himself. Corinna felt angered by the occurrence, which prevented her asking her uncle for permission to accompany him on his visit to O'Brian's plantation the next day, and felt guilty that she was not more sorry for the unfortunate slave concerned. Lionel sauntered off into the garden to smoke a last pipe, he said, and Corinna managed to waylay Julian as he was about to climb the stair to his own chamber.

She caught him by the arm urgently. 'Wait, Jules.'

He stopped, a trifle surprised by the urgent note in her voice.

'Tomorrow, when you go to see Oliver, I must be with you. Speak to Uncle for me, please.'

He had mounted the first few steps, turned, and came back to her in the hall.

'Corin, I don't think that is a very good idea.'

'Don't you understand? It may be my last opportunity to see Oliver.'

'Yes, I see that, but it will be a tricky business managing to see him apart from the others—in fact I can't really see how it can be managed—and if you are there the deputy governor will feel it necessary to entertain us, and it will obviously be less easy to get near the slaves.'

She bit her lip in desperation. 'I'm as concerned as you are to see that Oliver gets Lionel's instructions, but I'm sure he will want to see me.'

'I don't doubt it.'

Corinna swung round as she heard her husband's dry comment. The fingers that were clutching Julian's sleeve bit into his flesh, so that he swore softly under his breath.

Lionel came closer, and Corinna released her hold on Julian.

'I can see how you all feel I shall be in the way,' she said huskily, 'but—but I might never see my cousin again.'

'Indeed you might not, and if the escape goes wrong no one will see Oliver again. Make no mistake about it. Plantation owners value their salves, but they also know that sometimes it is necessary to make an example of one in order to keep a firm control over the rest. Your presence on the deputy governor's plantation tomorrow could endanger the whole plot. No, it is quite out of the question.'

'But——'

'Please go on up, Julian. You need your sleep if you are to have your wits about you tomorrow. You might have to think very fast to take advantage of any opportunity which presents itself.'

Julian frowned doubtfully. He was concerned for the pleading expression and note of desperation in his sister's voice, but recently he had come to recognise that Lionel's word was law, and reluctantly he bent, kissed Corinna on the brow, and mounted the stair again.

'Things will work out well, Corin,' he said awkwardly. 'You can leave it to Uncle and myself to see to it and Noll knows what he has to do.' He looked doubtfully at Lionel's stern face before adding, 'If there's time I'll give Noll your love and good wishes.'

Corinna felt herself trembling, and caught at the newel post for support as she watched him reach the stair top and move towards his own chamber. She jumped as Lionel put a supporting arm round her waist.

'Come, my dear, you too should be in your bed. It might be some while before your uncle returns to the house.'

She allowed herself to be supported up the stairs and led to their chamber, where Lionel summoned the young black maidservant Edward Webster had put at his niece's disposal for the length of her stay. Rose had excused herself from the supper-table, complaining of a headache. Like Corinna, she found the heat exceptionally trying, and a meal had been served to her in her own room. Lionel withdrew while the young slave cheerfully set about her task of readying her new mistress for bed.

Usually Corinna was interested in the girl's chatter, and had become gradually used to the patois she used, but tonight she was only anxious to get rid of her, and dismissed her as soon as possible.

When Lionel returned it was clear that he was angry. He held himself rigidly as he stripped off his silk dressing-robe and climbed into bed, and she had come to know the ominous glitter that shone in his golden-brown eyes when he was irritated or infuriated.

Her body was trembling again as she forced herself to sit quiescent when he sat regarding her, a black scowl on his face.

'Well,' he said at last, softly, after so long that she thought she would scream with the prolonged wait for his accusation, 'it seems that your feelings for that cousin of yours run so deep that you would endanger his life for the opportunity of seeing him again. I thought you had learned better.'

Her tongue cleaved to the roof of her mouth with fear of him, but she managed to speak at last.

'I thought you would understand how I feel. I have known Oliver all my life. Yes, I *am* fond of him, but not as you think. Is it so wicked that I should want to see him one last time?'

'I suppose that would depend on what you wish to say to him.'

'I have told you all, over and over again, that I merely wish to bid him goodbye.'

He was silent, and she said impatiently, 'Don't you believe me?'

'I don't know.'

Her face flushed with angry colour. 'I thought you had come to trust me.'

'The devil you did.' There was a hard smile on his lips as he folded his arms, still coldly regarding her. 'I think you know little about men, my dear. No man entirely trusts his wife. I am no exception. Where you and Oliver Hunt are concerned I am adamant. I forbid you to meet him.'

'And if I defy you?' Corinna's breath was coming very fast.

'It would not be good for you — or for him.'

The angry colour faded from her cheeks, and she clutched convulsively at the bed sheet. 'What — what do you mean?'

'I think I make myself very plain. If you disobey me I shall punish you — severely — and I shall see to it that Oliver Hunt has no opportunity to be again in your presence.' It was so coldly and deliberately spoken that the words sent a deadly chill through Corinna's body.

'You mean that you would — try to kill him?'

'I mean that I would succeed.'

She took a hard breath. 'If you feel so, why have you taken steps to help Oliver?'

'Certainly not for Oliver's sake, I assure you. I simply tried to ensure that he is out of your sight and your mind. Had he died at Tyburn you would have mourned him. I want no ghost coming between us in my bed.'

'You are so deeply jealous of Oliver?' she said wonderingly.

'Does that surprise you? I have told you, Corinna, I wanted you from the moment I was old enough to desire you as a woman, and I had no intention of allowing your foolish infatuation for that young cub to prevent our marriage or to continue to dominate your thoughts. He will go free, find some suitable mate, and you will forget him. Once he is on board Lenoir's vessel, that will be an end of your association. I shall return you to England, and there will be miles of land and water between you. I think there is little likelihood of the King granting any pardons in the near future. For Oliver's sake you must try to put him out of your mind.'

Her eyes brimmed with tears as he drew her hungrily into his arms. She wanted to surrender to him, but some rebellious streak in her forbade it, and she struggled ineffectually in his grasp. His hands tightened on her cruelly, so that she gasped with pain and went limp. His lips pressed hard on hers and her eyes closed in submission to his iron will. He did not continue to hurt her, but his lovemaking was masterful and demanding, as if he was determined to impress on her his utter domination.

She lay wakeful afterwards, tearless now, but suffering an agony of desolation. She longed to tell him the truth, but the secret was not hers to impart, and others could suffer from the consequences. Despite his stated desire to have Oliver free and far from the island, where he could not come within Corinna's sight, she was tortured now with a fresh fear. Lionel's jealousy was so strong that only by destroying Oliver completely could he be sure of his possession of her. There was no truth in his gnawing doubt, but she would never be able to convince him of that. Oliver was in danger and must be warned. How could she be sure that, once aboard the Frenchman's vessel, that pirate would not have instructions from Lionel to kill his rival? It would be so easy, and she would never know the truth of it. However hazardous it would be to go against Lionel's will, she alone must be the one to see Oliver and convince him of his danger.

CHAPTER TEN

JULIAN and Ned Webster went out early next morning to spy out the route the escapees must follow to the hidden cove. Rose seemed much improved and sat with Corinna on the shaded stoop while the men were occupied. Lionel left the plantation early, giving Corinna no idea where he was bound, and she judged he had some assignation with the privateer, Marcel Lenoir, possibly in some tavern in Bridgetown. She chafed under the necessity to sit ostensibly resting while she longed to be riding with Julian and Ned, so that she would know where Oliver was bound tomorrow.

Rose watched her thoughtfully as she set stitches in the stump-work embroidery she had brought with her from England. Corinna smiled as her eyes went to the exquisite raised work Rose did so beautifully. Rose had made every effort to teach her, but Corinna had no patience for the task. She could do tapestry well enough, but her nature was too restless to allow the long hours of concentration the finer work required. It had always puzzled her that Rose could enjoy such a pastime. Her nurse had always been a practical woman of action, but, when taxed for her reasons, Rose replied that such careful work kept her from being anxious-stricken and impatient, as her charge so often was.

When Corinna sighed for the tenth time within the hour, Rose laid aside her work and signalled for one of the young Negro house slaves to bring them cooling fruit drinks.

'I think you had better tell me,' she said, 'if you are planning some future foolishness; it is best if I am warned in advance.'

'Now why should you think that?'

'I know you so very well, my dear. Am I to be included in whatever it is?'

Corinna hesitated, her brow furrowed. She waited until the drinks had been brought and the girl dismissed before answering.

'Lionel and my uncle have planned Oliver's escape for tomorrow soon after noon.'

'Ah.'

'Lionel is to provide a ketch, and Julian is even now with our uncle marking out on the trees the path Oliver must take to the cove where the boat will be hidden. I wish I could be with them.'

'Naturally you do, but you also know when you would be more likely to be in the way than helpful. Has Oliver been contacted by anyone from this plantation?'

'Not yet. Julian and Uncle plan to visit the deputy governor's plantation this afternoon. Apparently my uncle does so often, so it will not be remarked on. Julian is charged with getting Oliver's attention and imparting the plan to him.'

'The whole thing seems fraught with difficulties.'

'It is. It depends on Oliver or Bart being freely available on the plantation and not kept locked up in some compound, then the opportunity must be seized to get either one or the other aside without the deputy governor noticing.'

'And you would have liked to be present?'

Corinna bit her lip and nodded. 'Lionel has forbidden me to accompany them.'

'Yes.'

'It must succeed, Rose. It *must*, and—and I have to see Oliver before he sails. It is imperative that I do.'

'My dear, that could be very dangerous for both of you.' She paused, frowning, then voiced the doubts they all felt. 'You know it will be very hazardous when the two make their break. Nothing must endanger them further.'

'Lionel has planned some elaborate scheme with that pirate captain who boarded the *Curlew* to keep the deputy governor from his own home and cause such a commotion that Oliver and Julian can make the attempt while all the guards and overseers are occupied elsewhere.'

Rose nodded, content. 'If Sir Lionel has the matter in hand, be sure he has thought it out to the last detail.'

'I know well enough how resourceful he is, and I also know Oliver would rather die than live out those long years in captivity, but—still I worry.'

'That is understandable.'

'Rose, you don't understand. Lionel is fiercely jealous of Oliver, and—and I cannot entirely trust him to—'

'See to it that your cousin escapes with his life,' Rose completed firmly.

Corinna's pallor and stricken expression showed her that her surmise was correct.

'I must go with Julian when he sets out to meet Oliver. He must be warned. The *Genevieve* is a pirate ship and—Captain Lenoir is an old friend of Lionel's. Who is to say what will happen when—when he is aboard?'

Rose said slowly, 'I believe your husband to be an honourable man.'

'In most matters, yes, but—'

'He believes you still love your cousin?'

'Yes.' The single word came on an anguished whisper.

Rose was silent, staring into the distance of blue-green hills.

'There will be terrible trouble for you if Sir Lionel should discover what you intend.'

'He should be well occupied in Bridgetown. Once Oliver is safely off the island he will cease to be so obsessed with the thought of us—together.'

'Aye, more than likely so. Best if I go with you to this tryst, and leave me to convince Master Julian. He will be stubbornness itself if he thinks you could be in danger and he responsible for you.'

Corinna breathed a slow sigh of gratitude and took up her neglected tapestry work.

That afternoon the two women were, again, left to fret over what could be happening on the next planta-tion, but at supper Julian was able to report complete success in the mission.

'It was more simple than I could have thought possible. Uncle was explaining how I probably would involve myself in the family sugar business, so I was able to request, quite innocently, if I might see some evidence of success in the accounting. On the face of it it seemed an outrageous liberty, but apparently men here are so proud of their business acumen that Mr O'Brian readily agreed that I should examine his books and called for an overseer to conduct me to the counting-house shed. Oliver and Bart were there, and the overseer carried off Bart to make a count of some bales and left me with Noll. Bart gave a little start of surprise on first seeing me, but recollected himself almost at once and bent over Noll—I imagine to whisper to him that I was there and he must show no sign of recognition. We were left together for fully half an hour, and I was able to explain what we planned.'

'He is aware of the risks?' Lionel questioned sharply.

'Oh, certainly, and instantly assured me he was ready to take them.'

'How did he look?' Corinna put in.

'Look?' Julian looked puzzled, and impatiently she pressed him again.

'Does he look ill? Has he taken some sickness from that dreadful voyage?'

'He looks a bit thinner, but he's none the worse for that. In the old days, in Swithland Woods, we often played tracking together. He knows some of our blazing signs. I think he will manage to follow the route we've marked out and will be at the cove when the ketch arrives.'

Corinna had often accompanied the boys when they had gone on such expeditions; now she was determined to go with them this final time.

That night Lionel was very gentle with her, holding her close with the care that he might bestow on some expensive figurine of fine Venetian glass. Corinna felt unaccountably guilty that, even lying outwardly quiescent, she was planning to defy him. As if aware that something was troubling her, he murmured against the luxuriant tresses of her hair, 'You must not concern yourself for Oliver. These recent experiences will have matured him greatly, changed him beyond recognition. He will have learned a sense of self-preservation and will win his freedom. I have no doubt of it.'

'But the overseers will be armed. Julian said as much. He saw them on the O'Brian plantation. He could be fired upon. You warned me of that.'

He chuckled, bending to kiss the soft hollow of her

neck. 'O'Brian's men will be occupied with other matters.'

'He will not be harmed? His—his imprisonment could not be traced back to you—or to Uncle Ned?'

'I doubt it.'

She pulled sharply away from him and sat up in the bed.

'You could all be in danger. I had not thought of that.'

Her heart hammered in sudden doubt. Indeed, she had been so wrapped up in her desire for Oliver's freedom that she had given no real thought that, for her sake, Lionel was again going into danger. While they had sat discussing the plan round the polished table they had laughed, as if it were all a great joke, but it was not. Marcel Lenoir intended to abduct the deputy governor and hold him prisoner until he received ransom money. Things could go terribly wrong. The privateer could be taken in the attempt by the Governer's militiamen and, if so, could he be trusted not to implicate Ned Webster and Lionel, to say nothing of Julian?

She caught convulsively at the bed sheet.

'Anyone implicated in this affair could hang.'

'Certainly, but Lenoir knows his business. O'Brian will be freed and the men from the *Genevieve* back on board before the Governer's militia can be alerted.'

He was so sure of himself. Had Julian alone embarked upon this wild prank she would have castigated him for rank foolishness, but she had blindly accepted Lionel's plan without a qualm. Because she wanted Oliver's freedom so much that she would risk her husband's life? No, because she had so deep a trust in his ability.

He touched his hand to her ribcage, as if he could

sense her fear and feel the frightened drumbeat of her heart.

'Is this sudden panic for Oliver or Julian or—for me?'

It was lightly, mockingly spoken, but she could read a wistful note in the question and, for once, did not answer teasingly.

'For all of you, Lionel, most of all for you.'

He pulled her down to him again, his lips caressing the ivory contour of her shoulder.

She spent the morning in a state of dry-mouthed fearfulness. Julian paced the drawing-room after they had breakfasted, impatient to be off upon his mission. Lionel, as usual, ate well, without appearing in the least discomposed. Ned Webster said nothing, remained quietly confident, but Corinna noted that he ate very little. Perhaps, like her, he found the food as sawdust in his mouth.

He had been assigned the task of visiting the O'Brian plantation and carrying the deputy governor off into Bridgetown on some pretext of consulting with his man of business there and requiring O'Brian's advice as to the outcome of the talks. The consultation over, he planned to entice him to one of the taverns and there leave him.

He had grinned sheepishly when Corinna had asked how he was to keep himself clear of suspicion.

'O'Brian has little head for his favourite tipple, rumbullion. I've seen him often in this state. Provided I keep his cup primed he will be in no state to question my motives when I get up and leave him. Likely he'll be so drunk he'll remember little of what *does* occur, least of all seek to put any blame on me for his misfortunes.'

He, too, professed himself so confident as to the

outcome that Corinna was forced to put on a false smile of encouragement.

The hot, sticky heat of the morning wore on slowly. Corinna thought she would scream aloud with frustration, and found Rose's warning eyes on her.

When her uncle left the house and Lionel followed to order his horse saddled, Corinna went with him to the stable door.

'Is — is it necessary for you to go into Bridgetown?' Her voice was husky with emotion. One part of her screamed for him to be far from the plantation while she went with Julian to the trysting-place, but the other stabbed her with fear for his safety.

He turned to face her, the teasing smile for once absent from his lips. 'Yes, my dear, very necessary. You do want everything to go well with the prisoners?'

Mutely she nodded her head.

'Do not let your night fears torment you now. I shall leave all fisticuffs to Lenoir's men, who are experienced and well paid to accomplish the business competently. Yet because they are as they are — arrant ruffians — it is essential that I am there to ensure they are in the right place when necessary and do not let us down.'

Her fingers clutched at his velvet sleeve. 'Promise me you will take no risks.'

He tilted up her chin. 'I promise. In the old days when I roamed the high seas with Lenoir I had no beautiful and loyal wife to return to.'

The word 'loyal' pricked at her heart-strings when she thought of her intended betrayal, but he would never know. He had told her that Oliver would be changed, that he would know how to guard himself once aboard and among that ruffianly crew. When she saw with her own eyes his embarkation on the ketch she would be able to put him from her heart once and

for all. She would return quickly to the house and pray
for her husband's safe arrival. Somehow she would
make up to Lionel for these long days of doubt. Free
of the strings which bound her to Oliver, she could
surrender to the joy of being his wife. Even if he
returned her to England, to the seclusion of his
Yorkshire manor, she would accept gratefully, and
soon, please God, she would bear his child.

She reached up on tiptoe to kiss his mouth, then
raised her hand in salute as he mounted and rode from
the yard.

Rose was waiting in her bedchamber.

'Julian took some persuading, but has agreed. I have
laid out your habit. Julian suggested you travel in
breeches, but I think that unwise. You could possibly
be seen, and I fear Sir Lionel would be more angered
than ever were he to discover the truth.'

Rose herself was garbed simply in a sensible gown.
She helped Corinna to change swiftly.

'Rose, would it not be better if you stayed here. . .?'

'Julian says he does not intend to return to the
house.'

'No,' Corinna faltered, her gaze embarrassed. 'He
told me he wishes to go with the others.'

'Young fool,' Rose snorted. 'If he had any sense he
would make his fortune here with his uncle.'

Corinna fervently agreed, but thought it politic not
to voice her concern. She bundled her hair beneath the
straw hat with the curling brim to shade her from the
fierce sun. Today the rain had mercifully held off, and
it would be easier to traverse the scrubland and jungle
to reach the coast. She knew Rose would not be
dissuaded now she was aware that Corinna would be
forced to make the return journey alone, so nodded
that she was ready and the two women descended to

the hall, where they found Julian impatiently awaiting them. He had dressed in planter's garb of frieze breeches and holland shirt, a leather waistcoat topping it, riding boots and, like the women, a wide-brimmed straw hat. Over one shoulder he carried a seaman's canvas bag, presumably containing valuables and a change of linen and outer clothing. This confirmed Corinna's opinion that he would not be turned from his purpose. He looked approvingly at Corinna's service-able brown riding skirt and the loose linen shirt she had purloined from Lionel's valise. So attired she would find the journey less difficult. But his Corin had always known how to dress for their childish excursions, and he had been able to trust her not to delay them. He grinned crookedly at Rose, who raised her eyebrows comically in reply.

'I can understand why you wish to see Oliver, but you must both keep up. We mustn't be late at the meeting-place. I know you can, Corin, but what about you, Rose?'

'I've scrambled my way through more wasteland and forest than you can remember,' she retorted tartly.

'But that was when you were young.'

'I should hold my tongue, if I were you, young Master Julian,' she snapped. 'Even now you are not so old that I couldn't fetch you a good blow round the ear.'

He grinned at her again. Rose had had the rearing of him, as she had of Corinna, and he knew the worth of her threat.

They set out on foot, since horses were of little use when once they had struck off into the dense under-growth which lay between the two adjoining planta-tions and the coast.

Something struck Corinna, and she turned to Julian.

'I have just thought we have seen little of Pierre Barbizet since we arrived on the island. Lionel has been served by one of the young male house slaves. Julian, have you any idea where Barbizet might be?'

Julian grinned at her. 'I have no real notion, but I would suppose him to be with Lenoir, probably liaising between the Frenchman and Lionel. Do you know Barbizet was once one of Lenoir's crewmen?'

Corinna checked in her walk, startled. She recalled her earlier suspicions regarding the wizened little French valet.

Julian continued, 'During the voyage out we had time to talk. Indeed, I learned much of my sailing craft and navigation from Pierre. He was once Lenoir's sailing master. It is a wonder to me that he has settled down in Lenoir's service to so tame a life at courts.'

'Then they must have met when Lionel sailed as a privateer.'

'Oh, Lionel has told you?'

'He has told me very little, only that he sailed for a while under letters of marque, and I do know what that means.'

Her tone was grim, and Julian looked crestfallen.

'Gentlemen like Lionel think no dishonour in such an occupation.'

'I am well aware of that. It enables them to restore their fortunes. But I hope and pray, Julian, that you and Oliver will not live to rue the day you took up with a scoundrel like Lenoir.'

'Oliver has no choice——'

'But you have. Oh, I know it is considered acceptable to prey on Spanish shipping as they, in their turn, prey upon the hapless Indians of New Spain, but I imagine Lenoir is less scrupulous as to his selection of targets. I could not bear to think of you sacking towns and pillaging merchant ships. Can you stand to watch the slaughter of innocent women and children?'

There was an uncomfortable silence. 'I saw dreadful sights on the march, Corinna, and was a witness to the brutality of men, and most of them Royalist troops.'

'Surely that should make you shun such bestiality?'

They were walking briskly now past the small garden which marked the boundary of Ned Webster's land, Rose only a few paces behind.

Julian stopped and faced his sister. 'Lionel has discussed my decision with me. He advises me to take passage with Lenoir to Tortuga, then to take ship to the North America coast, or to Virginia.'

Corinna's heart lifted. 'And you plan to do that and will try to persuade Oliver to join you?'

'I do not know if Oliver and Bart would be safe in British territory. Like it or not, Corin, we may have to face the fact that Oliver will always have to make his way as a fugitive. It may be a choice of that life or a hangman's noose.'

Corinna shivered, in spite of the all-pervading heat which was causing Lionel's shirt to cling to her unpleasantly and sweat to trickle down her back in small rivulets.

Julian tramped on down a narrow track between palmetto and overhanging branches of tall exotic and free-growing plants unknown to Corinna, the two women following. So far they had been lucky not to encounter slaves from the household. Corinna thought her uncle had issued instructions for work well away from their route which would keep his slaves fully occupied for the afternoon. At any rate it would be almost an hour yet before most of the workers stirred after their noon meal. Ned Webster was not so inconsiderate as most owners, who expected their slaves to toil through the hours when the heat was at its greatest power.

Julian continued to keep Corinna informed as to his knowledge of Barbizet's antecedents and entry into her husband's service.

'Pierre was born near Reims. His father was a tenant farmer whose landlord took the opportunity to turn the family off the land when his father died. Pierre's mother died of grief and the resulting squalor of her life as a laundrywoman in the town. Pierre decided to make his fortune at sea and walked the whole of the way to Marseilles. God knows what miseries and difficulties faced the boy on the way. He took service aboard a French merchantman, but was vilely treated before the mast, and when their ship was attacked off Cartagena by Lenoir he accepted the invitation issued to all the crew and joined Lenoir. He was involved in a brawl in Tortuga, and there Lionel saved his life. Pierre gave me no details as to the cause of the quarrel — over some woman, I imagine — but he had laid his opponent low, and the man threw a knife secreted somewhere on his person. Lionel called a warning and tackled the fellow. After that Pierre took service with him. When Lionel decided to return to civilisation he brought Pierre with him. That is all I know, except that I have had evidence of the little man's considerable and varied abilities, especially in the healing of wounds. He told me he gained experience working with the ship's carpenter, who, apparently, is usually the only doctor available and capable of amputating limbs when needful.'

Corinna shuddered and, turning in a narrow part of the way, saw Rose's horrified expression. Neither woman spoke aloud their fears that Julian was going into such perils. What sights had Lionel seen and

played his part in during his life at sea, what terrible
experiences known? She knew, only too well, that her
father and Lionel's—Sir Richard Summers—had
undergone many hardships during their time in exile.
Such men needed to harden their hearts and make
their fortunes in the best way possible. Lionel had now
turned his back on such a life, and she could not
believe he would have taken part in any act of bestiality. Even the smiling Lenoir struck her as more honourable than most men of his kind. She told herself that
she must believe the best of the pirate or she would
have no peace of mind concerning her brother and
cousin.

Julian stopped again, holding aside branches which
had grown right across their path to allow the women
passage.

'We must be cautious here. The track borders the
deputy governor's plantation over to the right of us.
About a quarter of a mile ahead is the place where I
plan to meet Oliver. I think you should make your
goodbyes there and wait while I guide him to the cove
and come back for the two of you. I think it is safe
enough. Lionel tells me there are wild pigs in the area,
but they rarely approach men.'

Corinna passed no comment. In any case she fully
intended to accompany the men to the coast and see
Oliver embark with her own eyes.

It was while the three of them stood, hesitating, that
they heard the crack of a musket. With an inarticulate
cry Julian yelled at them to crouch down.

'Stay low under that bush. Damn it, the overseers
must have been alerted.'

He plunged forward, crouching low, as Corinna
caught at Rose and the two clung together, uncertain
what to do. There followed a second musket crack, a

sound of crashing and loud voices, as if heavy bodies were thrashing through the undergrowth. Again Julian gave a cry and Corinna froze, knowing instinctively that something was wrong. For only a moment longer she stayed where she was, then, freeing herself from Rose's grip, she thrust forward after her brother. The crashing noise had stopped, though the voices continued, but appeared to be moving further off. There was yet another shot and a hoarse cry, then Corinna found herself catapulted over her brother's prone body. She picked herself up and hastened back to him.

'Julian, were you hit?'

'No.' He gave a muffled oath. 'God's wounds, do I have to be the clumsiest fool in creation? Sounds of musket fire fill me with arrant fear after that ghastly retreat from Sedgemoor. I make no apologies for that, but I fell down instinctively and now I've hurt my confounded ankle. Did you hurt yourself falling over me?'

He kept his voice purposefully low, and she reacted in kind.

'No, no, just knocked the breath out of me.' She knelt down, brushing back her hair, for her hat had fallen into the dust of the track. Retrieving it, she jammed it on hard and, remaining in a crouching position by her brother, lifted her head slightly to listen to the sound of the pursuers ahead. 'You think they are after Oliver and Bart?'

'Who else?' Julian replied grimly. 'Damme, I thought Lionel's ruse would have kept them from this corner of the plantation. Let's pray Noll and Bart managed to get clear and are in hiding ahead somewhere.'

He was rubbing hard at his left ankle and, hearing

no more voices near by, Corinna knelt to examine the damage.

'Do you think you have broken it?'

'God knows. I can't feel any snapped bone near the flesh, but it hurts damnably.' He struggled to get up and put weight on the injured limb, while Corinna offered the support of her arm. Rose had joined them now quietly, and she stooped to feel Julian's ankle with gentle probing fingers.

'I do not think the bone is broken, but it is swelling badly already. It would be unwise to put weight on the foot. You can't go on, Master Julian.'

'Rubbish, woman, I must.' He gritted his teeth and attempted to move forward, gave a strangled cry, hastily cut off, and sank down again on the track.

'You'll not make the meeting-place in time, Jules,' Corinna said crisply. 'You must stay here and I'll go on and warn Oliver. I know the tracking markings. I can guide him to the cove.'

'No, no, you mustn't go near the cove. Lionel would kill me if he knew you were endangering yourself. Noll will have the sense to find my tracks when he realises I can't join him.'

'But does he know your marks as well as I do?' Corinna questioned practically. 'When we were children we played that game very often and used the same signs. Noll came with us sometimes, but now isn't the time to take risks and hope for the best.'

Reluctantly Julian leaned back against the bole of a palm-tree. His face looked pale and even more sweaty than usual. Obviously he was in great pain or he would have forced himself to go on. Disappointment at his inability to join his comrades as he planned vied with his fears for Corinna's safety, but both were overlaid with the need to get his cousin safely to the ketch and freedom.

He reached into a pocket of his waistcoat and produced a piece of paper.

'This is the plan, but you must follow the track marks.' He stabbed a point on the scrawled map. 'Here you must veer off the track and push through the scrub to the coast. It's a steep drop to the cove, but if you reach the top of the rise Noll and Bart can make their own way from there. Best if they wait till they see the ketch in position or rounding the bluff before they go on down.'

She nodded impatiently and thrust the plan into the waist of her habit skirt.

'What am I to tell Noll about — about the possibility of you joining him?'

He shrugged. 'Tell him I'll try to get to Tortuga and hear word of him, but he is not to wait for me. He must see to the safety of his own hide at all costs, and, Corin. . .'

'Yes?'

'In God's name be careful. If there is further pursuit and you're shot at lie down in the bushes and, if it comes to the worst, surrender to the overseers. These fellows will not hold their hand because you are a woman. Do you understand?'

'Oh, Jules, of course I understand,' she said testily. 'Do you think I have no sense? I'll take no risks with any of our lives. Rose, you should stay with Jules.'

Rose hesitated. She knew she could only delay her nursling, and Julian, her other charge, was lying here hurt and unprotected. She nodded gloomily.

'Hasten back. I shall wait only an hour at most before coming after you.'

Corinna rose to her feet and scanned the area of

track ahead. Julian handed up to her a cutlass he'd thrust through his waistband. 'You may need this to hack your way through. The vegetation is very dense in parts, and it's doubtful if Noll or Bart are armed at all.'

She set off resolutely, stopping once or twice to listen for betraying noises to her right, where she knew the boundary of the deputy governor's land lay, but, for some reason she could not determine, the pursuit appeared to have gone elsewhere. She told herself optimistically that perhaps the searchers were not in pursuit of the two fugitive rebels. Black slaves could well have taken this opportunity to make a bid for freedom while their master was from the plantation. If so they could confuse the issue and Oliver and Bart would have a better chance. The track led uphill and sometimes she found it difficult to detect the distinctive cut tracking signs among the glossy leaves and twining lianas of the undergrowth. She was breathing hard before she saw the meeting of ways ahead marked on the plan and knew she was near the trysting-place. She stood still to consider and drew into cover while she waited to see whether the two she sought had reached the place before her.

After a few moments a man withdrew from the undergrowth and surveyed the path, one hand raised to his eyes to shade them from the sun, fierce even here in this shaded place. He wore the remnants of velvet breeches and a tattered holland shirt. Corinna gave a great sob of relief at the sight of matted brown hair and a straggle of beard which could not hide Oliver's well known countenance from her.

She stepped out into the path and held out her arms. 'Oliver, oh, thank God, I thought you might have fallen foul of those overseers.'

He stood and stared at her and was joined by the taller figure of Bart Spicer. Oliver's eyes widened and he looked beyond her, back along the track.

'Corinna, I had not thought. . . Dear God, where is Julian?'

He drew her clumsily against his heart, one hand wonderingly pushing back her concealing hat, looking long and earnestly into her eyes. She gave a little embarrassed laugh.

'Poor Jules stumbled when he heard those shots just now and badly twisted his ankle. Rose is with him. I came on to guide you to the cove. Oh, Oliver, are you sure you are well?'

Lionel was right. He was greatly changed. The youthful lines of his face were replaced by a hollow-eyed gauntness. The mouth, which she remembered as constantly smiling, was held in, as if against pain. There was a feverishness about the way he held her, about the way his red-rimmed eyes roved about her face, her body, as if striving to convince himself that she was really here in the flesh.

Bart Spicer gave a brief, bitter little bark of laughter.

'Aye, we're well enough as we're like to be in this hell-hole. The pursuit had naught to do with us. Some black making a run for it, like as not, thought what he could hope for in freedom save starvation heaven alone knows.'

Corinna drew herself from Oliver's clutching hands.

'You two, at least, have a far better chance than any of them, poor souls. We must hurry to the cove and get you away before your escape is noted and the pursuit is on for you. Come, Oliver, I have the plan and I'm familiar with Julian's tracking signs. We have no time to waste. The seaman Lionel hired will not want to wait. They could well take off without you.'

Bart was clearly impatient to do as Corinna urged.
'She's right; we must get clear of this plantation.'

Corinna glanced briefly at the plan and then indicated which path they should take. It was very overgrown, as Julian had said, possibly used only by animals, the wild pigs Julian had mentioned. Perhaps there was a spring near by and the creatures went there to drink. She handed the cutlass to Bart.

'You'll need this to hack your way through in places. Make for that tree over there, the one with the trailing creepers.'

Bart needed no further urging but set off, brandishing the weapon. Oliver could not take his eyes from Corinna.

He said tonelessly, 'Julian says you married Summers.'

Corinna turned back to him, her eyes widening. 'Yes, you knew we were betrothed.'

'I thought you would seek to postpone the ceremony.' He sounded childishly sulky, and Corinna felt sudden impatience with his lack of response to their need for haste.

'We have no time for recriminations, Oliver. We must go—now.'

They pressed on, Bart mechanically hacking at the twining creepers which stretched along the track, almost obscuring it in places. Corinna hitched up her skirts, her eyes alert for tracking signs on the trunks of trees ahead, unconcerned for the rough places and roots along her way. Once she fell full-length and Oliver lifted her and held her close again. He murmured her name thickly.

'Corin, dear God, you are not hurt?' His lips pressed on her throat, and she forcefully wriggled free.

'No, no, of course I am not hurt. I'm no doll, Oliver.

Remember the hunts in the old days. Did a fall lay me low? Now let's get on.'

When Bart's arm tired Oliver took over, until the undergrowth thinned out and they were faced by a slight rise of the ground. Corinna, breathless after scrambling along rough ground, scanned it thoughtfully and looked down at her plan again.

'This is it, I think. We need to climb here, and soon we should see the cove below.'

Bart indicated that she and Oliver should draw into cover again.

'We must take care now we aren't seen against the skyline from the shore or out at sea. You two stay here while I go to investigate.'

He began to slip down the incline, while Corinna turned hurriedly to Oliver.

'We have very little time now.' There was a little catch to her voice at this moment of parting. 'We — we might never see each other again. Go with God, my dear. My mother and father send their love, and mine too.' She reached up, and her fingers brushed tenderly the unshaven cheeks and chin. 'Oh, Oliver, you look so thin. Were you badly treated in that terrible prison in Taunton, or on the ship did you fall ill?'

He gave a little mirthless laugh like Bart's earlier.

'It was not pleasant. I think Bart and I must have been made of stern stuff, because neither of us ailed. So many succumbed. Of course we were fortunate we were not wounded when taken.'

'Julian was lucky that Lionel was able to get him away from Bridgwater.'

His mouth tightened again at mention of her husband's name.

'Aye, I'm grateful to him for that. We feared Jules

would hang. I didn't want to leave him there, Corin, but. . .'

'I know. You had to. I blame you for nothing, Oliver.'

'Summers, he is good to you?'

She avoided his searching eyes. 'You have a new life ahead of you and you must make the best of it. One day, I pray God, the King will grant some pardons and you may be able to come home again.'

He nodded abstractedly. 'Julian wants to come to sea, he says.'

'Yes, he will try to join you in Tortuga, but you must not wait for him if there is opportunity for passage to the American Colonies.' She handed him a leather bag. 'There are some jewels here, family jewels, nothing Lionel will miss. Sell them and set yourself up there if you can.' She faced him urgently. 'Oliver, do not stay with this privateer, Lenoir. Do not trust him. I'm afraid. . .' She could not put her suspicion into words. If Oliver distrusted Lionel he might refuse to leave, fearing for her happiness, and she could not risk that. Desperately she plunged on. 'The man has been paid well for carrying you from the island, but none of these pirates can be relied on. Watch yourself.'

His brows drew together as he put both hands on her shoulders and drew her close to him again.

'I have learned to defend myself, Corin. I can protect you too, if need be. You need not be afraid.'

'Protect me?' She stared up at him, bewildered. 'You must not concern yourself about me, Oliver. Look to your own future now.'

His hands tightened on her shoulders. 'But you came. . . I thought—believed you would come with us. Tell me that is why you came.'

She went icy cold, even when sweat drenched her body.

'Come with you?' She forced the words incredulously. 'How could you believe such a thing? I am married to Lionel Summers. Julian could not have led you to believe that——'

He brushed away the thought. 'No, no, he said nothing of it. But you came. . .'

'Only to warn you, Oliver, in case—in case. . .'

'In case your husband had arranged for my timely death.'

'No—I don't. . . No, Oliver, but he does suspect our feelings for each other. . .'

'He knows you love me?' His tone was triumphant.

'Oliver, I love Lionel.' She said it simply, determinedly. 'He is my husband. I am pledged to him——'

'What can pledges mean now? You said yourself there is little time. I need you, Corin. I've always loved you. You know that. I know life will be hard for us, but I swear I will keep you safe. We have this one chance. You must come with me.'

She shook her head. She was frightened by the red gleam behind his brown eyes, the intensity of his words, forced out so fiercely. She struggled in his arms.

'Oliver, you have to let me go. Yes, I love you as my cousin, as my brother, but everything is changed now. . .'

'Because you are Lady Summers and wish to preen yourself in luxury at court.'

'No, Oliver. I told you in Barrow I could not marry you.'

He bent his head so that his face was very close to hers. His breath was hard on her cheeks. His lips forced down hard on hers, bruising them, demandingly, as if she were some army whore. She felt the scrape of his half-grown beard on her soft flesh and was more afraid than she had ever been in her life. This was not the Oliver she had known but some stranger whose experiences had taught him to regard women as cheap playthings, to be taken on the moment and soon discarded. She renewed her frantic struggles, but he shook her again, mouthing demands, entreaties. As if from a distance, over the pounding in her head, she could hear somebody calling urgently. She kicked out sharply with one foot and Oliver swore roundly, then she staggered back. Her head made contact with the tree bole behind her. There was agonising pain and then — blackness.

CHAPTER ELEVEN

ROSE, seated with her back to a palm-tree, facing Julian, who appeared to have fallen into a doze, shifted her position restlessly. As if aware of her unease, Julian opened his eyes and sat up, wincing sharply as stabs of red-hot pain shot through his injured ankle. He followed Rose's gaze upwards to the position of the sun showing between the glossy foliage above them.

'Shouldn't she be back by now, Master Julian?'

Julian grunted in reply and consulted his pocket watch. He moved to stand up, and yelled out this time in real distress.

'I must have fallen asleep. She's been gone close on three hours. I can't understand it. The ketch should be well away by now and Corinna back here with us. Rose, can you fashion me a makeshift crutch from one of those fallen branches? I must try and get to the cove and discover what happened.'

Rose's face paled. She had been fearful this past hour, but doubtful of disturbing Master Julian. She'd sat, anxious and distraught, listening to the rustling in the undergrowth which had alerted her to the sound of animals passing though — nothing, fortunately, she had judged large enough to be a danger. There had been no further sounds of men from the nearby plantation and nothing to make her fear the escape had gone wrong, but now she was as worried as Julian. She scrambled up and held out a hand to help him to his feet.

It was soon clear to her that he would be unable to

walk, not even back to the plantation. Before resting
Julian had removed his boot, and the ankle was puffy
and swollen. Even with her help he would not be able
to go after Corinna.

'You must stay here while I go, Master Julian. No, it
is useless to argue. You would only delay me, and if
we wait too long the light will go.'

Julian sank down again, his face contorted with pain.
Quickly he pointed out the nearest tracking sign and
gave her details of others and where she must look for
the marks.

'If the two men made it to the meeting-place they
must all have gone to the cove by now, so you should
find signs of disturbed undergrowth where the trailing
plants have been cut back. If Oliver hadn't come,
surely Corinna would be back with us by now. Hasten,
Rose. If she lies injured on the track we shall need to
summon help from the house.'

Rose needed no more urging and set off at once. It
did not prove difficult to follow the signs, and the track
showed distinct signs of the passage of several people.
Rose's alarm grew as she was afraid that whatever
calamity had menaced Corinna must have been on the
return journey when alone.

She arrived, panting, at the rise above the cove and
found evidence of footmarks in the soft, sandy soil as
well as other, more ominous signs where it appeared
men had struggled. Twigs had been displaced and
creepers torn free. Rose looked round desperately and
then mounted the rise and peered down into the little
cove below. It was an idyllic spot, soft sand, gentle,
lapping blue water, but quite deserted. Far in the
distance she could dimly make out a tiny black sail and
knew the ketch had left the cove, possibly a full hour

before, and put out to sea to rendezvous with the privateer's ship.

Rose thrust her knuckled hand hard against her lips to prevent herself crying out. No sign of Corinna either here or back along the track. Had she been injured the men would have left her here or — taken her with them?

The full import of the idea hit her like a blow between the eyes. Had Corinna decided to leave of her own will? No, that was impossible. Corinna had a real fondness for Oliver, but she knew the truth — that she could never be his. However, Oliver did not. He had loved his cousin and wanted her. . . But he would not, *could* not be so perfidious that he would force her. . .

Rose waited for no more. She ran back along the track and breathlessly imparted the news to Julian. He stared back at her, bewildered.

'No, no, you must be wrong. Noll would never do such a thing. It's just possible that Corinna decided——'

'No, Master Julian. I will not believe that. I tell you, she has been abducted. Your uncle and Sir Lionel must be told at once.'

'She might be lost, lying hurt. . .'

'And if so must be found before sundown. Master Webster will organise a search, but I fear she is aboard that ketch. I will send back help for you. I've no time to get you back to the house.'

Rose, her heart pounding, burst into the hall as Sir Lionel was mounting the stair. He turned instantly at sight of her, came quickly to her side, put one hand on her shoulder, and waited till she had breath enough to speak.

'Lady Summers, sir. She — she went with Master Julian and myself to meet Master Oliver. We — that is Master Julian and me — we waited in the shade for her to go on ahead. Master Julian, he hurt himself, you see, and couldn't go on, and then — and then — she didn't come back.'

Golden eyes flashed fire and his brows drew together in a scowl, then he led Rose gently to a chair.

'Sit for a moment and get your breath.' He moved to a console table and returned with a glass of rum. 'Drink it down. Yes,' he commanded, 'do as I say. I want you able to talk and to think clearly.'

Rose swallowed the strong, fiery liquid and gulped and coughed, but her colour was returning to normal and she was beginning to think more rationally, though the fears for her nursling which had kept her running headlong down the treacherous path, heedless of danger, were returning in force.

She clutched at his velvet sleeve. 'She is gone, sir, I'm sure, on the ship.'

'The ship?' His tone was as incredulous as Julian's had been and harsh with anger. He crouched down by Rose's side. 'I think you must tell me just what happened after Master Webster and I left the house.'

'She had always meant to see him, sir. I knew she would go alone if I did not persuade Master Julian, but. . .' Rose plunged into her story, and he continued to listen without interruption. When she paused at last, she saw that fury struggled with alarm in his emotions.

'Julian thinks she might have lost her way back?'

'Indeed, sir, but I cannot believe that. There should be a search, but — '

'Just so. It seems likely that she is, as you say, aboard that ketch.'

He stood up slowly, and Rose watched him warily.

'It might be that — that, as Julian half suggested, she decided to go with her cousin.' The words were spoken very deliberately.

Rose said vehemently, 'I know that to be untrue, sir. She knew, you see, knew they could never be lovers. Master Oliver is her half-brother, son of Mistress Tabitha. I know; I helped to deliver Mistress Corinna.'

He turned to face her, and those golden-brown eyes blazed suddenly tempestuous light. 'Half-brother?'

'Yes, sir; they told her, you see, the day of the betrothal.'

'But in the wood they. . . I saw them. There was nothing brotherly about his manner with her. . .'

'He doesn't know, sir. They made her promise she would not tell him, to save Mistress Tabitha's good name.'

'Then that is why she changed her mind so unaccountably and agreed to accept me?' The tone was harsh, uncompromising.

'Yes, sir, that might have been the reason then, but not later. She loves you, sir. You have to believe that and go after her.'

There was a sudden movement from the outer door, and Lionel turned to face Ned Webster, who was poised there, riding whip gripped tightly in one hand. The two men stood and stared at each other, then Lionel made an imperceptible movement of one hand.

'She is *your* daughter, then, yours and Tabitha Hunt's?'

Ned Webster inclined his head and came further into the hall. His gaze took in Rose's distressed state and travelled back to Lionel's stern features again.

'I heard the end of what Rose was saying. When Corinna and I were riding, a day or so ago, she told me she knew of our true relationship. We spoke of her feelings for Oliver. She had always been fond of him. Their lives had always intertwined. It was natural she should have wanted to wed him, to continue to feel safe and content on her own land that she so loved, but she is fully aware now that those feelings were those of an inexperienced girl. She has become a woman and fallen deeply and irrevocably in love with her husband. Since she felt partly responsible for Oliver's involvement in that doomed rising, she had to be sure he gained his freedom. Once that was obtained, her only desire was to be a good wife to you, Lionel.'

Lionel said bleakly, 'She went with Julian to meet the prisoners and has disappeared from the area. Rose believes Oliver abducted her. There were signs of a struggle. You've come straight from Bridgetown. Is there news of Lenoir?'

Rose had vacated the chair at Ned Webster's entrance and stood uncertainly, biting her lip. It was an attitude foreign to her nature, but she was helpless to aid Corinna until the men decided on the best course of action.

Ned Webster sank heavily into the chair and rubbed distractedly at his chin. 'I saw Lenoir briefly before I left the town. It seems the business between O'Brian and him was concluded amicably. O'Brian needed certain commodities which Lenoir could provide and willingly agreed to a small ransom, and Lenoir freed him, once he was sure the time we needed had passed, and the two men sat on drinking rum together.'

'Then Lenoir is not abroad the *Genevieve*?'

'No, he told me he's left his sailing master in charge and intends to rejoin the ship in Tortuga. He gave no details, but I assumed he had business of a personal nature here in Bridgetown. You know the man is tolerated because of the cargoes he brings in. There would be no objection to his presence in the town. I take it he would then sail to Tortuga on one of the other vessels he owns when it comes into harbour in a couple of days.'

'We can't wait for that. Where was he when you saw him last?'

'In the Black Boar tavern. The *Curlew* is in harbour. I saw Jack Greenwood——'

'Good.' Lionel moved towards the stair foot. 'Send a man into Bridgetown with orders to find them both — Greenwood and Lenoir — and ask them to meet me at the Black Boar in a hour. You'll need another couple of fellows to go on that track and bring in Julian. The idiot has injured his ankle, may have broken it.'

'You intend to follow the *Genevieve* on the *Curlew*?'

'It's our only chance. She can make excellent speed, as she's more than likely without a full cargo.'

'But she's not equipped for battle.'

'We must hope it will not come to that. If Lenoir is with us his crew will heed his orders. If not——' grimly '—then we must think again. It will not be the first time I've faced heavy odds at sea. 'You'll come with us?'

Ned Webster rose at once. 'Do you need to ask? Corinna is my daughter.'

'Good,' Lionel said again, and turned finally to Rose. 'Be ready to go into Bridgetown within the hour. I take it you'll want to be with your mistress when we find her?'

Rose gave both a hurried curtsy of acknowledgement and ran upstairs to change her torn and dusty gown and pack for herself and whatever she thought Corinna might need.

Corinna stared up wonderingly at the swinging lantern above her head. She moved cautiously and realised she was lying, fully dressed, upon a wooden bunk. Her

head still hurt, and she lifted a questioning hand to feel
sticky wetness between her fingers. She tried to remember. She had been fighting her way through the creepers with Oliver and they had reached the rise above the
cove. And — Oliver had wanted her to go with him and
she had tried to explain how much she loved
Lionel ——

With a great fearful start she sat up on the bunk and
felt the motion of the great ship beneath her. She was
at sea, and, if she were any judge, not aboard the small
ketch Lionel had hired to carry the escapees from the
island. This was a large sailing ship. The Frenchman's
ship had stood off the coast, waiting for Oliver and
Bart, to carry them to freedom.

Then Oliver had carried her down to the cove and
the ketch. He had abducted her. She thrust her fingers
against her lips to quell the cry of alarm. It was dark,
but for the lantern, hours after she had fallen against
the tree in their struggle. It was all coming back to her
now. She had tried to ward him off and had stumbled.
He would not have wanted to leave her there, unconscious, and had decided to take her with him. She drew
in a hard breath. She was alone in the cabin. Where
was Oliver? How much time had passed? Were they
far from land? Dear God, how could she return to
Barbados?

She could hear few sounds from on deck. There
would be a watch, of course, on the bridge, and the
helmsman, possibly the captain. She gave a faint shudder as she thought about the black-clad Frenchman,
Lenoir, an assumed name to conceal a true identity,
one chosen to reflect a personality, captain of a black
ship known throughout the Caribbean for black deeds,
a man whose reputation she had feared and warned

Oliver against. And if the captain was such a man, what of his crew?

Panic welled up in her and was rigorously quelled. Lionel would consider her faint-hearted. She must keep calm, remember that Lenoir had been Lionel's friend and would, once he heard her tale, restore her to her husband.

Thoughts of Lionel made her heart pound in her breast. Where was he now, at this very moment? What was he doing? He must be aware that she had been taken. A more terrible thought struck her. Would he assume she had gone willingly with Oliver? He had every reason to believe the worst. If so, would he leave her to her fate?

No, Ned Webster, her true father, knew her love for her husband, and so did Rose. *They* would convince him. They must.

Frantically she considered what Lionel's reactions would be to her disappearance. He had wanted her, desired her, but did he love her? She thought back to the time in the arbour when he had proposed. He had been arrogantly confident that she had been given to him, a possession, a chattel. He had made love to her, taught her the meaning of passion, told her she was beautiful in his eyes, but she could not gauge the depth of his emotions. He was a courtier, bred to the niceties of fine phrases and flattery. Would he have said as much to any woman who pleased him for the moment? She was his wife and must be treated with consideration, with courtesy, but love. . .?

She had known for weeks now that she loved him, not for his practised lovemaking alone, which filled her with delight, not even for the knowledge of his courage and practicality, which saved Julian for her, and his readiness to free Oliver. It was for the little, loving things which had grown between them, the way his auburn hair curled into the nape of his neck when the fashionable periwig was discarded, the times they had talked intimately on the ship, the manner in which he held her close to his heart after lovemaking, stroking her hair; the moments that had been hers alone. She needed him, wanted him desperately, but did he love her enough to forgive her now? Had any other man stolen her away, yes, he might have accepted it, but Oliver?

He would rescue her, she was sure, would take her back, outwardly behave towards her as if nothing had happened, but could he love her? For the moment she must thrust thoughts of Lionel to the back of her mind and concentrate on the problem of convincing Oliver that she could not stay with him.

Oliver! He had seemed so terribly changed. Though he looked gaunt and ill, he had fought with the strength of a madman, and, with a madman's hold on one thought only, had refused to accept that she no longer wished to be his.

Firmly she told herself that she had always before been able to control Oliver. Whenever he had come up with some hare-brained scheme which augured a risk of punishment for all of them when it failed, as Oliver's schemes frequently had, she had been able to convince him of her arguments against the plan. Now that her life — and more than her life, her reputation — depended on Oliver's subjection to her will, she must remain in complete control of her thoughts and emotions. Surely the pirate would not seek to hold her in despite of his former comrade's wishes? She tried to recall where she had been told the ship was bound — Tortuga. Was not that some vile stronghold of the Brotherhood of the Coast? But she would be safe with

Oliver to protect her, and Lionel would come soon to claim her. . .

The door was thrust open, and Corinna sank back against the rough pillows of the bunk. By the light of the lantern the man held she saw that her visitor was Oliver. She gave a great sigh of relief.

He came slowly forward, as if fearful of waking her.

'Corin, my dear love, how are you? I was afraid — but the ship's carpenter, who cares for the injured aboard, said you were not gravely hurt. You came to just for a moment in the ketch, then you dozed off again. The wound has been bathed and the worst of the bleeding stopped. They told me I should leave you to sleep.'

She sat back against the pillows and tried to smile gamely back at him.

'Oliver, you mustn't be afraid. I am well enough, have taken worse tumbles and hurts before now at Barrow. My head aches and the wound is oozing blood still, but it will soon heal.'

He'd come close to the bed now and was bending over her solicitously, his lantern put down on a sea chest. She reached out and took his hand.

'Oliver, my dear, whatever possessed you to bring me here, to the ship? I take it I am aboard the *Genevieve*, Lenoir's vessel.'

'Yes, I couldn't leave you, Corin. Bart helped carry you down to the cove and lift you aboard. What else would you have had me do? All will be well. No harm will come to you, I swear it. Don't you trust me?'

In the soft light from the lanterns he looked more his old self, younger, more vulnerable. The gaunt lines of the features were obscured, and he had taken the trouble to shave and comb his hair. His brown eyes shone with love for her, and she caught back the great lump of pity for him which welled up within her.

Nothing had changed for Oliver. He had loved her at Barrow, taken her image with him into battle, carried memories of her to sustain him through the horrifying days in hiding, in prison, in that awe-inspiring courtroom where he had been doomed to die, and now she must tell him she could never be his, never return his love, that he must give her up and try to forget her.

She touched the bunk at the side of her in invitation, and he sank down. She reached up gently and touched his cheek.

'I shall always be very fond of you, Oliver, and since hearing the news that you were taken and in danger I have done everything I could to speed your rescue. Without my husband, Lionel, that could not have been accomplished.'

His mouth set in a sulky line, and she touched his lips fleetingly.

'You have to return me to him, Oliver.'

'I love you. You are mine; you'll always be mine,' he said stubbornly. 'Now we have the opportunity to do as we please. Your father cannot rule you here. In the colonies there will be no one to question whether we are truly married. Will God consider it sin in us, to live together and love, as we were meant to do?'

She shook her head. 'I keep trying to tell you, Oliver. That cannot be. Things have changed.'

'You want to go back to him, to become respected, a wealthy court lady? Life in penury in Virginia or elsewhere in the Americas would be too much hardship?'

'If you were my true husband, Oliver, no hardship would be too great to bear.'

'Then you no longer love me?' His eyes had gone hard again, like opaque pebbles in the subdued glow of the lantern light. 'I could make you love me again, prove to you that he is nothing to you.'

Suddenly she found herself seized with the hard strength she had not known he possessed. There was that strange intensity in the movement which she had noted on the rise above the cove. He was forcing her back against the pillows, pressing her down into the bedding. His body was hard across hers, his hands flat on her shoulders. His mouth sought hers. He had been drinking. She smelt raw rum on his breath. Obviously he had been carousing with the privateers, celebrating his freedom. Trying to reason with him would be useless.

She made a desperate effort to thrust herself upwards, to dislodge him, but he had the strength and determination of a desperate man, and she felt herself drowning in the embrace.

He was panting hard as he drew away from the kiss. Just in time he had recollected himself, remembered how much he loved her, how dearly he would have sold his life to protect her from harm such as he had now intended.

'Forgive me, Corinna, oh, my love,' he murmured shakily. 'I want you too much to harm you; you know that. Just tell me that you will forsake him, go with me, love me. . .'

She turned her face from him, tears streaming down her cheeks, soaking the rough linen of the sheet.

'I can't, Oliver,' she moaned softly. 'Oh, my dear, how can I make you understand? I *did* love you, will always love you—but not in the way you want. We cannot love, Oliver. I wanted you never to know, but I see I have to tell you. That day, the day you asked me to be your wife, I—I told my father and mother.' She drew a sobbing breath. 'They told me—they told me that—that we are brother and sister, Oliver. Your mother, Tabitha—she is also mine.'

The silence which followed seemed interminable, then, as he said nothing, she turned to face him again. He had withdrawn himself slightly from her and sat staring, his eyes wide with shock. She struggled into a sitting position.

'I know it to be true, Oliver. She told me, your mother—and mine.'

He made some slight, incoherent sound.

'I thought at first that my heart would break. I knew, even when I was denying the truth of it to myself, that what they said was so, and I knew when they asked me not to tell you or Julian that it was the only way to save your mother from pain. But I knew, Oliver, I knew. You must believe it, my dear, and let me go.'

He said slowly, 'Does he know, your husband?'

She shook her head mutely. 'He fears I still have feelings for you which—which could destroy our marriage. That—that is why I came to the cove to warn you.'

'And do you still hold those feelings for me, the ones he fears?'

She could not look at him, sat, head down, moistening lips which had become unbearably dry.

'No, Oliver,' she said at last, in a hoarse whisper. 'I have come to terms with it, learned—learned to love my husband. What we had—was very fine, a wonderful companionship which had not time to develop into full-blown love. We were as we truly are—brother and sister—my dear, and I think we should always have felt like that. Perhaps it is as well that we—I found out when I did. It saved us from what might have been an unfulfilling marriage, which we would both, in time, have regretted.'

'*You* might have done,' he said harshly, 'I never. I love you as man loves woman, will always love you like that.'

She said chokingly, 'I shall pray that you learn to. . . replace me in your affections with someone else — if you cannot forget me. Oliver, it would break my heart if I thought you could never do that.'

He sat moodily silent again, his fingers toying idly with the baldric which carried his sword. At last he said, 'Who was the man?'

'My father, you mean?'

'The man who betrayed my father.'

'There was no real betrayal, Oliver. Your mother had been promised to Saul Hunt when she was scarcely more than a child. When — when my father came upon the scene she could no more prevent herself from loving him that she could stop herself breathing. He was Edward Webster. He would have married her, I think, but he did not know, was fighting in the Dutch Wars, and when he returned your mother was wed and soon you were conceived.'

'And he still loves my mother? For that reason he helped in the escape?'

She hesitated. 'I don't know. He — he has never wed. . .'

'So Rose knew, too, suckled you with Jesse. She must have been in on the secret. And Jules, does he know?'

'No, and mustn't. If — if there is ever a chance for you to return you must never let them realise that you know. You must forgive your mother, Oliver. She loved Ned Webster as — as you say you love me.'

The strangeness had left his expression now. He

resembled the old Oliver, young, innocent of guile, but deadly tired.

'So you must be returned to Barbados. Will he take you back?'

It was a bald question, and she winced at the harsh reality of his tone.

'I don't know that either. I only know that I have come to love him—very dearly.'

'Will you tell him?'

'I think perhaps I must, that he deserves to know. Whether he will believe that I. . . I don't know if I can convince him, whether the damage has been too great. . .' She broke off with a little despairing gesture of her hand. 'I only know that I have to try.'

He nodded. 'You realise that it won't be easy, convincing Bart and the others of the need to turn back.' His teeth bared in a mirthless grin. 'As usual I behaved like a fool, a childish, besotted fool, and God knows whether it can all be made to come right, but, like you, my love, I must try to *put* it right. Stay within the cabin. I don't have to tell you that there are those aboard who might not wish to part with you. I'll come for you when I have news.'

As the door closed on him she heard the click of the key and understood that her imprisonment was for her safety. She lay back exhausted. Her head still ached abominably, as much with the effort of struggling to convince Oliver as from the original accident. She wished she could have gone with him, faced them out. Oliver was as much in danger from his friend as from the privateers, who had no reason to obey his wishes. Would they be prepared to turn the ship, to sail openly into the English colony where any or all of them could be accused of piracy? And, if not, what hope had she of being restored to Lionel?

Her reverie was broken abruptly some half-hour later when she heard the key turn in the lock. Whoever was preparing to enter her cabin was impatient and swore as it refused to turn at first. Corinna stared at the door fearfully. Her visitor did not sound like Oliver, who surely would have called to her first.

She had done her best with her appearance. Her skirt habit was soiled and torn, also woefully marked by sea water. It must have trailed in the water when she was carried to the boat. She had no comb and her hat had disappeared. She let down her hair and combed and smoothed it with her fingers as best she could, then simply drew it back from her face and fixed it in position with two or three pins which remained to her.

She stood up gamely as the key ground again in the lock and turned at last and the newcomer stepped in. Bart Spicer stood framed in the doorway, one hand on his sword hilt, the other on his hip. Like Oliver he had shaved and washed and been provided with a fresh shirt and canvas drawers such as seamen wore. Both men, she had noted, had very quickly been given weapons. Apparently the members of Lenoir's crew had accepted the new recruits readily enough. She had never really liked Oliver's college friend. The man had always seemed to her sullen and envious of the fortunes of Julian and Oliver, for his own people came of merchant stock. She had credited Bart Spicer with inculcating the enthusiasm for the Monmouth Rebellion. The man was fiercely anti-papist, she knew, had made no secret of it, but she had privately considered he longed for change in government for his own advantage. Perhaps she had been unfair to him. Oliver and Jules were not children and had made up their own minds. She knew that her resentment of Spicer's sway over his new-found friends had been

rooted in her whim to have them to herself over that
last vacation from Oxford.

Now she stared into Spicer's broad, tanned face with
a sense of foreboding. He had a shock of dark curls
and black, dancing eyes, a fleshy nose and the loose
mouth which spoke of sensuality. There was no doubt
he would be termed comely, even handsome, by the
women of his acquaintance, but Corinna had always
been a little wary in his presence.

'Well, well,' he drawled, 'Noll's wench, and not, I
hear, best pleased to find herself with him?'

'Where *is* Oliver?' Corinna demanded.

'On deck, where, I imagine, you'll want to join him.
I was dispatched to fetch you.'

She opened her mouth to remonstrate, thought
better of the idea, and waited in icy silence, her head
high, until he moved clear of the doorway to allow her
to proceed. At the foot of the companionway he put a
hand on her arm to help her ascent, and she hastily
shook him off.

'I can manage.'

When she emerged upon the poop deck she was
blinking in full daylight. She hesitated at the head of
the stair, looking anxiously round for Oliver.

There were three or four men she did not know near
the helmsman. Oliver turned hurriedly at her approach
and moved to come towards her but one of the crewmen, a small, fat, bandy-legged man, detained him
with a hand on his shoulder. He said something in
French that Corinna did not catch, and the other men
laughed. She could see that a black scowl darkened
Oliver's brow.

Before she could utter a word she was seized by her
escort and thrust forward towards the gaudily dressed
individual, who stood lounging, his back to the taffrail,

close to the helmsman. This she took to be Lenoir's deputy, his sailing master or lieutenant.

'Here she is, *messieurs*,' Spicer said pleasantly, 'Milady Summers, and Noll Hunt's light of love.'

Oliver gave a snarl of rage.

'Mind your evil tongue, Spicer.' He struggled with the privateer, who still held his arm and was looking to his superior for further orders.

The man made Corinna an insolent bow and continued to lounge, his gaze passing smilingly from one Englishman to the other, as if the sight of them at odds offered him fine entertainment.

Spicer's easy manner did not relax under Oliver's reproof. He shrugged nonchalantly. 'What else would you call a woman who inhabits your mind to the exclusion of all sensible thoughts? To add to it, she follows you to the meeting-place, though I imagine her husband knows nothing of the rendezvous.'

'I'll cut out your heart for this. . .' Oliver's apparent friendship with Spicer had totally been replaced by hatred. Whether their association had become increasingly strained over the weeks of imprisonment or the bad feeling had simply developed during this exchange of opposing views, Corinna could not tell. She was becoming alarmed, more for Oliver's safety than her own. Surely Spicer's opinion would be backed by the privateers, and Oliver isolated by his overweening desire to obey her wishes and return to Barbados.

Spicer appealed to the ship's master. 'Who would be foolish enough to contemplate returning to the English colony simply to take a runaway wife back to her husband? We'd put ourselves in peril, and what profit would there be in such a course? If Hunt here were not so besotted with the wench he'd see the futility of it, as I do. He did the right thing by her. She was hurt and he couldn't leave her, so we carried her here. What else could she expect? Now, it appears, they have quarrelled and she has had second thoughts about deserting her husband. Are we to be held responsible for her change of heart? I say we sail on to Tortuga. There she could be held aboard ship under guard until word could be sent to her husband and a suitable ransom obtained. If the man isn't prepared to pay — and who could blame him? — then, if what I hear of the town is correct, there will be plenty more who would jump at the chance, and the bidding should be high.'

The ship's master signalled to his subordinate to keep a tight hold on Oliver, who was straining every muscle to launch himself at Spicer. As if at his master's unspoken command, a second ruffian joined Oliver's gaoler, taking his other arm so that he was helpless.

Corinna faced the master, chin high, disdaining to struggle vainly in Spicer's hold. The Frenchman stroked his chin, his bold black eyes continuing to smile.

'Monsieur Spicer, there seems much good sense in what you suggest, but we can do nozing without ze consent of our *capitaine*.' He gave a Gallic shrug. '*Naturellement*, it would be foolish to turn the ship. We must, as you say, sail on to Tortuga. Once in port we shall come under the jurisdiction of Captain Lenoir. For ze present I zink milady Summers, she should be returned to 'er cabin, and——' his smiling gaze passed to Oliver again, whose face was suffused with scarlet, revealing his rage and frustration '—I do not zink that Monsieur 'Unt here should be confined with 'er. Per'aps it would be better if he be held in ze brig, *non*?'

Corinna's lips trembled at the thought of separation

from her one champion, but she kept her voice level as she appealed to Oliver.

'Please do nothing foolish and endanger yourself, Oliver. Sir Lionel will see to it that any insult to my person will be paid for in full, and no man will dare to do me harm.'

'Confound it, Corinna, you came to help us. How dare this perfidious hound insult you so?'

Despite his struggles, Oliver's captors began to urge him towards the companionway, presumably to convey him to the ship's brig in obedience to the master's orders.

A sudden shout distracted the attention of all of them.

'Monsieur Richard, ship on the port bow, making towards us at speed.'

The master gave a surprised oath and gestured for Corinna to be held tightly until he could ascertain if there was threatened danger. A sailor proferred a ship's glass and he moved forward and trained it on the vessel looming up on his port side.

There was an imperceptible shift of interest from the protagonists and the unfortunate lady towards the sea. Men lifted hands to shade their eyes, and the helmsman looked expectantly towards the ship's master for orders.

'She bears down on us fast,' the French commander said crisply. 'She 'as the lines of a merchantman, per'aps the *Curlew*. If zat is so then *c'est possible* zat Captaine Lenoir is aboard with Sir Lionel.' He turned towards Corinna, his black eyes snapping with excitement and alarm. 'You bring ze great trouble upon us, *madame*.'

'That is not my fault, *monsieur*,' Corinna replied. 'I did not ask to be conveyed aboard this ship.'

The Frenchman muttered darkly below his breath. 'Hold your course.' This to the helsman. 'It would be useless to outrun her, and if we anger ze *capitaine*. . .' He left the rest unsaid.

Striding to the ship's waist, he gave out urgent orders.

'We rendezvous with ze approaching vessel. Make no move to attack, and wait until we are hailed. Have ze grappling hooks ready to allow our *captaine* to come aboard, if it is as I say.'

Spicer kept a firm hold on Corinna's arm, but his grip was no longer painful. She half turned to find him watching the approaching vessel, which was looming up tall on the port bows fast now, his brows drawing together in alarm. The men holding Oliver also were intent on the manoeuvres of the following vessel and loosened their grip on their captive. With a howl of rage, Oliver tore free and sprang at Spicer. Taken by surprise, the man was forced to release Corinna, who half stumbled and almost fell to the deck. The blood was pounding in her ears as she struggled to rise and come between the antagonists, but Oliver, enraged, was far too quick for her. He had drawn his sword and advanced on Spicer, who was forced to defend himself and draw his weapon.

The *Genevieve's* crewman hurriedly drew apart from the two. They were not unused to such hasty quarrels and had learned by experience to keep well clear of combatants; besides, they were more intent on what was likely to happen to their ship to concern themselves with two brawling Englishmen. Corinna gave a sobbing breath and retreated to the taffrail, her eyes on the steel blades attacking, engaging, parrying. She was concentrating now only on Oliver's possible fate, and took no heed of the noise of the grappling hooks as the ships drew together or even the arrival of the three men who climbed the ship's ladder and mounted to the deck.

She could see that Oliver had no chance. Spicer's skill with the weapon far outmatched his, and he was soon disarmed. He gave a hoarse cry and bent to retrieve his weapon. Ruthlessly Spicer struck him down. Oliver gave one shrill scream and sank to the deck, his hand still reaching blindly for his sword. His other sought vainly to stem the blood which pumped from the wound in his chest.

Spicer took no further heed of him and sprang towards Corinna again.

'You damned wanton,' he panted hoarsely. 'You were the ruin of your lover and now you come between us and threaten my life. If I had any sense I'd finish you too.'

A cool voice said evenly, 'Any move towards my wife, fellow, would be extremely unwise.'

Corinna did not wait even to look at her husband, but ran to Oliver's side. He was straining gamely to get up, but she pressed him back against the deck, tears streaming down her cheeks.

'Oliver, oh, my dear, you mustn't try to move. Stay still till we see how badly you're hurt.'

Pierre Barbizet detached himself from the little group by the ship's ladder and came to the fallen man. Corinna was sitting on the deck now, Oliver's head and shoulders supported against her heart. She stared distractedly at the little French valet.

'Please, please tell me he is not gravely hurt.'

'*Excusez moi*, milady.' Barbizet knelt to make his examination. Blood was oozing from the corner of Oliver's mouth and his breath was coming in hard rasps. Corinna watched Barbizet's skilled fingers gauging the depth of the wound. He turned towards Lionel, who waited, silently, and gave one small regretful shake of the head, then he turned again to his patient, tore free part of his own sleeve, and made an improvised pad for the wound.

Lenoir's deputy hastened to his captain's side and began a flood of explanations in rapid French. Corinna sat on, holding tightly to Oliver's hand, but now she was looking up towards Lionel, and her eyes appealed to him for understanding.

Spicer was breathing heavily. Already his erstwhile companions had deserted him and deliberately moved away. He gave a harsh rasp of breath as his eyes passed over Oliver's supine body.

Lionel moved to tower above Corinna where she sat supporting her burden.

'Are you unhurt?'

She made a brief nod of assent and did not seek to avoid any sign of censure in his golden-brown eyes. He inclined his head, looked down gravely at Oliver, then moved to face Bart Spicer.

'Sir,' he said coldly, 'I think you owe me satisfaction.'

Spicer stared back at him dazedly and made no answer.

With grave courtesy Lionel explained, 'You have offered my wife insult and threatened her life and safety; also you have injured my kinsman.'

Spicer said hoarsely, 'It was not my wish she should be carried aboard ship. Afterwards, to return her would have placed us all in danger.'

Lionel's steady gaze did not waver. 'From what I hear from the ship's master it was your suggestion, and yours alone, that she should be taken to Tortuga and subjected to be humiliation of ransom or worse, offered for sale to any ruffian who would look on her with lust.'

Spicer swallowed and looked huntedly towards his fellow crewmen for support, but they all remained grimly silent.

Captain Lenoir addressed Lionel in French, and Corinna lifted her head to try to follow the exchange, but it was too fast and she gave it up and returned her attention to Oliver, who remained unconscious.

Lionel's voice, deadly calm, again addressed Spicer. 'We will settle this matter now, if you please. You have, it is true, been recently engaging in sword play, which gives me a slight advantage, but I feel you will get as good a chance from me as you gave your antagonist.'

There was a little hiss of contempt from a crewman nearest the pair. All had seen Oliver cut down while attempting to retrieve his weapon. In a battle for control of the ship every member of that rascally crew would have defended himself by any means available, but they had their own code of conduct in settling private affairs, and this Englishman had broken it. Besides, had not the two men been recent comrades? Was this the treatment meted out to a friend?

Still Spicer made no move, and Lionel prompted him again very quietly. 'Draw and defend yourself, fellow. You must do that, you know. Must I request someone to draw your weapon and place it in your hand?'

Spicer drew away from his tormentor until he backed up against the taffrail. Lionel had not so much as removed his velvet coat, and was wearing his periwig. His hand was steady on his rapier hilt, but he had not yet drawn.

Corinna came abruptly out of her grief-stricken stupor to give a frightened cry.

'No, Lionel, no, not on my account. Too much blood has been shed already. Lionel, please. . .'

He had his back to her and did not turn.

Oliver, slowly coming to himself, caught convulsively at her hand and she knew she could not leave him. In all events, Lionel would not heed her. Instinctively she knew that. She mastered a little sob of panic, caught Barbizet's eyes, and subsided to await the outcome.

Spicer was staring with red-rimmed eyes at the man who seemed determined to kill him. He was rested now, and his lips parted in a contemptuous grin. Did this fashionably clad coxcomb think he could beat him with the small sword? He had made short work of enemies on the field at Sedgemoor, aye, and dealt with quarrelsome cronies in camp. Well, since needs must, better quickly. If he triumphed it was less likely that this French captain would do him harm in recrimination.

Sneeringly he drew his sword, saluted his opponent mockingly, and adopted the 'on guard', position.

Oliver's feeble grip on Corinna's hand tightened as his head lifted and he could see the combatants preparing to engage.

'Dear God, Corinna, I hope Summers knows how to handle himself. Spicer has killed two men in camp in stupid brawls over gambling. He. . .' He broke off, choking, and blood bubbled afresh from the side of his mouth.

'Hush,' Corinna whispered, 'I'm sure Lionel knows what he is about.' She spoke with considerably more confidence than she was feeling, and her gaze went fearfully to where her husband stood in the glitter of morning sunlight, his blade touching that of his opponent, one hand on his hip. Even from this distance she could see that he was smiling, his pose graceful and unconcerned, but there was that cold glitter about the eyes that told her he would not be satisfied until Spicer lay dead at her feet.

She was unable to cry. There was a terrible numbness in her of body and mind which made her unable to move or speak. She could lose Lionel and she knew, without asking Barbizet, that Oliver was going to die. She had an unbearable sense of inconsolable guilt for what was taking place before her eyes.

Again the crew members had drawn aside to give the duellists room to manoeuvre. Lenoir had taken up a position to monitor events. He briefly touched the crossed blades with his own and the men stepped back, saluted each other once more, and engaged blades. Oliver had forced himself into a half-seated posture, his eyes following the progress of the combatants. They began like dancers warily circling each other, weight balanced evenly on the balls of their feet. Again Corinna watched in horror as the flickering blades touched, parried, counter-parried. This time the men were more evenly matched. Though she knew little of the art, she recognised that Spicer's style was sheer braggadocio. His tactics were to rush in quickly on to the attack in an effort to confuse his opponent. Though he had been recently fighting, he now appeared rested and was not breathing heavily, and he was more suitably attired for combat than Lionel. His holland shirt made movement easy and was not confining, and his sleeves were rolled high. In contrast Lionel was encumbered by his full-skirted coat and long embroidered waistcoat. Corinna wondered, fleetingly, why he had not removed them, and sighed inwardly. Was Lionel out to impress her? If so, he had no idea how much she was enduring an agony of suffering now. She prayed inwardly. Dear God, do not let him die because of any foolish conduct of mine. I should have been

content to remain at the plantation and let Oliver go
from my life forever. If I had done so, none of this
would have happened. Oliver would not now be dying
in my arms and Lionel in grave danger.

Her eyes scanned the small group near the ship's
ladder. Behind Captain Lenoir stood her father. He
took his attention briefly from the duellists to offer her
a little encouraging smile. Then it was that she saw
Rose on Ned Webster's left. Her former nurse watched
like the others with her habitual expression of imper-
turbability, but Corinna could see a small tic moving
by her jawline, and knew Rose was as frightened as
she was.

Now Corinna realised that Spicer was tiring. He was
heavier built than Lionel and the extra weight was
telling, but she also understood that desperation could
make him reckless and one of those sudden lunges
could take Lionel by surprise. There was so little sound
on deck that she could hear the lapping of the water
against the ships' sides and Oliver's laboured breathing.
Her fingers tightened comfortingly on his wrist and she
whispered a swift prayer for him that he would not
suffer unbearably in passing.

Spicer's mouth was stretched in a hard grimace now
and his expression was no longer contemptuous. He
seemed intent only on parrying Lionel's blade. Her
husband appeared as fresh as he had been when he had
climbed to the head of the ladder. Inexorably he was
pressing his opponent back towards the taffrail.
Spicer's expression became hunted, and he struggled
to resist the inevitable pressure to retreat before the
other's blade. Corinna swallowed as he realised that
Lionel was now playing with his victim. She was sure
that, at any moment he chose, he could disarm Spicer.

All at once the affair ended. Lionel's blade arched,

flicking golden light from the sun. Spicer gave one gurgling cry and fell backwards, his body toppling over the low rail to the sea below.

There was a moment of continued silence, then Lionel unhurriedly wiped his blade upon a handkerchief proffered to him by Lenoir, and sheathed it. He was still breathing totally without effort.

She made a little inarticulate cry as he came steadily back to her and dropped to his knees by Oliver.

She was unaware of the gentle buzz which resumed around them. Her free hand reached out for and caught Lionel's, and her eyes, swimming with tears, appealed for his forgiveness.

He smiled reassuringly. 'I have one or two scratches, nothing of consequence. I am sorry that you were forced to witness that, but it was unavoidable. He was a scoundrel, you know. Once he took to a life of piracy, no woman or vulnerable man or child would have been safe from him. I know the type only too well.'

Oliver croaked, 'He has been going to the bad since we joined the Duke's army. He — he had an unreasonable envy of any man with pretensions to gentility. After — after Taunton and our experiences in that unspeakable gaol the — bitterness had grown in him. . .'

'Don't try to talk.' Lionel's voice was gentle, but a command nevertheless.

Oliver gave a ghost of a laugh. 'It can make no difference if I rest now. We all know that and — and I've little time.' He released Corinna's hand and grasped at Lionel's. 'Tell me you love her.'

'With my whole heart and soul.'

'You will not hold her — responsible for — any of this?'

Lionel gave a slight regretful shake of the head. 'I swear I will not.'

'It's — it's best this way. Even now that I — I love her, will go on loving her till the moment. . .' Again he gave that ghost of a laugh, then, like Spicer, he choked on his own blood, and fell back in a paroxysm of harsh coughing.

Barbizet squatted down, one hand feeling for the failing pulse, the other pressed against the chest. He did not need to even shake his head for Corinna to understand Oliver was going. She gave a little helpless sob and bent her head yet nearer to kiss the closing eyes.

Oliver said faintly, 'Summers — take her home — home — to Barrow. . .'

Lionel's throat worked as he saw Corinna desperately clutch at her cousin's hand again, and watch fearfully for the failing breath, then, as his hand slackened in hers, she gave a final despairing cry and fell forward across Oliver's body, the dam bursting at last, and the dreadful storm of weeping gushing forth.

He waited for a moment, then he rose and went to confer with Lenoir. When he returned to her the worst was over and she was looking helplessly for someone to tell her what to do about Oliver's slack form still lying against her breast. Stooping, he lifted her gently to her feet and signalled to Pierre Barbizet to do what was necessary for the decent arrangement of the dead man's body. Corinna was facing him, her two hands pressed against his chest. There was a strange, unreal look about her eyes, and he drew her close, lifted her in his arms, and made for the companionway, where he was joined by Rose, who followed him down.

When he laid Corinna on the bunk in the small cabin which an embarrassed member of the crew pointed out to him, he made to leave her with her nurse, but she caught at his sleeve blindly in a effort to prevent him. Lionel nodded towards the door, and Rose withdrew discreetly.

Corinna's head was turned from him and he said at last, 'Would you not rather have a few hours to yourself? Rose has brought a change of clothing. . .'

'Please. . .please stay—if only for one moment. I—I must try to explain.'

She still kept her head averted, as if she dared not look full at him, and he could feel the trembling of her slender form under his hand.

At last she whispered brokenly, 'He—he was my brother.'

'I know.'

She turned, shocked, to face him. 'You knew—from the beginning?'

'No, Rose told me yesterday at the plantation. She was afraid that I might believe you had left of your own accord.'

Corinna let out a pent-up sigh. 'I promised my mother—Dorcas. She wanted so much to keep the truth from Saul Hunt. He is—a hard man where morals are concerned.'

'Yes.'

'I could not tell Oliver the reason—the reason why I went back on my word to him.'

'You accepted me for want of another excuse?' His words were slow, deliberate, chilling.

'Yes—at first. Then, gradually, I began to see you as you really are. I—I fell in love. I knew—after our marriage night—that I could never love another man as. . .as I do you. I don't expect you to believe that. It must seem to you that I was wanton or, at the very least, foolish in the extreme to go to Oliver like that, but I thought Julian would be there. . .'

'And Oliver did not know your true relationship and thought — that you were prepared to go with him?'

She gave a stiff little inclination of her head and her lips trembled again. 'In the cabin he — he tried — he thought he could make me love him — leave you — and — and then I had to tell him.'

'Ah. Then it was that he quarrelled with Spicer about, returning you to Barbados?'

'Yes.'

She picked at the rough blanket beneath her distractedly. 'Lionel, I wanted so much to tell you, that last night on the plantation you were so jealous and I feared — I feared. . .'

'That I would arrange for his timely disappearance.'

This time she said nothing, neither did she look at him.

His voice was brusque as he said, 'Yes, I was jealous of Oliver Hunt. Despite the fact I won you as my bride I thought you would always belong to him. You should not have feared that I would ever have harmed him — he meant too much to you — but I confess I did want him far from England. Now I think I am beginning to understand how your heart was torn between us.'

'I felt responsible for his plight, Lionel. Oh, I know he was a grown man and made his own choices, but that night when you confronted us in the arbour, after he discovered I was to wed you after all, he was in such a state I think he was ready then to sacrifice his life willingly in the Duke's cause rather than face up to the loss of me. I wanted to be sure that he was free and happy — and now — now. . .' She broke down again and Lionel sat down by her side and gathered her head to his shoulder.

'You cannot see it now, Corinna, but I think perhaps this was all for the best. His life at Glebe was finished and he was not the man to settle to a life of privateering. He had no stomach for it. When you have had time to grieve you will be glad for him that he is at rest.'

She shook her head, her eyes blurred with tears and wetting the fine cut velvet of his coat.

He stood up. 'I'll leave you now with Rose. It would be best if we buried Oliver at sea, and this evening you will be better prepared for the ceremony.'

'At sea?' Her expression was anguished.

'Do you not think that preferable to his burial on Barbados, the island of his humiliation as an indentured servant? The sea is fresh and clean and bears no taint of tyranny.'

She considered soberly and then briefly inclined her head. 'I — think he would prefer that.'

'Julian will not be here, but that cannot be helped. All Oliver would have wanted to be present was the woman he loved above all things. You will be very brave, my love?'

'Yes.' Her reply was so low that he had to stoop to hear her.

'I'll make the arrangements with Marcel and then we'll board the *Curlew* and make for Bridgetown.'

As he reached the cabin door she said anxiously, 'You haven't said if — if you forgive me.'

He gave a little crooked smile. 'There was never any question of that. You see, like Oliver, I love you beyond everything I hold dear. I always have.'

They were two days out on board the *Curlew* on their way back to England. Corinna sat pensively looking at her reflection in the mirror. Rose was resting in her own cabin and Lionel was on the quarterdeck. Rose had wanted to prepare her for bed, but Corinna had dismissed her.

She had borne up well during the simple, dignified ceremony when Oliver's mortal remains had been committed to the sea. Lionel had stood very close to her and he had rarely left her side since, during the two short days on Barbados while they had completed their preparations for departure, and she had taken loving leave of her true father. Their final parting on the harbour had been painful, since she thought she might never see him again. To her relief Julian had decided, after all, to remain with his uncle on the plantation. The terrible events on board the *Genevieve* had convinced him finally that a life at sea held no promise of happiness or fulfilment for him.

Lionel had been very gentle with her, and their time together on the *Curlew* since they set sail had been precious to her and cleansing. Already the agony of her grief was fading, though she faced the prospect of revealing the story of Oliver's fate to his parents with grave misgivings. She knew in her heart that Lionel was right. Oliver was a true English gentleman farmer. Exiled, he could never have been happy. His life had ended really with the death of the Duke whose cause he had espoused and, in time, she believed Tabitha and Saul Hunt would come to the same conclusion. The full truth as to the reason for Oliver's quarrel with Bart Spicer which had led to his death must never be revealed, but Corinna trusted to Lionel's good sense to offer some cogent reason for the duel which would not besmirch Oliver's memory.

She was restless alone in the cabin. Lionel had forgiven her and he loved her, he had said so, but these last days he had behaved more like a brother to her

than the passionate husband she had known on the
voyage out, and she was beginning to be fearful that
that state of affairs which had filled her with such joy
on the outward voyage might not return.

On impulse she seized her cloak and hastened out of
the cabin, up on the companionstair to the quarterdeck. Lionel was leaning down over the stern rail,
watching the moonlight's silvery path over the parting
water in the ship's wake. She hesitated, biting her lip
uncertainly, then he turned and saw her.

Etched against the ship's lantern light, his tall form
looked dark and vaguely forbidding, then she saw that
his arms were opened wide to receive her, and she ran
into them eagerly, her face uplifted for his welcoming
kiss.

He held her so close that she thought she would not
be able to breathe, and the rapid pounding of his heart
against her own stirred her body to rapturous response.

'I thought — I thought — you would never love me
like that again,' she murmured hoarsely, and he gave a
little triumphant laugh.

'Oh, Corinna, my wife, you still have so much to
learn about your husband. I thought you needed time
to come to terms with your sorrow. You have been
through so much. . .'

'Through it and out to the other side, with your help,
beloved. Lionel, I do love you, truly. Promise me you
will not banish me to your country house.'

His kisses nuzzled her hair, blowing wild in the sea
wind. 'Corinna, my heart, I intend to show you off to
every envious fellow at King James's court, but not
before spending some months alone together in
Yorkshire, where I will prove to you my adoration. If
you think I would trust you out of my sight again you
still have not my measure.'

His teasing smile roved over her. 'Where is Rose?'

'In her cabin. She pleads a headache.' Corinna stifled a laugh. 'Poor Rose. I think she fears a return of her *mal de mer*, but she did offer to help me undress before she retired.'

'Then I must be your tiring servant.'

'Barbizet?'

'Knows better than to press unwanted attentions on his master.'

'Good,' she murmured wantonly.

Laughing again, he gathered her up into his arms and strode towards the companionstair.

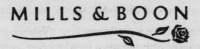

MILLS & BOON

New Look
Legacy of Love

A few months ago we introduced new look covers on our historical series and we called them 'Legacy of Love'. We'd like to hear just how much you like them.

Please spare a few minutes to answer the questions below and we will send you a **FREE** Mills & Boon novel as our thank you. Just send the completed questionnaire back to us today - **NO STAMP NEEDED.**

Don't forget to fill in your name and address, so that we know where to send your **FREE** book!

Please tick the appropriate box to indicate your answers. ☑

1. For how long have you been a Mills & Boon Masquerade/ Legacy of Love reader?

Since the new covers ☐   1 to 2 years ☐   6 to 10 years ☐
Less than 1 year ☐   3 to 5 years ☐   Over 10 years ☐

2. How frequently do you read Mills & Boon Legacy of Love books?

Every month ☐   Every 2 to 3 months ☐   Less often ☐

3. From where do you usually obtain your Legacy of Love books?

Mills & Boon Reader Service ☐
Supermarket ☐
W H Smith/John Menzies/Other Newsagent ☐
Boots/Woolworths/Department Store ☐
Other (please specify:) _____

4. Please let us know how much you like the new covers:

Like very much ☐   Don't like very much ☐
Like quite a lot ☐   Don't like at all ☐

5. What do you like most about the design of the covers?

_____

_____

6. What do you like least about the design of the covers?

_____

_____

7. Do you have any additional comments you'd like to make about our new look Legacy of Love series? _____

_____

_____

8. Do you read any other Mills & Boon series? (Please tick each series you read).

Mills & Boon Romances ☐	Temptation	☐
Love on Call (Medical Romances) ☐	Duet	☐
Favourites (Best Sellers) ☐	Don't read any others	☐

9. Are you a Reader Service subscriber?

Yes ☐   No ☐

If Yes, what is your subscription number? _____

10. What is your age group?

16-24 ☐   25-34 ☐   35-44 ☐   45-54 ☐   55-64 ☐   65+ ☐

THANK YOU FOR YOUR HELP

✉   Please send your completed questionnaire to: ✉

Mills & Boon Reader Service, FREEPOST,
P O Box 236, Croydon, Surrey CR9 9EL

NO STAMP NEEDED

Ms/Mrs/Miss/Mr: _____   CLL

Address: _____

_____   Postcode: _____

You may be mailed with offers from other reputable companies as a result of this application. Please tick box if you would prefer not to receive such offers. One application per household.   ☐